IN BLOOM

IN BLOOM

FERN MICHAELS
LORI FOSTER
CAROLYN BROWN

WHEELER PUBLISHING
A part of Gale, a Cengage Company

LIBRARY OF CONGRESS CIP DATA ON FILE.
CATALOGUING IN PUBLICATION FOR THIS BOOK
IS AVAILABLE FROM THE LIBRARY OF CONGRESS.

ISBN-13: 978-1-4328-9689-8 (hardcover alk. paper)

Published in 2022 by arrangement with Zebra Books, an imprint of Kensington Corp.

Printed in Mexico
Print Number: 01   Print Year: 2022

TABLE OF CONTENTS

Amazing Gracie

FERN MICHAELS

May 2022

Gracie checked the supplies for the next flight, making sure there was plenty of booze, pretzels, sodas, and coffee stocked. The new crew would arrive in time to set up the hot meals and everything else that went along with a nine-and-a-half-hour flight from Dallas to Dublin. She'd just finished four twelve-hour days of flights and was ready for a break. At thirty-two years of age, she had spent most of her adult years traveling the world. But now she was looking forward to working domestic flights again, relishing their simplicity. A couple of drinks, snacks, a crying baby once in a while, and even the occasional grope from passengers who had had too much to drink would be a breeze compared to what was involved in international flights.

She recalled her first international flight after spending two years working domestic.

She'd known immediately that it was her jam. Plans for flight training to become an airline pilot had gone down the tubes when she found out that twenty-twenty vision, even with glasses or contacts, was required. She'd had laser surgery in high school to correct her vision. A year later, however, she had to have a second surgery. Fearing another vision issue, Gracie knew it would be wrong to endanger hundreds of passengers should she become an airline pilot. Being a flight attendant may have been her second choice, but she took pride in her work and enjoyed traveling the world and making new friends. Since she was responsible only for herself, it was the ideal life.

Though there was a long list of responsibilities involved in prepping for overseas flights, she was diligent in her duties, which included checking equipment, learning how to use a defibrillator, and performing CPR. She was trained to handle the situation if a woman went into labor. And she had even been trained in how to handle the death of a passenger or, heaven forbid, a member of the crew. Fortunately, no one had ever died on one of her flights, though she once had to assist in delivering a premature baby boy to a young woman traveling alone with a toddler. It was a frightening experience, but

Gracie's instinct and professional training had kicked in, and when they touched down in Dallas, both mother and baby, as well as the toddler, were fine. When she walked down the aisle to inform the passengers they had a new baby on board, she was filled with pride from helping bring a new life into the world, and they'd clapped vigorously for her and the doctor who, luckily, had been on the flight.

Now that she was head flight attendant, once all the passengers were seated, Gracie would explain and demonstrate the emergency procedures and inform the passengers about the length of the flight, something most of them already knew. She would also inform the passengers that if there was a headwind, the time in the air might be greater, also explaining what to do should the aircraft encounter turbulence. Once they were airborne, the captain would repeat her instructions. After he was finished, her work began. Working in first class was simple. She enjoyed making her guests comfortable so they would have the best flight possible.

Before commencing her duties in first class, Gracie would walk through the plane, looking for anyone who feared flying. Long experience allowed her to identify such passengers in an instant, and she took extra care to see to it that their every need was met in the hope of easing their fear. Her older sister, Hope, didn't like to fly, so she had a bit of knowledge about fear of flying. Many of her fearful passengers found themselves able to relax after she distracted them. Being able to help them was extremely satisfying. She had always been a people person, never met a stranger, and could talk for hours if the situation called for it.

Her mother often told her that she should have studied law, since she had the ability to speak so eloquently and endlessly. Her sister Hope was a talker, too. When they were together, they could yak, as her mother referred to it, for hours on end. Hope worked as a nurse anesthetist and had the same passion caring for her patients as Gracie had for seeing to her passengers' needs.

Gracie had taken two weeks of vacation time to head to Amarillo for the upcoming Mother's Day weekend. She had done this every year except last year, during the Covid-19 pandemic, since moving to Dallas to begin her training as a flight attendant after spending two years earning an associate's degree in marketing. Her passion for the sky was much greater than her desire to earn a bachelor's degree, much less a master's degree, as her sister had.

Hope still lived in Amarillo, and she, too, would take two weeks off just to spend time with Gracie and their mother. The three women would do all the girly things they always did. The only difference this time around was that Hope could truly relax. Having divorced Roy Gates, she now had the freedom to do as she pleased. Roy was an okay guy, but he was fifteen years older than Hope and way too controlling.

Their mom, Ella, was as sweet as the iced tea she served up, which Gracie craved all the time. Gracie could not recall ever having the sort of teenage issues with her mother that some of her friends had with theirs. There had been no reason to. Her mom doted on both her and Hope. If Gracie ever met anyone to share her life with, and if she was lucky enough to have children, she would raise them exactly as her mother had raised her and her sister.

Ella's husband, Gracie's father, had died two years after Gracie was born, and Gracie knew that her mom could have dated. Instead, she chose to devote her life to her daughters. There were times when she wished that her mom would find someone to love, someone with whom to share her life. The thought of her mom living alone for the rest of her life always made Gracie sad. But her mother assured her that she was happy, and that is what really mattered. And there was still time for each of them to meet the man of her dreams. Gracie couldn't help but laugh at the thought.

"What's so funny?" Jessica asked.

Gracie gathered her luggage and a freshly dry-cleaned uniform from her small storage space at the front of the airplane. "Wondering if Mom will ever date, maybe marry again."

Gracie and Jessica shared an apartment in Dallas. They practically knew one another's life stories after six years of flying and rooming together.

"You never know. She's still young enough; plus, she's gorgeous. She could be Hope's twin rather than her mother."

"Yep, they look like sisters; they get that a lot. Don't know what the heck happened to me. An odd strand in the gene pool, I suppose." She smiled. Gracie was tall, with a slim, athletic build, her eyes an unusual mixture of gray and green, her hair thick and long, the color of a shiny copper penny.

"You look like your father."

"I know; don't know why I let my thoughts stray. I'm tired, ready for a trip home. Wish you could go with me. Mom and Hope adore you."

"It's all good. I'm headed to London, and I have the entire weekend to myself. I didn't want to take the extra time off because Tina is still out on maternity leave. Us older, more experienced gals are hard to find these days."

Gracie rolled her green eyes. "Hey, just because we aren't twenty with plenty doesn't mean we're out of the game yet." Twenty with plenty was their private joke, referring to younger women with great bodies to match.

Jessica winked. "Nope. I'm not out of the game." She offered up a snarky grin. Jessica was the opposite of Gracie. Average height, short blond hair, eyes so dark that one couldn't distinguish the iris from the pupil.

"I assume you have a date for your weekend in London," Gracie teased.

"I never kiss and tell," Jessica replied. "Though if there's any hot romance going on, I'll send you an e-mail."

"As long as you leave out the details," Gracie joked. "Even if you say you never kiss and tell, we both know that's a crock of balogna!"

"Bologna doesn't come in crocks, Gracie."

They both burst out laughing, as this, too,

was a private joke. Jessica used *a crock of shit,* but Gracie rarely swore. She thought it unladylike and knew that if she slipped while on duty, a passenger might hear. In addition, she didn't want to tarnish her professional image. She was no goody two-shoes, but there were certain behaviors she preferred to avoid. Cursing at work was one of them.

"So you keep reminding me," Gracie said.

"You gonna take a hopper to Lubbock?"

Gracie glanced at her watch. "Yes, and I need to be at Gate C in fifteen minutes. Be safe in London. Send me a text when you arrive, and I'll do the same."

Jessica laughed. "I will, *Mother.*"

Gracie rolled her eyes, gave her friend a one-armed hug, then raced through Love Field to Gate C, dragging her luggage behind her. The flight was just over an hour if all went as scheduled, which she had no reason to believe would not happen. She'd arranged for a rental car in Lubbock for the drive to Amarillo.

She usually made it in two hours, not making any stops along the way. There wasn't anything she cared to see on the trip from Lubbock to Amarillo, which she had made numerous times, and she always made sure she had an audiobook for the drive.

Reading was one of her favorite ways to relax, and she had made sure to visit the local library. She had been a member of her hometown library ever since she was a toddler. Audiobooks were great, but there was nothing like holding a book. Feeling the different textures of paper and experiencing the scent she couldn't quite put a name to were a big part of her life. On downtimes during a long flight, she always had a book with her.

As soon as she rounded the corner to Gate C, she spied another flight attendant she had worked with in the past. "Hi, Elsa," Gracie said.

"Hey, yourself. Girl, I hope they have a couple jump seats on this flight, I can't wait to go home," Elsa said. "Those twin boys of mine are going to forget they have a mother."

Gracie knew what she alluded to, and knew if she had to give up her seat, she would. As far as jump seats went, there was only one on this aircraft. "Let me check, be right back."

She spoke to the ticket agent, a young guy, and explained her situation. "The flight isn't full, so you and your friend are good to go."

"Thanks." She hurried back to where Elsa stood.

"It's not a full flight. Let's hurry before someone decides to book a last-minute trip to Lubbock."

Elsa shook her head. "I doubt it. Even though I call it home, I cannot see taking a vacation there."

"Same with Amarillo. It may not be Dallas, but it is where I was born and raised. Home is where your heart is, anyway." She might have sounded corny, even to herself, but she didn't care because it was exactly the way she felt.

"Absolutely! Flying the world, I see a lot, so it makes going home seem like paradise." Elsa was a few years younger and had given birth to adorable twin boys four years ago. If Gracie had a family of her own, she didn't know if she would be able to leave them at all, let alone three to four days at a time.

Elsa followed close behind her as they rolled their luggage down the jetway, stopping as they neared the door to the aircraft. Waiting for the passengers to find their seats, Gracie and Elsa were able to sit together in the last row, seats that were usually the last to be booked. That day, Gracie would not have cared if she had to sit in the tiny restroom because she would finally be getting to see her two favorite people in the world.

CHAPTER TWO

Gracie parked her rental behind the house as she normally did. Her sister's cherry-red Thunderbird convertible was shaded by the copse of oak trees next to Mom's practical white Honda Accord. She smiled at the familiarity of it all. Home. Even though she had a great apartment in Dallas, Amarillo was what she thought of as her true home. She opened the car door, and before she could put a foot to the ground, Hope and her mother came bustling out the back door.

"Look at you," her mom said. "My lovely girl; I have missed you so much." Gracie hugged her mother, smelling the familiar lilac perfume she always wore. "It's been way too long, sweetie."

Hope stood behind their mother, her smile as wide as the state of Texas. "Hey, Poo."

Gracie embraced her sister. "It's so good to be home, I've missed y'all so much." She looked at Hope. "Poo? Really, sis? It's been ages since you called me that. I'll let it slide this time." She laughed at the nickname given to her by her sister when she had been a toddler.

"It's been tough for everyone, Gracie. I've missed you, sweet child, more than you'll ever know. I've made a fresh pitcher of tea just for you girls. We have two weeks to make up for lost time." Her mom was always sweet yet very succinct with words. After years of teaching second graders, speaking to them on a level they understood, she hadn't changed at all.

The past two years had been hard on all of them. The entire country had practically shut down during one of the nation's worst pandemics since 1918. Flights were canceled; hospitals all across the nation and beyond had become the epicenters for hope and, sadly, too many unnecessary deaths. Hope had contracted the deadly virus at the hospital, though she had never been sick enough to require a hospital stay. *Thankful* did little to describe what Gracie had felt during that time.

"I've missed your tea, Mom. You can't imagine," Gracie said, her eyes pooling with happy tears. "And you."

"Oh, sweetie, I think I can." Ella took a tissue from her pocket to dry her tears.

"Last night's weather forecasters predicted we're going to have one of the hottest days on record today, so let's get out of this heat."

Amarillo was hot and dry a big part of the year. Gracie had spent many of her teen years lounging in the backyard, her nose in a book while she worked on her tan. Fair-skinned, she never achieved the bronzed glow her friends had. Her efforts had been for naught, as all she came away with were more freckles and two splotches of bright pink on her cheeks. Her mother had warned her that she would regret this in her later years. *So far, so good,* she thought as she followed her mom and Hope inside.

Memories of her childhood rushed at her like a tidal wave. The kitchen, the hub of their home, looked exactly as she remembered it.

Almost.

White cupboards with wood-and-glass-framed doors wrapped around the large U-shaped kitchen. The family collection of Corningware filled the cabinets according to color, reminding her of a box of crayons. Her mother had replaced the old Formica countertops with white marble, and of course, all the appliances were modern and up to date. Pots of herbs in primary colors sat along the windowsill. Red-and-white-checkered curtains hung in the window above the kitchen sink, and as far as Gracie knew, these were the same ones she had seen on her last visit. The only new addition was an island in the center of the kitchen.

"Wow," Gracie said. "Mom, it's beautiful. You should start a Pinterest page, share your talent. Maybe let those tour groups have a peek inside."

Her mom chuckled. "Since retiring, I've had to keep busy. Stuck inside all last year, I decided to make a few changes here and there. I had Rick build the island and added a few knickknacks here and there. No to the tourists; you know how I feel about them."

"His work is pristine as usual." Gracie had seen his work. He owned a woodworking shop on the outskirts of town. Word of his creativity had spread to a production company for a major network with a popular decorating show. He made an appearance about once a month. Gracie was thankful he had taken time off to work with her mother.

Hope took a pitcher of tea from the refrigerator and filled imitation Ball jar glasses with ice and tea. She plunked a lemon slice in each, then slid them across the new island.

Gracie sat on one of the new barstools.

"I've dreamed of this," she said, after she'd drained her glass. "I've tried making your tea a zillion times, but I can't seem to get it just right. What's the secret you've been hiding, Mom?"

Hope gave her mother a sharp look.

"Oh, it's just years of practice, I suppose," Ella said, but her words seemed strained.

Odd, Gracie thought. "Whatever it is, you've definitely mastered sweet tea." She reached for the pitcher to refill her glass, but Hope had a death grip on its handle, so tight her knuckles were white.

"Jeez, sis, loosen up. Mom can make more tea." Gracie forced a laugh, but she couldn't help but think that Hope was ticked at their mother for some reason. She had to get the lowdown later tonight after their mother went to bed. This was usually the time when they had their best sisterly yak sessions.

Out of the blue, her mother said, "If you must know, it's the pot."

Hope's dark eyes widened as she turned to look at their mother. Gracie raised her eyebrows. "Pot?"

"I've had it for years; it's been handed down for at least three generations." Her mother sipped her tea, her light brown eyes twinkling. At sixty-seven, her mother was fit and petite, like Hope. She wore her dark brown hair cut in a modern bob and could easily pass for a woman ten years younger. What little makeup she wore enhanced her high cheekbones, and her apricot lipstick was applied carefully as always. Gracie thought her mother was stunning.

"Mother, are you all right?" Hope asked, all traces of indignation gone, her professional instinct on full display.

"Hope!" Gracie raised her voice a notch so that Hope had to look at her.

"What?" Hope gave her a snarky look.

She tilted her head toward the stove. "*That's* what she meant. I never gave it much thought until now."

Hope followed her gaze. Gracie could see that her sister finally realized what her mom referred to. "The pot. It's the one you always use to boil the tea bags in," Gracie said, to clear the air.

"It is. As I said, it's been handed down from generation to generation. I think that in its years of use, maybe the tea has somehow permeated the enamel into the cast iron."

"You had me for a minute. I thought you were smoking pot," Hope said.

"Actually, Mama smoked it when she was going through chemotherapy. Said it helped her more than her pain medication. She had such a terrible time taking all those pills. I'm not one to judge. It gave Mama a little relief."

Her mother was truly the most nonjudgmental person she knew. She was kind and compassionate, and Gracie adored her mother. Probably more than most daughters, as they had always been extremely close. Hope, who was much older, had less patience with their mother, as she saw her almost on a daily basis. With Hope's divorce and the hours she spent working at the hospital, Gracie figured her sister was long overdue for a bit of downtime.

"Mimi smoked pot. Wow, if I had known that I would've been the coolest kid in high school."

"Gracie! Shame on you. I hope you're not hinting that you and your friends smoked marijuana." Her mom spoke in her *you-are-in-big-trouble* voice.

"Nope, never tried the stuff. I would get fired in a heartbeat if illegal substances were found in my pee." Gracie watched Hope. She bit her bottom lip to keep from laughing. "We're tested occasionally."

"There's definitely a lot of controversy on medical marijuana," Hope interjected, trying her best to act serious. "Some patients with terminal diseases swear it helps them

25

with anxiety, pain, and sleep. I've read a few published articles, and opinions vary. If I were terminally ill, and I'm not, before you ask" — Hope eyed her mother — "if pot helped, I guess I might give it a shot. Not much to lose with a diagnosis like that. I had no clue Mimi smoked the stuff, but she was pitiful at the end."

"Yes, she was, but let's not bring negative vibes into this house today," their mother said. "We've had enough bad news this past year, so let's spend our time together doing fun stuff. It's been ages since we stayed up half the night playing Monopoly. When you two are rested, I'll challenge you both to a game."

They had spent many nights throughout the years playing their favorite board game. Gracie recalled a game that had lasted an entire weekend. As usual, Hope won, but they usually had a blast when they were into the game.

"I'm certainly ready," Gracie said. "I need to beat Hope at least once in my life."

"Game on, Poo," Hope acknowledged.

"Let's stop with the Poo stuff already! I'm thirty-two; time to call it quits."

"Never," Hope said.

Ella spoke up. "Girls, let's not get into

that stinky old story again." She winked at Hope.

"Thank you, Mother."

"Not so fast now. You're not the one who cleaned the poo out of her hair," Hope reminded their mother.

"What was I, two? I had no clue what I was doing. We didn't have a dog. I didn't realize what I was doing. Right, Mom?"

"You were just a tiny little thing, but I would have thought the smell might have warned you away."

"I should have never volunteered to babysit you that day," Hope added.

"I suppose I would've said no if the situation were reversed. You're the oldest. Babysitting a little sister who is sixteen years *younger* than you is kind of a normal chore. Right, Mom?" Gracie smiled at them both. She couldn't imagine the horror Hope must've felt when she found her in the front yard playing with a very large pile of the neighbor's dog poo. According to Hope, she had called her "Poo" while being hosed down outside. From that moment on, Hope nicknamed her Poo, and the nickname had stuck.

"Gracie, let's talk about something else before I gag at the memory," Hope suggested. "Mom ordered Taylor's BBQ for supper tonight. They're delivering at seven-thirty. It's been ages since I've had their brisket. I can't wait to dive in tonight."

"Oh no, Mom! I'll gain ten pounds while I'm here. I won't be able to fit into my uniform, but I can't wait, either. Your iced tea and Taylor's BBQ rank at the top of my list of favorite foods and drinks."

"She ordered banana pudding, too. With extra whipped cream," Hope added, an evil grin on her face.

"Their banana pudding is to die for, which both of you know I can't resist. Guess I'm going to be jogging a bit more than normal," Gracie teased.

"When do you find time to jog?" Hope asked. "I barely find the time to exercise these days."

"Mostly through airports when I'm running late. My off days, I jog at the greenway near my apartment."

"She does have the legs for it," their mother said.

"Meaning?" Gracie questioned.

"Long and shapely," Hope answered for their mother.

"Well, thank you both, that's sweet." Gracie had often wondered why she didn't resemble her mom or Hope. They were petite, with dark hair and whiskey-brown eyes. However, she knew she looked like her father. He had been tall, but she didn't remember much more about him other than what she had been told. She was barely two when her father succumbed to a rare disorder, Huntington's chorea. She hadn't known much about the disease until she was older. Knowing that there was a fifty-fifty chance she had been born with the defective gene, her mother assured her she had her tested when she was a baby. Neither she nor Hope had inherited the defective gene from their father. Hope remembered much more from that time in their lives, but she rarely spoke of it, as it still upset her. She thought that this was why Hope had never had children, even though she didn't carry the faulty gene. Gracie couldn't blame her. It must be incredibly difficult for anyone to take the risk of having a Huntington's child.

Gracie had questions about her dad, and her mother was always happy to speak about him, but she would get incredibly sad as she recalled the last three years of his life. The disease had sent him into a state of depression, which happened to be a part of the disease itself. Mom told her that from there, he had become extremely forgetful — another effect of the disorder — and there were times when he could hardly walk.

What Gracie didn't understand, and wouldn't dare ask, was: If her father was so sick, how had she been conceived? Of course, she knew *how;* she just didn't understand how he could, for lack of better words, keep up with his husbandly duties in the bedroom if he were so ill. She supposed he'd had good days and bad days, and she was the result of a good day. She would talk to Hope about it when they were alone, though not now, not on her first night home after all this separation during the pandemic. She would know when the time was right.

They spent the next hour catching up on one another's lives and some of the experiences they'd had while forced to be apart.

Gracie yawned. "I'm still on European time. Y'all mind if I take a quick shower and a nap before dinner?"

"Not at all; I was about to suggest it myself. Your rooms are ready, sheets are freshly washed, and there are plenty of towels and supplies in the upstairs bath. And I added a little something extra for each of you."

"Thanks, Mom. You're the best." Gracie stood up, stretched, and then leaned down to kiss her mother.

Hope blew their mom a kiss, then raced

upstairs. She liked to be first in everything, as she was highly driven in every area of her life.

Ella shook her head and placed a finger to her lips. Hope did not like it when they spoke of her competitiveness.

"I know, not now. Don't worry, Mom," Gracie said, before heading upstairs to her childhood bedroom. Upsetting her mom was not in her DNA.

CHAPTER THREE

Gracie's childhood bedroom had gone through a complete makeover after she moved to Dallas. Gone were the purple curtains, the silken purple comforter, and the three lava lamps she had received for Christmas the year she turned fourteen. They were a mixture of her then-favorite colors: purple, pink, and baby blue. Ugh, she couldn't imagine wanting such a color scheme now. Years ago, her mother had asked her if she could donate the items to charity. Gracie remembered her response quite clearly. "Absolutely not! Burn them." They were hideous. She had never asked her mother where the ugly linens and curtains had wound up. Hopefully in the garbage, never to be seen again.

Her mother's decorating skills were obviously in service to Gracie's adult self. The curtains were a soft cream color with matching blackout shades. Her twin bed had been replaced with a wrought iron full-size bed. She knew that her mother had painted the bed to match the drapes, and it truly looked like something from a magazine. Next to the bed was an antique table her mother had refinished, again in the cream color. The bed was covered in a red-and-white floral-patterned quilt. This, too, had been made by her mother. A red vase with a single white rose sat on the small table beside the bed. A white lamp, its shade in the same pattern as the quilt, certainly created a relaxing space. Her mother enjoyed decorating, and it showed. The room was perfect. A dresser had been sanded and stained, then sanded again to give the piece the look of age. It was obvious that her mother had kept busy this past year. Gracie's luggage was still in the car, but she knew she had sweats, T-shirts, and underclothes here. They would do for now.

She opened the top drawer and found that her extra clothes were folded neatly and smelled like they had just been washed. There was a new cotton nightgown with matching robe and a little note from her mother. "These are designed to keep you cool on hot nights." Gracie touched the soft lingerie. She would sleep in this tonight. Smiling, she took what she needed to the bath, not sure what to expect when she opened the door.

"Whoa," she said when she saw that the room had also undergone a complete make-over. The single shower stall had been replaced by a much larger one, with white subway tile and glass doors and a seat, which Gracie thought a fantastic idea for shaving her legs. A single pedestal sink with an oval mirror and new light fixtures had definitely modernized the bathroom. The biggest surprise beneath the window was a soaker tub. Pale cream sheers that allowed the sun in washed the room in a golden glow.

Thick bath towels in a celery green were placed on an antique shelf beside the tub. Soaps, mesh sponges, bath salts, shampoo, and conditioner were in place on the second shelf, along with body lotion and two of her favorite gardenia-scented candles. Was there anything her mother hadn't thought of? Gracie couldn't imagine doing all this. She wasn't nearly as talented as her mother in the decorating department. Hope, though, had a bit of decorating talent. Yet most of her skills, as a certified nurse anesthetist, were spent making sure that patients were pain-free and would wake up from surgery without remembering anything that had occurred during the procedure. Gracie sometimes wondered why Hope had not gone on to medical school and become a doctor — a full-fledged anesthesiologist. Hope was as close as she wanted, Gracie knew, as they had talked about this before.

Though Gracie wanted to fill the tub and climb into steamy water, she opted instead for a quick shower. She did plan to enjoy the tub a few times before heading back to Dallas.

As soon as she finished her shower, she felt like a new person. She would take a nap, too, because it was going to be a late night trying to catch up on one another's life. Zoom was great, but it would never replace being with the people she loved.

It was after four when she finally fell asleep. A raucous outburst of laughter woke her. She glanced at her cell phone on the bedside table. Close to eight. Gracie made fast work of brushing her hair, pulling it on top of her head, and securing it with a clip. In the bathroom, she splashed water on her face before going downstairs.

Hope and her mother were in the kitchen.

"It's about time you woke up," Hope said, as she removed foil from an aluminum container. "You're lucky the delivery was late."

Gracie took a seat at the new island. "I agree."

"Friday nights are their busiest," their mom explained, as she brought a stack of plates to the island.

"Sorry, I was wiped out. Anything I can do to help?" she asked.

"We've got this, Poo," Hope teased. "You needed the rest."

Gracie let the Poo reference slide. It was silly for her to even care what Hope called her at this stage in life, though it was fun to mess with her when she used the old nickname.

"I must say, I needed it. It was early when we arrived in Dallas. It takes a couple of days for my internal clock to get back to normal."

"I don't see how you can spend most of your time in the air," Hope told her. She filled a plate with ribs, brisket, and potato salad, handing her sister a fork and a knife.

"If I ate like this every day, they wouldn't be able to get the plane off the ground," Gracie teased. "I love flying, you know that."

Hope sat next to her, a plate piled high, and a smaller plate with the jalapeño corn next to it. "No way will you eat all of that," Gracie said to Hope.

"You're right. I'm going to save some for later."

The smoky scent from the BBQ filled the kitchen. Tea bags simmered on the stove in the family pot. Between the three of them, they could consume three to four pitchers a day.

Gracie dug into her food, not caring that barbecue sauce was smeared on her cheeks. "Do they ship this stuff?" she asked no one in particular. "I think once a month I should treat myself."

Hope's mouth was so full she looked like a squirrel with nuts packed in its furry little cheeks.

"I'll find out for you," Ella said. "They ship just about anything these days. Clara had Maine lobsters delivered on her wedding anniversary last month."

Clara had lived next door to them ever since Hope was a baby. She had a son, Jackie, probably in his early fifties, still living at home as he had been born with a mental disability and wasn't able to live on his own. He was sweet and kind. Gracie remembered that he would always mow the grass in the summer and do any other chore he could just to be helpful. She remembered him fixing the chain on her bicycle once when it broke, and another time teaching her to count to twenty in Spanish. Gracie had nothing but good memories of Jackie. He was like an older brother to her.

"Jackie still there?" she asked out of curiosity.

"He is. He helped me refinish the furniture, always sees to it the lawn is kept up. A good fella," their mother said.

"Sad he hasn't had much of a life," Hope added, while stuffing her mouth.

Gracie looked at her mom, then turned to Hope. "Why would you think that?" She wiped away the sauce on her face, focusing her attention on the conversation rather than the food.

"It's obvious. He's a middle-aged man, his parents are in their seventies, and who knows what will happen when they're no longer around? I don't understand why they didn't insist on his going to live in a group home. They do have them. He could be with people like himself."

Gracie dropped the napkin she held and, raising her voice, asked, "Are you serious? You think Jackie is less of a person owing to a few mental disabilities?"

"I didn't say that. Clara and Rob's life would have been easier. They always wanted to travel. If Jackie were in a home with people like himself, they would be free to come and go as they please. Who knows? Maybe Jackie could've met someone to love, too. I know what you're thinking," Hope said calmly, then took another bite.

"No, I don't believe you do. What if you had a child with mental disabilities? Would you just put them anywhere, a place with 'people like himself' so you could do what you wanted?" Gracie was upset. Jackie was as sweet as her mother's tea.

Hope's face turned several shades of red. Her mother's, too.

"Am I missing something here?" Gracie felt like she was going to explode. "Mom? Is this what you think about your neighbor, your dear friends' son?"

"Of course not. I don't agree with your sister's way of putting her thoughts into words. Clara has talked about this off and on for years, but she just couldn't bring herself to check him into a home or a special school. Rob would never allow it under any circumstances, according to Clara. Rob is totally devoted to caring for Jackie. He was a teacher for many years, so he's qualified to care for him. I'm sure that Rob has made arrangements for Jackie's future. But . . . I do believe a special school might've provided more opportunity for him to make friends who were like him. And

I don't mean that in a cruel way. Jackie doesn't have any friends his age, and certainly you can agree how sad that is?"

Gracie had lost her appetite. "I disagree. Everyone likes Jackie. If I had a child, no matter what the circumstances were, I would devote my life to their care like Clara and Rob."

No one said a word. Hope pushed her chair away and took her plate to the sink. She wrapped her leftovers in aluminum, crushing the shiny foil so hard, the food was most likely mush.

"Not your favorite topic, huh?" Gracie raised her voice. "Just so you know, I am ashamed of you. Mother, you should be, as well. Hope is in the medical profession. Surely she has the ability to understand Jackie's limits. He seems to. It's not like he can't read, write, do everyday chores. You said he helped you refinish some furniture."

Hope turned around to look at her. "I didn't mean it that way. Jackie is nice and quite capable; I agree with that. But what will happen when Rob and Clara aren't here to care for him? He'll be tossed into a state facility, and trust me, you wouldn't want your worst enemy to step foot inside one of those places."

"So, why don't you do something about

it? You're the overachiever. Or is it too messy to get involved?" Gracie shot back. They were sisters, but they had different views on many issues.

"Girls, let's not ruin our first night together. You two can discuss this another time. As adults," Ella said, in a firm voice.

Embarrassed, Gracie nodded to their mom. "I'm so sorry."

They both looked at Hope, who remained facing them. "Okay, I'm sorry, too, though I'm not exaggerating about the state institutions. They're bad. It's not my business, and there's nothing I could do, even if I wanted to. The state controls these hospitals. It would take years for them to make changes. Plus, a boatload of money."

"If you feel so passionately, then why don't you try? Surely you're in a position to get the ball rolling," Gracie said. The thought of Jackie being sent to a home, where he knew no one, where he would shrivel up and die, made her ill. "You know doctors, right? People you can speak to," Gracie pushed.

Hope took a deep breath. "I do."

"I'm not asking for Jackie. I'm asking for all those who don't have a voice. When institutions make choices for folks who aren't mentally able, don't you think they

41

need someone to speak up for them?"

"Do you mean a guardian or a representative?" Hope asked.

"I suppose," Gracie said. "I'll admit that I know absolutely nothing about this, about how it works."

Hope nodded. "Maybe I can speak to the hospital's director. I won't make promises I can't keep, okay?"

"Thanks, sis. I know you'll keep your promise. You've always been honest and up front with me." Gracie took another rib from her plate. "Now, can we finish eating?"

CHAPTER FOUR

It was after ten by the time they cleaned the kitchen. With fresh glasses of iced tea, they took their usual seats in the front room. While Gracie reclined on the sofa, Hope sat in the rocking chair where, as Ella often told them, she had spent many hours rocking them when they were babies. But that night, sitting in her recliner, she did not remind them.

"This is nice," Hope said out of the blue. She tucked her legs beneath her, one hand on the side table to occasionally give herself a push to resume rocking.

"I'm just happy to have my girls at home," their mom said. "Just like old times, right?" She laughed.

Gracie stretched her long legs across the arm of the sofa. "It is. But it's even better, because it's been the longest we've gone without our annual Mother's Day ritual."

"I thought you both would want to do

something different this time, so I have a surprise for you two," Ella said.

"Hope and I should surprise you," Gracie said. Though she hadn't had time to shop for a gift, she planned to slip out of the house the next day and find something special. If she had time, she might see Rick, maybe commission him to repair the formal dining-room table. It, too, had been in the family for generations. Years of hot dishes, water rings, and a few gashes had created the need for repair. It would take a while, especially since Rick worked on the decorating show that everyone she knew watched, but she had only caught a few shows, and none with Rick as the guest carpenter. Gracie would visit him, or at the very least call, ask his opinion, see if he could fit the job into his schedule.

"Why are you two so quiet?"

"Speaking for myself, I'm enjoying this. As much as I love to talk, it's nice to just sit with your thoughts. I don't do this often enough. Flights are pretty much back to normal. You all know what my job entails. I do love to fly, love all the perks, but I think being home beats the heck out of a week in Paris."

"The world traveler," Hope said. "I would so love to go to Paris."

"You should go with me, you'll get a deal on the tickets," Gracie teased. "When you fly on an international flight with our airline, you won't even think about your fear — well, not really, but it's not as bad as you imagine. The plane is huge. It's almost like you're just sitting around watching a movie, reading. Like now. Relaxed. Of course, when you're fearful, your focus is either on landing or crashing."

"Gracie! You know better," their mom admonished. "Hope is terrified. You remember the one time we flew to Houston for Aunt Stella Mae's funeral? I thought we were going to have to attend another."

"Y'all stop talking about me. I will fly when and if it's a do-or-die situation."

Gracie sat up; she needed a little challenge. "So, what would you call a 'do-or-die situation'?"

"It wasn't attending Aunt Stella Mae's funeral. I could've sent flowers, a card. I didn't even know her that well. She didn't know us either. Besides, she was blind. We could've paid someone to visit her, and she would never have known the difference."

Gracie couldn't help herself. She burst out laughing. "Oh, Hope, I am so glad it was you that said that and not me!" She tossed her head back, laughing so hard that tears streamed down her face.

Hope started laughing, too. "Remember when Uncle Joe used to talk about rearranging the furniture?"

"You two grown women should be ashamed of yourselves. I didn't raise you to be disrespectful. Uncle Joe was a mean old drunk who really wasn't your uncle. At one time, before the booze took over his life, he was a friend of your father's. I can't believe you girls heard that kind of talk."

"Mom, we're grown women talking about what we heard. I can't help it if we overheard him." Hope struggled to suppress her laughter, biting her cheeks.

It didn't work, as they howled like two high-school kids. "I am so glad it was you that brought this up." Gracie managed to spit out the words. "I thought the same thing myself; I just never" — she slid onto the floor, laughing so hard she could barely finish her words — "had the guts to say it!"

Ella couldn't help but laugh at the two younger women. They were adults, and even though she didn't like to speak ill of anyone, living or dead, she knew that both of them had a streak of orneriness and, often, a warped sense of humor.

"So" — Gracie blew her nose on the edge of her T-shirt — "what's that 'do-or-die' situation we were discussing?" Her eyes were still pooling with tears of laughter.

Her thoughts traveled to a woman on a flight just three weeks ago. The flight was not a smooth one, the turbulence horrible. The pilot had turned on the seat-belt light, telling the passengers to strap in. Gracie spoke over the intercom, asking all passengers to please remain in their seats just as she always did after the captain spoke. As she was about to buckle herself into her jump seat, the plane hit the worst turbulence she had experienced in her career. Before she could finish buckling herself in, the restroom door flew open, and a very large woman landed in the small space in front of the toilets. Obviously, she hadn't locked the door and had flown off the toilet seat. Gracie was stunned, as she had just told all passengers to remain seated. When the woman flew out of the restroom like a large missile, her first reaction was to laugh. Biting her cheeks as Hope had just done, she helped the woman up and back to her seat without cackling. As soon as the captain told the passengers they were free to move about, she had hurried to the restroom, where she hid and laughed for at least five minutes. When she was able to control herself, she returned to the galley, where

Jessica was anxiously waiting for an explanation.

Jessica and Hope were the only two people on earth who knew of her fatal flaw. It was uncontrollable. Her brain misfired when anyone took a tumble. It didn't matter where they were or how old the person was. She could not control her laughter when she saw a person fall. It was a terrible reaction. When she tried to control herself, she would laugh even more. She had even talked to a therapist once about her flaw, and the therapist had laughed, which caused her to laugh at the therapist. It was part of her, and try as she might, she had absolutely no control over it.

"Gracie," Hope asked, raising her voice, "are you okay?"

"Sorry, I was just thinking about an incident that happened on a flight a few weeks ago. So, back to your 'do-or-die' situation. What would it be?"

Hope exhaled and raked a hand through her hair. "You're not going to let up on this, so I would say if I needed to get to *you,* since you're the only close family member who doesn't live within a couple of hours driving distance, I would fly then. But only in an emergency, so there you have it."

"Wow, I wasn't expecting *that.*"

"Now you know, so can we talk about something else?" Hope asked.

"Thanks, sis. I really didn't know."

"Why don't we call it a night? You two need to rest, and, honestly, I'm ready for bed myself," Ella said.

"Me, too," Hope said. "Tomorrow, we'll be fresh as daisies." She gave a slight wave, then headed upstairs to her room.

" 'Night," Gracie called. "Good night, Mom, I'm gonna call it a day, too." She kissed her mom on the forehead and went upstairs to her room.

It had been a crazy evening.

CHAPTER FIVE

Gracie checked her cell. She had a text from Jessica. Here safely.

With the time difference, Jessica was probably fast asleep, so she didn't reply. Jessica would know she had read her message when she looked at her phone, as it would say: Read 05/07/22 @ 12:38 AM.

What would the world do without cell phones, she wondered, as she turned hers off. Certainly, she depended on hers to keep track of so many things: her work schedule, appointments, e-mails from friends, banking. She couldn't imagine life without the technology.

Tired yet unable to sleep, she tiptoed downstairs to the front room. Built-in bookshelves covered an entire wall. She had to find something to read, as reading always relaxed her. Light from the streetlamp shining in through the large window provided just enough light so she could read the titles of the books. Her mom had everything from the classics to the latest fiction novels. She took a tattered copy of Barbara Taylor Bradford's *A Woman of Substance* off the shelf. She hadn't read any of her books but knew that she was one of her mom's favorite authors. As she scanned the shelves, she spotted a photo album, one she didn't remember having seen. She pulled it off the shelf and took her novel and the photo album upstairs.

She closed her door, switched on the bedside lamp, and sat down on the bed. She read the back of the book she had chosen and decided it was probably worth reading. But first, she wanted to scope out the photo album.

Tweed material in faded yellow, the edges scalloped from time. She opened the cover. There were pictures of her parents wearing swimsuits, her dad with his arm draped across her mom's shoulders. They looked so young, so happy. She turned the page, and there was another picture, one taken with one of those cameras that developed the picture instantly — definitely before her time — of her mom and dad again, only in this shot, her mother was very pregnant. Gracie thought she looked ready to explode. Carefully, she peeled back the cling wrap–

like covering and removed the picture to see if there was writing on the back. There was a date. May, 1974. The year and month that Hope was born. She continued to flip through the pages. All family photos of Hope as a baby; then there were a few of Hope and Dad. Flipping through the pages, she could tell a few of the photos had been removed. Many were of Hope along with her friends; she had to be in high school in some of them, and then the next picture was of Hope and her mother holding a tiny baby, whom she knew had to be her. She wondered if there were pictures of her with her father right after she was born. Knowing he had been ill when she was born made her sad for all the time she had lost, time they had all lost. She barely remembered him, as she had been only two when he passed away.

Something about her mom and Hope in the photo was strange. Neither was smiling, even though the occasion should have been a happy one. Gracie assumed her father had been ill at the time the photo was taken, or maybe he had taken the photo himself. She drew in a deep breath and closed the album. She would ask her mother about the pictures later. Too tired to start the book she had chosen, she switched off the light and instantly fell asleep.

A loud clattering jolted her out of a sound sleep. "What the heck?" She threw the covers aside, stretching her arm out to reach for her cell on the nightstand. She glanced at the time. "Dang," she said, when she realized she had slept so late. It was after ten, so she hurried to the bathroom, splashed cold water on her face, and brushed her teeth. When another loud noise came from the kitchen, she knew it was Hope's way of waking her up. It had happened often enough on their annual visits. Gracie laughed. She would have to think of a prank later, something she could do to Hope to tick her off, give her a good scare. Just then, however, all she wanted was a cup of coffee.

She spied a new red Keurig machine on the kitchen counter. "Nice thinking, Hope," she said, knowing the coffee maker was most likely a gift from Hope to their mom. Hope was a coffee addict. Mom still made coffee in a percolator on the stovetop.

"I thought so," Hope replied, handing Gracie a fresh cup.

"Thanks." Gracie slid onto a barstool, sipping the black coffee. "I don't know why I didn't think of this." No way was she going to tell Hope she had yet to purchase a gift for Ella. Hope was a planner and always one step ahead of her in that regard. Gracie had always been a last-minute shopper; more often than not, her gifts were purchased in airport shops across the globe. It worked with her hectic lifestyle. She had found many unique gifts over the years.

Her mother stood in front of the stove. "Isn't this fancy? I won't know what to do with myself when I don't have to wait for a pot of coffee to brew."

"Mom, I hate to inform you, but these coffee machines have been around for a while. No one uses percolators anymore," Gracie said. "Are you making mulberry pancakes?"

"Of course. Though these berries are from last year. You two get bored, go check the tree, as it's just starting to produce this year."

"I read somewhere the trees were outlawed a few years ago," Gracie said.

"They were in some states. They said they were a nuisance, because they produce so much pollen. The red mulberries, which are native to Texas — I don't think they're bad. At least I've never been asked to cut the old tree down. It's been on our property since the house was built."

"Gosh, I remember in the summer playing outside, I had to stomp on the berries that fell to the ground. My feet were always red," Gracie said.

"Hope did, too. I would've done the same had I been in your shoes — rather, your bare feet. Hard to resist, I suppose. It was terrible bathing you two, trying to remove the stains from your feet."

"I promise you won't catch me with red feet," Gracie said. She drained her coffee cup and brewed a second one. "Mom, last night I couldn't sleep, so I went in search of something to read. I found a photo album I must have missed when I was younger. I went through it, saw pictures I had never seen. I saw how huge you were when you were pregnant with Hope. And there was another with you holding me; I must've been a newborn, and Hope looked like she had just swallowed splinters. Actually, both of you looked sad."

As their mother poured pancake batter into a skillet, she stopped and turned to Gracie. "I haven't seen that old picture album in years. You found it with the books?"

"Between a couple other books, yes. Toward the end, it looked like some photos were removed, but I did get a kick seeing you pregnant, all beached whale-like," Gracie teased. "Exactly how much weight did you gain? If I ever marry and have kids of my own, I guess I need to know what to expect. Doesn't that sort of thing run in families?"

"That's rude to ask a woman how much weight she gained during pregnancy," Hope answered for her mother.

"Mom, how much, seriously? There may come a day when I'll need this information. I still have a few years left before my eggs are worthless. Maybe I should have mine frozen? Just in case Mr. Right doesn't come along in the near future. Something to think about." She said this more to herself than to Hope or her mom.

"Mom! The pancakes are burning," Gracie shouted the moment she saw smoke coming from the stovetop. She jumped up, grabbed the skillet, and tossed it into the sink. "Crap, you're going to catch the place on fire." She ran water over the burned skillet, sending smoke throughout the kitchen.

Transfixed, Hope did nothing but stare at her.

"Couldn't you see that Mom was burning this?" Gracie asked Hope, as she washed the skillet. "Mom, are you okay? You're acting strange. You too, Hope. What gives?"

Her mother turned away from the stove, her face flushed from the heat, but there was something else Gracie couldn't put a finger on. Had she upset her asking about her pregnancy weight? They were always open with one another. If Hope gained or lost a pound, they discussed it. If she had her usual monthly bloat, it wasn't a big deal for them when she said she looked like she was pregnant. They laughed at her, and she at them. Burning pancakes because she had asked a silly question didn't make sense.

"Honestly, I wasn't paying much attention, lost in my thoughts," Hope explained.

"They must've been deep," Gracie said to Hope, then focused her attention on her mother. "Does this happen often? Are we going to have to hire someone to come in and look after you? Cook your meals?"

"Gracie Lynn Walden, I can't believe you would ask such a thing! No, I do not need or want someone in my kitchen, thank you very much. I am sixty-seven years old; I am not ready to be put out to pasture yet."

Her mother was angry. Gracie knew her mother, and she wasn't angry about the pregnancy weight, or burning the pancakes, or asking her if she needed help. No, it had to be something serious.

The three of them were closer than most families. Gracie had known nothing but happiness in this house. She was sad that her father hadn't lived to see her grow and become the woman she was today, but they had no control over that. Mom seemed fine. She had taught elementary school and had just retired a couple of years ago. She had friends she socialized with. Of course, Hope lived nearby and saw her mother almost daily. Was her mother ill? Did Hope know that her mother was ill? Were they trying to keep this a secret?

Without another word, Gracie made herself another cup of coffee, took the plate of pancakes, heated them in the microwave, and then took butter out of the refrigerator and a bottle of syrup out of the pantry. She set three plates on the island, added forks, knives, and napkins. When the microwave dinged, she removed the steaming pancakes and placed them in the center of the island. Then she sat down.

"Now, I want both of you to tell me what the heck is going on? Mother, are you hiding something from me? Are you sick? You too, Hope. You're both acting weird, like I don't even know you. So what gives?" she asked.

Hope looked at her mother, as if they shared something private and didn't want to involve her. Finally, her mother spoke. "Gracie, nothing is going on except you're overreacting to a burned skillet. Your sister was lost in her thoughts, and if you must know, when you spoke about finding that old photo album, it brought back memories of your father."

"Really? You *really* think I overreacted?" She paused. Maybe she had been a little over the top. "It's my job," she offered as an explanation. "We're trained to act fast in an emergency. Smoke, fire is not something we want to see on an airplane. I suppose I went overboard. I apologize, Mom. I guess I really need to chill out. After breakfast, I think I'll go for a run, unless you have something planned."

"No, nothing, a run will do you good. Now, let's forget this and eat. I saved that last batch of mulberries in the freezer so I could make my girls their favorite pancakes. So, let's eat." They all bowed their heads, and Ella said a short prayer before they dug into the pancakes.

Out of the blue, Gracie remembered dinner last night. "We didn't say grace before dinner," Gracie blurted out. "Sorry."

"I think we were all overly excited last evening. It's been such a stressful time for all of us. For everyone. I'm sure we'll be forgiven if we miss saying grace now and then." Their mother smiled. "Though I appreciate the reminder, sweetie."

"Sure, Mom. Hope, do you have any plans today?"

"Absolutely none," Hope said with a grin. "I haven't been in this position in so long, I feel like a bird out of a cage. I want to catch up on my reading, I want to get my hair trimmed. Maybe a manicure and a pedicure. All the things a girl needs. I might even paint my fingernails hot pink."

"You should," Gracie insisted. "I can't wear polish at work, so I'm with you. What about it, Mom? You wanna join us?"

"Yes," she said. "Sounds like fun. I'll try a bright orange, it being spring and all. We need to lighten up, have fun just like we have all these years." She paused, took a bite of pancake. "I never tell you girls this, but it means so much to me that you take time away from your jobs, your lives to spend this time with me. I look forward to it more than you know."

"Mom," Gracie said in a syrupy-sweet voice. "We look forward to our time together as much as you. Right, Hope?"

"I do; even though I see Mom all the time, I don't get to spend this kind of time here. Relaxing, eating too much, sleeping whenever I want. I relish this time, Gracie. With you, too," Hope added.

"We're all good, then? On the same page, right?" Gracie questioned.

"We are," both Ella and Hope said at the same time.

They finished the pancakes, cleaned up, then went their separate ways.

Gracie remembered that she hadn't brought her luggage inside and ran upstairs, grabbed the keys to her rental, swooped down the stairs like she was a teenager, grabbed her things from the car, then ran right back up the stairs. Thankful she always had her running shoes with her, she quickly dressed in jogging attire, grabbed her cell phone, and went downstairs. In the kitchen, she removed a bottle of spring water from the fridge, then left through the kitchen door.

It was warm, but not uncomfortably so. Gracie rounded the house and looked to see if any of the neighbors were outside. Luckily for her, they weren't. Living at the edge of Amarillo's historic area, most folks knew one another but minded their business, as Hope would say. Not that she didn't want to see them, just not now. She looked a mess, and she needed this time to clear her head, allow her mind to relax. The episode in the kitchen had freaked her out.

She started a slow jog, heading for Polk

Street, the historic district a few blocks from her childhood home. Knowing they had all sorts of neat gift shops, she planned to spend time searching for a gift for tomorrow. Unsure of what her mother had planned besides church, she was up for just about anything that didn't involve work. Since her return to work, she had taken all the flights she could to make up for the financial loss when the airlines weren't able to fly owing to the pandemic. Between her and Jessica, they both had enough savings to live comfortably. So to say she was in need of a break was an understatement. Gracie jogged down Polk Street when she remembered she had forgotten her wallet. Maybe she would ask a salesclerk to hold whatever she purchased, then go home and drive back to pay. Yes, this was even better, because she would be able to hide her gift in the car. Of course, it all depended on some unknown clerk. But Gracie did have the gift of gab and knew how to use it to her advantage when necessary.

After half an hour jogging, she slowed her pace enough so her breathing was normal. She downed the water, then saw that Thompson's, a local stationery shop, had a bench for customers. She sat down and allowed herself to people watch, something she still enjoyed, even though she saw people from all over the world almost daily. Feeling content with herself and the world, she watched folks as they went about their business. When the sun started to feel too hot, she decided she had baked long enough. The weather in her hometown could change on a dime. It might rain, or maybe a windstorm or a tornado would pop up. Local weather wasn't ideal in the spring. She went inside to get a card before remembering she didn't have her wallet.

A pretty young girl, with long blond hair and eyes as blue as the sky, greeted her. "Let me know if I can help you with anything."

"Thanks, I'm just looking for a Mother's Day card," Gracie answered politely.

"Yes, ma'am, we've plenty left, so I'll just leave you to look around."

She walked down the aisle where the Mother's Day cards were displayed, then stopped. Gracie was bold. She returned to the register where the girl was typing on her cell phone. "Excuse me, miss," she said in her most eloquent voice. "I was out jogging and left my wallet at home. If I pick out a card, would you mind holding onto it for a bit? I'm just a few blocks away at my mother's house. Ella Walden."

"Oh my gosh, is she your mama?" the girl

gushed, her Southern accent pronounced.

"She is," Gracie said.

"She taught me and my brother in second grade. Mrs. Walden was one of my all-time favorite teachers. Would you mind telling her that Kelly Thompson said hi? She might remember me and my twin brother, Philip. We were both in her class together."

"Absolutely. Mom loves hearing from her former students. You should drop by her house sometime. She's just a few blocks away, the big white brick house in the historic district, the place with the red doors. Now, I have a favor, and if you can't do this, it's not that big of a deal. As I said, I need a card, and I forgot to bring my wallet. I went out for a jog, with my car keys and cell, but no cash. Could you hold a card for me while I run home?"

"Oh my heavens, no! Just take it with you. You can stop by whenever. Don't make a special trip. I know your mama, I know where y'all live. Daddy would never forgive me if I didn't let you take one. It's fine. You take a card, Miss . . ." Kelly paused.

"It's Gracie," she offered.

"Well, Miss Gracie, go on, find a special card for your mama, and don't worry about paying."

"Thanks, Kelly. I will, and I'll tell Mom

you said hello. As I said, she loves hearing from her former students."

"You're welcome," Kelly said, returning her attention to her cell phone.

Gracie read through several cards before finding one that said what she felt, or as close as a greeting card could proclaim. Really, her mother didn't care about material things. Mom would love a smile and a fresh-picked flower from her extensive gardens. Maybe she would get some red lipstick and kiss the inside of the card instead of signing it. Just for fun. They would all get a laugh out of that.

She took the card to the register. "Could I get a small bag?" she asked, not wanting to ruin the delicate paper inside.

"Absolutely, Miss Gracie." Kelly took a lavender bag and slipped the card inside before handing it back to her.

"I'll see you later; thanks for trusting me," Gracie said.

Kelly smiled, then went back to her cell phone. Probably on social media, as that seemed to be the entire focus of the world these days. Gracie had an account with Friendlink for friends she had stayed in touch with, but that was it. She would not allow herself to get caught up in the drama that social media thrived on.

Gracie viewed the many shops downtown, deciding to peruse the art gallery that had opened last year. Her mother had spoken very fondly of it during one of their many phone conversations. Gracie loved art of all kinds, but she was especially drawn to pieces or paintings that communicated a message, one she could feel. It might not be the message the artist intended, but she always came up with her own interpretation of the artist's work, what it meant to her.

Inside Artiste, Gracie was greeted by a gush of cool air with a tinge of sandalwood. High ceilings with track lighting focused on various paintings and sculptures, pieces so unique she had to stop and read the placards before she could understand what she was seeing.

She stopped when she spotted the paintings of a local artist, Callie Ramirez. On display in the middle of the studio were four mock walls holding eight paintings. Each painting depicted some aspect of Texas heritage, or at least that was Gracie's interpretation of what the paintings communicated. Each painting was of a farm, a lone barn. In the first, the colors were light, almost pastel in color. In each, the scene appeared to be the same as the one before, but the colors became much more vivid.

The last painting struck a chord in her. With vivid colors of a variation of the first painting, this particular one now had two little girls sitting on a fence. One had short brown hair; the other child had hair to her waist, the color an almost perfect match to her own. The little girls faced each other, smiling, as though they shared a secret. Bold colors, yet the scene was utterly tranquil in its simplicity. This could be her and Hope minus the age difference. She reviewed each painting several times, and each time she saw that another image had been added to the original. The final painting depicted a proud Texas farm, with vivid green grass, stacks of hay poking out of the barn window, and a tiny depiction of the flag of the Lone Star State.

No one had approached her, and she knew why. One had to soak up all the talent, the dedication of each individual artist in order to truly experience what pieces spoke to the buyer. It was a feeling, not a sudden urge to buy a new clock, where you hardly gave the purchase any thought. Clocks were practical and functional. Art was different. It spoke to her soul. She had to have the last picture.

"Excuse me," she said, knowing the curator would appear.

"They're quite simple though extraordinary," said a man with a heavy French accent. It was not something she heard very often in Texas.

"They are," she answered, still mesmerized. "Are they sold together?"

"*Non,* no," he said.

"You're French?" She stated the obvious.

He laughed. "I am."

"The last painting, it's stunning. I would like to purchase it as a gift." She didn't want to think how much that would set her back, but she was in decent financial shape.

"When do you want to take the painting?"

"Today, if possible. I'll need to get my car first." She cleared her throat. "And my wallet. I've been jogging and didn't think to bring a credit card when I left the house. Can you hold the painting for me?"

The man was probably around Hope's age. He was tall, with dark hair that reached his shoulders, and quite handsome. Showing a brilliantly white smile that reached his eyes, he said, "I will, but only for you. Only for a short time. As this is Callie's first showing, and normally, I would not allow a purchase before the artist makes an appearance, but I will make an exception for you."

"I wouldn't want to get you into trouble with her," Gracie said.

Again, the man smiled. "*Non, non,* Callie is my wife."

"She's very talented," Gracie said. "Is it considered *mal élevé* if I ask how much you're asking for the painting?" Her French was not the best, but she thought using a bit of his language might make him feel more . . . *French* in the Lone Star State.

"No, though I appreciate that you ask me in French. You have much Southern accent like Callie." He motioned for her to follow him to the back of the store. "Not ill-mannered at all. Practical, I think."

She followed him to his office, where they negotiated a price on the painting, one she was quite happy with. After Gracie assured him that she would return within an hour to pay for the painting, he told her to make it two hours, as he had to pack up the painting, *correctement.*

Gracie knew the French he used meant *properly* in English. Once this was agreed to, Gracie jogged back to the house as fast as possible. She didn't want her mother or Hope to suspect she was up to something.

"Right," she huffed, as she stopped to catch her breath. They always knew when she had something up her sleeve.

CHAPTER SIX

As she usually did, Gracie entered the house through the back door. She placed her keys on the island in the kitchen and grabbed another bottle of water to take upstairs. She needed to shower, get dressed, and leave before her mother or Hope saw her. They would definitely know she was being sneaky. Hope could look at her and know she was hiding something, as she wore her emotions on her sleeve. If she told even the slightest fib, her face would turn as red as a mulberry.

She was in and out of the shower in five minutes. Having no time to dry her hair, she twisted the drenched strands into a soppy wet topknot. She would let it air dry as soon as she picked up the painting. In this heat, it would dry in minutes.

She chose a navy sundress patterned with tiny bluebonnets, a birthday gift from her mom last year. She put on red handmade Magdalena wedges from Bali ELF, a gift

70

from Jessica that she had yet to wear. She was glad she had thought to bring them on the flight, as she knew she wouldn't have had time to run home and pack for her trip to Amarillo. Slipping into the soft handmade shoes, she wiggled her toes, amazed at the comfort. She located her purse, made fast work of adding mascara and lip gloss, then swooped downstairs without making a sound. Her keys were where she had left them. Still no sign of Hope or her mother. She hadn't thought to check to see if they were in their rooms. Carefully, she eased the back door open, making her escape.

Hope's and their mother's cars were parked in the usual places. Gracie opened the door of her rental, started the engine, and rounded the circular drive onto the main street without incident. They were probably taking a nap or lost in the extensive gardens. The drive to the gallery took little time, but it took forever to find a place to park. Finding nothing close to Thompson's or Artiste, she drove to the parking garage on Buchanan Street.

First, she returned to Thompson's. Kelly was at the register with a customer. Gracie stood back, waiting for her to finish her sale. As soon as the customer left, she went to the register.

It was obvious that Kelly didn't remember her.

"Gracie, Mrs. Walden's daughter," she said to jog her memory.

Kelly's sky-blue eyes brightened in recognition. "Of course, I didn't recognize you. You look awesome," Kelly told her.

"Nothing like a shower and a change of clothes," she said, thinking she must have appeared really hideous before. "Just wanted to thank you for letting me take the card. Take this." She held a twenty-dollar bill out to her, more than enough to cover the cost of the card.

Using a handheld scanner, Kelly said, "It's three dollars."

Gracie put the twenty on the counter. "Just keep the change; you trusted me."

Kelly seemed unsure. "I don't think I should."

"I insist; it will make me feel better," she added. "For allowing me to take the card without paying first." Gracie pushed the money toward Kelly. "Have a great weekend," she said, then swooped out the door before the young girl could say anything.

The art gallery was just a few stores down. As soon as she entered, she was greeted by the cool air scented in sandalwood. "Mister . . ." It occurred to her that she didn't know his name, so instead she said, "Hello?"

"Back here," a male voice called out.

Gracie went to the back of the gallery, easily locating the office. The Frenchman held a large wooden crate. "You are back soon." He gazed at her, a slight grin on his handsome face.

"What?" she asked.

"You look very ladylike. This is okay to say?" he asked.

"Sure. Thanks," she said. Gracie wasn't one to be easily offended. In her training, she had learned how to deal with an unruly man, or woman. In no way did he appear to be flirting with her. Frenchmen appreciate all women; at least, she thought so. Callie was a lucky woman.

"You're parked where?" he asked.

"At the parking garage on Buchanan."

"You can't carry this that far, I will deliver to your house," he said.

"No! Sorry. This is a gift for my mother. I was going to keep the painting in my car until tomorrow morning."

"Non, Non, Non! Tu vas ruiner la peinture!"

She understood *non* meant no, but she was clueless as to the rest of his words. "I don't understand."

"My apology. Keep the painting in your vehicle; the heat will destroy Callie's beautiful work."

"I didn't think of that. Are you open tomorrow?" It might be possible for her to slip away after church and pick up the painting.

He shook his head. "Callie and I, we have children. Big celebration planned for tomorrow."

Gracie felt like an idiot for assuming the gallery would be open on a holiday. "Okay, then, I guess I can take it with me now, and I'll bring it inside. I can keep it upstairs or in the shed. As I said, I want it to be a surprise."

"Bring your car to the back entrance, and I will load it for you."

"All right, I appreciate this. I, uh, didn't get your name," she said. He had been kind and helpful, and she wanted to send a card thanking him, and of course, Callie.

"You may call me Lucas Beaulieu," he said. "Now, you get your car. Meet me in the back, and you shall have your surprise for *la mère.*"

"Thank you. I'll only be a few minutes," she replied.

"Use the back entrance; it's closer to the car park," he offered.

She nodded, then left through the door he held open for her and walked the few blocks to the parking garage. As soon as she opened the car door, a blast of heat hit her. She cranked the air conditioner as high as it would go. Now she understood. The painting would have melted if she had kept it in the trunk.

Ten minutes later, she thanked Lucas Beaulieu for everything, promising to bring her mother back to the gallery so she could see more of Callie's work.

As soon as she pulled into the drive leading to the back of the house, she saw that both cars were still parked where they had been when she left earlier. Not wanting to take a chance getting caught bringing the large package inside, she quickly thought about what she would say when asked where she had been. Not that she couldn't come and go as she pleased, but she just wanted to keep her surprise a secret. Hope tended to be a bit on the nosy side.

The second she entered the kitchen, Hope was waiting for her. "Where have you been?" she asked. "Mom thought you were still out jogging. I told her you usually don't take the car on a jog."

Gracie answered as truthfully as she could, given she wanted to keep her secret. "Thompson's. I wanted to get a card for tomorrow. They always have the best selection."

"They do, though I haven't been there since all this virus mess. I practically lived at the hospital." Hope took two glasses from the cupboard. "Mom and I were just about to have an iced tea. You want a glass?"

"Sure, thanks. Let me go change clothes. I thought this dress would be cool, but it's sticking to me like glue. Be right back."

"We'll be on the side patio."

The house had several outdoor areas they used. Mom tried to stay away from the front of the house as much as she could, because their home was on a local historic-area tour. She was a private person in many ways. Gracie often thought her mother went a bit overboard trying to maintain this appearance for the tourists, because most of the guides knew she lived in this house, which had been built by her family in the 1930s. Amarillo was not a small town, but it wasn't Dallas, either. She guessed that the population was a couple of hundred thousand, give or take. Though she had always felt Amarillo had kept its small-town flair.

Now that the coast was clear, Gracie returned to her rental, removed the painting from the back seat, and took it to the shed, which sat under a large tree and remained cool, where she hid it in a tall chest. Then she went to her room and focused on changing into a pair of denim shorts with a white tank top. Kicking off her shoes, she slid her feet into a pair of flip-flops she had picked up at some airport.

Gracie saw her mom and Hope on the patio in deep conversation; Hope looked ticked off. Not wanting to interrupt, she stood off to the side, where they wouldn't see her. If they were having a spiff, she had to let them do their thing before making her presence known.

Hope spoke, her voice much louder than normal. "You tell her, that will be the end of all I've accomplished."

Gracie backed closer to the edge of the house. She couldn't help herself, wanting to hear what they were arguing over. *And I accused Hope of being nosy,* she thought.

"It's time, Hope. You and I both know it. You heard what she said this morning. She was not overreacting to the pan catching on fire. Neither were we. We know why. It's time she knew, too."

She waited a couple minutes to see where their conversation would lead them, but just as she was about to press herself closer to the wall, she heard Hope say, "She's coming out soon, let's pick this up later."

Gracie felt like an intruder in her own family. What were they hiding from her? Should she ask them? Tell them she had overheard their conversation. *No,* she thought, *this has to be handled delicately.*

Plastering a smile on her face, she stepped away from the brick wall. "I'm ready for that glass of tea," she said. It was the first thing that popped into her head. With no skill at acting, she thought now was time to start.

"There's my girl," Ella said, in her normal, sweet way. "I told Hope you must have gone for a drive. You ran out without telling us you were leaving."

"Sorry, Mom, I had to pick up a couple of items in town. Was I gone that long?" she asked, tilting her head to the side in what she hoped looked as though she were mystified by the time she had been gone.

"An hour," Hope said. "She was gone for one hour, Mother. She's a grown woman, remember?"

"Jeez, if I had known you two were going to make a big deal out of my leaving without telling you, I would have added both of you to the tracking app on my cell phone. Should I do it now? Just in case."

Hope's brown hair was damp with sweat; her upper lip, too. A sure sign she was stressed.

"You look like shit, Hope." She wanted to shock them, get their attention. Knowing it was rare for her to curse, Gracie felt sure they would know she suspected there was something they weren't telling her.

"Gracie Lynn, that's not like you to curse. You know how I disapprove. Are you upset with me? Did I do something to anger you?"

"I don't know, you tell me," she responded.

Hope looked at her mother. "Well, Mom, are you upset with little Gracie?"

She had never seen Hope so ticked. Ever. She was a calm person, never any drama. Until then.

"Hope, if you're ticked off at me, tell me. You, too, Mother. I'm an adult. Whatever secret you two have, you can tell me or not. I don't care either way, but don't drag me into the argument I heard the two of you having."

Watching them, Gracie knew she had hit the nail on the head. Her mother's face turned as white as the brick on the side of the house. Hope clamped her mouth shut.

"I'm sorry you had to hear that. Hope and I, well, we've had a disagreement over . . . Clara. It's nothing, really, Gracie. Just a little difference of opinion on Jackie's future, more of what we discussed last night."

In thirty-two years, Gracie had never known her mother to lie. As sure as the sun would rise in the morning, she knew at that moment that her mother was deliberately lying to her. "Okay, if that's what you want me to believe, fine."

She took a drink of tea and waited for one or the other to explain herself. Nothing but silence, except for the northern mockingbird's mimicking singsongs, a hummingbird's tiny wings flapping in a nearby feeder, and a loud bullfrog croaking in the bushes. A car passed by, windows down and blasting music. An ice cube clinked in her glass. Still, no one said a word. Gracie normally had the patience of a saint. She had to in her line of work. But not then. They were acting like two-year-olds. She took another drink of tea and watched the struggle between Hope and their mother.

Pushing her chair back, Gracie stood. "I'm going inside, just so you know."

Let them stew for a while. She went inside to her room. Checking her cell, she saw that she had missed a call from Jessica. She would return the call when she was in a better state of mind. She leaned against the pillows, saw the book she had picked out last night, flipped it to the first page, and within minutes was absorbed in the life of the fictional character, Emma Harte. She was on chapter two when she heard a light tap on her door. She closed the book and slid it beneath the pillows.

"Come in," she said, still reclining on her bed.

Hope.

"I'm sorry you had to witness me and Mom arguing. We're normally like two peas in a pod, but we do have our disagreements more often than you're aware of. I see her almost daily, and I think our relationship is changing."

Gracie sat up. "Changing how?"

Hope shook her head. "That's just it, I don't really understand it myself. It's like we've become these two old spinsters with no life. I work. Mom makes nice. Repeat."

"First, neither of you are spinsters, and secondly, you like your work, right? Mom likes to be . . . *mom.* What is wrong with that?" Gracie asked, more curious about Hope confessing that her relationship with their mother was strained than she was when she had overheard them earlier.

"Lots of things, Gracie, so many that it would take years for me to try to explain them. It's not like we don't get along; we do. But there are issues, private issues, between us that you don't need to hear, but that's a whole different story. Just things from my childhood. When Dad was sick, home wasn't the happiest place. Mom took care of Dad's every need, and trust me, he needed constant care. Toward the end — I know you won't remember this, because you were just a toddler — but Dad was like the walking dead. No, scratch that, because he couldn't walk. Mom tried to put on a good show for me and her friends, but I knew she was about at the end of her rope. I was just getting in her way being here, so I spent a lot of time hanging with friends, drinking, partying too much for a fifteen-year-old. I know now that I was just trying to get Mom's attention. I think I was jealous of all the time she spent taking care of him."

"Oh, Hope, that must've been so hard for you, especially at that age. I don't remember him at all, though I've never said this to anyone. I have a vague idea of him, seeing his pictures, hearing y'all talk about him. I wish life weren't so cruel. I guess in a sense I was lucky, since I was so young when he died."

"You were two. Cutest baby I had ever seen." Hope had a faraway look in her eyes. "You ever wish you could do things over?

Fix the mistakes you made, take away the hurt you caused."

Gracie had never seen this side of her sister. "Honestly, I don't really have any regrets. Yet. Who knows? I'm sure I've made some stupid mistakes, but that's all they were. So what if you did a little partying when you were young. Isn't that what teenagers are supposed to do?"

Hope reached for her hand, placed hers on top. "I guess it is, but I felt guilty leaving Mother here to do everything. I still do. I wish I had paid more attention to her."

"Dang, Hope, you were a kid! It wasn't your responsibility to take care of Dad. Why didn't Mother hire help? It's not like she couldn't afford to. Maybe taking care of Dad's needs was her way of letting him know she still loved him, in spite of his illness."

"After he died, you know what I felt?"

Gracie shook her head.

"I was glad. I felt so much relief. Then I started feeling guilty. Mom changed. For the better. She had cared for him so many years, I think that when he died, she was relieved. Not just for herself, but for him, too. I know she would never admit it, but she knew he was better off. They were young, had no life together; at least if they did, I didn't know about it."

Gracie didn't want to say what she was about to say, but Hope needed to hear this. "They had to have a little fun now and then. How else would you explain Mom's getting pregnant? Dad must've shared a few private moments with Mom once in a while."

Hope didn't say anything for a minute. "Now that, I wouldn't know."

"I wouldn't expect you to know something so intimate," Gracie stated. "Hope, when you spoke to Mom about the end of all you've accomplished, can you tell me what you were referring to?"

"It was just a stupid comment, a figure of speech. We disagree sometimes. We've been known to get a bit hot and heavy at times, but it isn't anything you should concern yourself with. As I said, Mom and I have our moments; you're just not here to witness them."

Gracie gave a half laugh. "I suppose I should be glad I'm not around much. It's odd that I've never heard you two in a shouting match before."

Hope removed her hand, stood up, and stared out the window that overlooked the gardens. "You're lucky to have this view," she said, staring out the window. She continued to speak. "Gracie, we don't have 'shouting matches,' as you seem to think. Once in a while, we just knock heads. Mom is honest to a fault. She has her opinion, and I have mine. Don't let our disagreements ruin your stay. I don't want a dark cloud hanging over you or Mom. We're fine."

Gracie wanted to believe Hope, just as much as she wanted to believe that her mother hadn't lied to her. Not being naïve, she had questions she wanted to ask, but she held back. It wasn't the time. Tomorrow was Mother's Day. Having disagreements with the two people she loved most in the world would have to wait.

CHAPTER SEVEN

Saturday evenings had always been game time at home. But Gracie wasn't in the mood that night. As far as she knew, there were no plans for the evening, so she decided to take advantage of the new soaker tub. She took her book and the new nightgown and robe her mother had given her to prepare for a relaxing soak. Maybe they all needed a bit of privacy that night. It had been so long since they had spent quality time together, maybe all they needed was to find a new rhythm, a new way to bond. She didn't think a game of Monopoly would be in the works that evening.

Just as she went to the bathroom, her mom came up the stairs. "Gracie, come with me. Please don't ask any questions. Get your purse, your phone, and a fresh change of casual clothes." Before Gracie could absorb her words, her mother raced downstairs. Clueless, she did as her mother asked, but she wouldn't leave the house without having some idea where it was that she wanted to take her, if that was even a remote possibility this late in the evening.

In the kitchen, Hope was sitting at the island, a small travel bag in her lap. Her mother was opening and closing the kitchen drawers in search of who knows what.

"Are you two going to tell me what's going on? This is beyond weird."

Apparently, her mother had found what she was looking for. "My watch." She dangled the Timex she'd had forever for them to see. "I take it off when I'm washing dishes and couldn't remember what drawer I'd put it in."

"That's a relief," Hope said, her voice laced with sarcasm.

"What are we doing, Mom?" Gracie held up the small tote bag with her change of clothes.

"I wanted this to be a surprise. Given the day, I can't keep this to myself. In about" — she looked at her watch, now fastened on her wrist — "ten minutes, we are going to have a spa day, or evening. This is my gift to both of you. We need a bit of pampering, don't you agree?"

Gracie couldn't help herself; she burst out laughing. "Mom, you certainly surprised me; I thought we were . . . I don't know what I thought. Hope, did you know Mom had planned this?"

"No, of course not. I'm as shocked as you are," Hope told her. "Truly, I had no clue."

"I've ordered a limousine to drive us to Salon Susannah's. After that, we're going to the Ale House for a late-night dinner. That's why I asked you both to bring clothes."

The Ale House was a local, family-owned business, their menu upscale, their service top-of-the-line. Reservations had to be made weeks in advance.

"I'm impressed," Hope told her. "You must have been planning this for a while."

"Actually, it was just a few weeks ago. I touched base with the spa, and they were open, happy to arrange a special evening for us. So many local businesses were closed for so long, now that they're open, people are getting back to work. I'm proud of our city, its ability to bounce back. I want to make sure I do my part helping these good folks stay in business. I made a few calls, and here we are. So, are you two ready to go? I told the folks at Luxurious Limos we would be waiting in the back drive."

Gracie imagined that a limo trying to park might have a hard time maneuvering, what with three cars in back taking up most of the space, but this wasn't her gig.

The limousine's lights shone in the kitchen window as soon as the limo turned into the drive.

"Our carriage awaits, girls."

Gracie and Hope looked at one another, each rolling their eyes at their mom's corniness. "Come on, Cinderella." Hope raised her voice several octaves. "Our prince is waiting."

Their driver introduced himself. "I'm José, and I'll be escorting you lovely ladies tonight."

José was dark-skinned and had a trace of a Spanish accent. He wore his black hair in a modern cut, along with the five-o'clock shadow that seemed to be in style. Tall, with broad shoulders and a slim waist, he was a handsome man. He held the door for them and winked at Gracie when he saw her scoping him out. He was beyond sexy, his dark eyes flickering with amusement. He held the door for them. "Please make yourselves comfortable. Mrs. Walden, nice to see you again."

The inside of the limo was very upscale. White leather seats, soft lighting, relaxing music playing. A chilled bottle of champagne awaited them.

Gracie took a moment to take in all the

luxury. "I'm impressed, Mom. You getting all fancy on us, or what?"

Ella laughed. "No, just wanted us to enjoy being together. I don't know about you, Gracie, those Zoom calls are great, but having you both here with me, I thought we could all use a little extra pampering."

"And I was just about to have a soak in the tub with your favorite author," Gracie said. "But I think this is worth the sacrifice."

"Barbara Taylor Bradford?" Ella asked.

"*A Woman of Substance.* I was hooked on the first page, but I can read anytime. I would much rather be here with you and Hope."

"I'm going to have a glass of that champagne. You two want to join me?" Hope asked, taking the bottle and reading the label. "Cristal — you really are spoiling us, Mom. I know this stuff is very expensive."

"Absolutely," Gracie said. "It wouldn't be a girls' night out without Cristal. Mom, you do know your champagne. Who would've known? Do you want a glass?"

"You said it's not a girls' night out without champagne, so of course I'll have a glass."

Hope filled each flute of champagne. "Let's make a toast."

"Do you mind?" their mother asked. "I would like to."

"Go for it," Hope said.

"To my best friends, my daughters, may you each continue to follow your own paths to happiness and have an excellent massage tonight." Ella held her champagne flute high; Gracie and Hope clinked their glasses together, then their mother's.

"I can't believe you pulled this off without either of us finding out. You do have a way of keeping secrets," Hope said.

Gracie chuckled. "That she does. Well done, Mama." Gracie's eyes pooled with tears. Such an extravagant gesture, when she should be the recipient of so much more. Raising two girls on her own, keeping the Walden family together. "Mom, do you ever regret not getting remarried? Having someone in your life?" She took a sip of her champagne.

"I think she's had a few dates," Hope said, a grin on her face. "You're not here all the time."

"Hope, it's not your place to discuss my private life, but if you must know, Gracie, I've been seeing a gentleman for a while."

Gracie finished her drink and poured herself another. Hope held her flute for a refill, followed by Ella. "So who is this gentleman? Someone we know? Have you met him, Hope? I assume you have, since you know about him."

Hope sipped her champagne. "Like Mom said, this is her news. Not mine to tell, and no, I haven't met him."

Gracie focused her attention on her mother. "So, are you going to give us a hint who the lucky guy is?"

"We can discuss this later." Ella nodded toward the front of the limo. "We may have ears."

"Mother, have you ever ridden in a limo?" Hope asked.

"No, I haven't."

"They have a window that separates us. Yes, they can hear us if we call, but I don't think José cares what we're saying. Limo drivers are kind of like doctors in the sense that they have a code of ethics that prevents them from discussing what they may or may not hear."

"Yes, I think that's the case, too," Gracie added, when in reality, she didn't know if what Hope said had any merit. "So, tell us who the lucky guy is," she encouraged.

"I will later, I promise. Let's forget about everything for a few hours, please? I want to relax. Both of you need to take this time and enjoy it. Let's leave our troubles behind, just for a little while. Can we agree on that just for tonight?"

"Sure, Mom," Hope said. "Let's forget about *everything.*" She placed extra emphasis on her last word.

Gracie just nodded. It had been so long since she had consumed alcohol that the champagne had left her feeling slightly woozy.

Five minutes later, the limo stopped in front of the spa. José parked, then opened the door for them. "Ladies." He held out a hand to each of them, making sure they were steady on their feet. "Enjoy your evening, Mrs. Walden. I'll be waiting to take you to your next destination."

"Thank you, dear. I'm really happy you're driving tonight. I'll send for you when we finish."

Gracie had a major buzz and hoped that she didn't pass out too soon. She wanted to enjoy the spa experience.

Inside, they were greeted by a stunning woman, whose long blond hair reached all the way to her waist. She was dressed in a smart, black, skintight dress, and her heels were so high that it was obvious she practically stood on her tiptoes.

"Welcome to Susannah's, ladies. I'm Kelsey, your hostess. We have a few requirements we like to attend to before sending you on the most soothing experience we have to offer. Please, have a seat. I'll be right back."

They sat in plush pale green chairs. In front of them was a small table. A plate of strawberries, sliced pineapple, and several other fruits sat on it. Another platter held several varieties of cheese, olives, an assortment of crackers, and tiny little cakes. A pitcher of sparkling water, filled with slices of lemon and oranges, was there if they wanted a drink. "I don't think I could eat before a massage," Gracie said, eyeing the snacks.

"Me either," Hope added. "But this is part of the deal, right, Mom? I guess you forgot to tell them we had dinner plans?"

"Yes, it's part of the package I chose, but you don't have to eat this. I do think I'll have some water, though. They say you should be hydrated before getting a massage." She filled a glass and took a few sips, then sat back in the plush chair.

Kelsey reappeared with three clipboards. "If you all would look over this form and sign at the bottom, we can get started."

"Of course," Ella said.

The form asked if they had any known allergies, any issues with latex, and if they were on any medication. Kelsey took the forms, looked them over, and said, "You all check out perfectly. Now we've prepared the salt room for your massage. We have dividers in the room for your privacy, but if you want them removed to chitchat, we'll do that now." Kelsey looked at them.

"Keep the dividers," Hope said. "No way am I stripping down to my birthday suit in front of those two." She laughed. "Seriously, whatever works, I'm good."

"Then we'll leave them as they are," Kelsey said. "Now, if you ladies are ready, please follow me."

Kelsey led them to a locker room, where they could undress and store their belongings. "Robes and slippers are in the lockers. As soon as you all are ready, Catherine will take you to the salt room. Enjoy."

As soon as they had changed into robes and slippers that would fit a giant, Catherine appeared. She wore light green scrubs, her brown hair in a high ponytail. "Good evening, ladies, if you will follow me, we can get started."

"I guess it's now or never," Hope said.

Gracie just nodded. She wasn't feeling too hot after having had two glasses of champagne.

They followed Catherine down a long hallway, the dim lights making it difficult to see. Twice, Gracie had to grab onto Hope to prevent herself from tripping. As soon as they entered the salt room, which looked more like a cave, Gracie relaxed. The walls gave off a pinkish golden glow, which must be the Himalayan salt, as the form they filled out had stated.

The room was divided into three sections by partitions. Massage tables were set up, and each area had a small table that held supplies for the masseuse.

Catherine continued her spiel. "Just choose a table, get comfortable, and we'll get started. If there is anything else you all might need, just tell your therapist, and she'll let me know. Bathroom, a drink — we'll see to your every need. Enjoy your massage."

Finally alone, Hope spoke up. "Shall we have a coin toss for the beds?"

Ella shook her head. "I swear, you are the most competitive woman I know. Just pick one."

"I think Mom should have the first pick. After all, it's her treat; plus, tomorrow is Mother's Day," Gracie said.

"Yep, you're right. Mom, hop to it," Hope directed.

As soon as they were settled on their chosen tables, three women entered, each introducing herself in soft tones not much more than a whisper. Gracie thought this all part of the spa experience.

As soon as they went over what type of massage they wanted, they relaxed. No one spoke or cracked jokes as the magic hands of the masseuses soothed knotted muscles and stiff necks. Next, each had a facial. From there, they were led to another room, where they had a manicure and a pedicure. When they were finished with their treatments, they showered and spiffed up, and Ella called José.

CHAPTER EIGHT

As promised, José was waiting for them as soon as they exited the spa. They each glowed after their massages and facials, with their nails and toes painted in bright spring colors.

Gracie wore a pair of Seven jeans and a Danise satin top in emerald green with a scooped back, her creamy skin showing. She wore the soft leather shoes from Jessica, not caring that they didn't match. She was so much taller than Hope and their mom that if she had chosen heels, she would have towered over them. She wore her hair loose around her shoulders.

Hope had brought a simple red sundress that highlighted her shapely arms and tanned skin. She wore beige flat sandals. Her dark brown hair had a just-washed shine, as they had all showered after their massages. The oil softened their skin but also did a number on their hair. Gracie had washed and dried hers again, using the blow-dryer the spa had provided.

Ella was dressed in a pair of black slacks and peach shell top. She had dried her hair, and her style was a shorter version of Hope's. Gracie thought they must see the same stylist. They looked more like sisters than mother and daughter. And she stood out like a sore thumb. Sadly, she wished she had had the opportunity to know her father, to see herself in him as her mother did. Photos just weren't the same.

José held the door for them as they climbed inside the luxury vehicle. Gracie saw another bottle of Cristal on ice. She was just starting to feel like herself and decided not to partake in any more toasts that night.

Of course, Hope took the bottle and opened it with the expertise she showed in everything she did. "Gracie?"

"No thanks."

"Mom?"

"Just a little," she said. "I don't want to get too inebriated."

Gracie laughed at her mother's use of the old-fashioned word for *drunk;* at least, she thought it old-fashioned. Like Gracie, her mom rarely indulged, so Gracie was surprised when she agreed to another flute of the fancy champagne.

"You two watch yourselves. It wouldn't look nice if y'all were to stumble through the doors at the Ale House," Gracie cautioned, ever aware of the safety of others. The last thing in the world she needed was to see either of them fall through the doors or trip. If that were to happen, her uncontrollable laughter would be worse than their misstep.

"I don't believe either of us had too much to drink, but I'll certainly make this my last sip of champagne tonight," their mother said.

"This is good stuff. A shame to waste. I'll just have a bit more before dinner," Hope announced as she filled her flute to the top, the creamy bubbles overflowing and sliding down the sides of the sleek flute.

Gracie kept quiet. If Hope wanted to get smashed, that was her business. As long as she didn't stumble or fall, Gracie didn't care.

Ten minutes later, José pulled the limo beneath the canopy at the Ale House, where one would normally stop to have the vehicle taken to the valet parking area. A limo probably didn't scream "park me," but nonetheless, a young man wearing a crisp white shirt, black bow tie, and dark trousers came to the driver's side window. After a few unintelligible words with the man, José opened his door and quickly came around the corner to open the door for them.

"Ladies," he said, as he took each of them by the hand, helping them from the limo. "Again, Mrs. Walden, I will wait for your call. Please enjoy your dinner."

It was almost eleven-thirty. Gracie wasn't even hungry, but she would try to eat something light. Ella had truly gone out of her way to make the start of their annual trip memorable.

Inside the dimly lit restaurant, they were greeted by a man wearing the same outfit as the parking attendant with a burgundy vest added. The man was much older, very tall, and had steel-gray hair and pale blue eyes. He greeted them as though he knew them.

"Good evening, ladies. You must be the Walden girls?" He had a twinkle in his eyes.

Hope was half-lit. "Yep, that's us. Though we're far from girls." She burst out laughing. "Maybe old women," she had to add.

Gracie was mortified at her sister's words. "She's, uh, had more champagne than she is used to," she offered in explanation. "Sorry."

"No, please, no apology is needed. Now we have your table as requested; if you'll follow me."

Her mother gave Hope a dirty look. "Let's not start something we can't finish, okay."

Gracie was clueless why her mother said this, but maybe Hope knew. Or if she didn't, in her state, she probably wouldn't care, anyway.

They followed the maître d' to a corner table that allowed a bit of privacy. The soft lighting created a romantic glow. Fresh flowers were placed in the center of the table. Tiny candles at each place setting flickered, and soft Celtic music played in the background. The well-dressed man pulled out their chairs, seating them one at a time. Soft linen napkins, held in place with rings of baby's breath rather than a traditional napkin ring, were more than Gracie expected.

"Mom, this place is top-of-the-line. How come you've never told me about it?"

"I guess it's not a topic we usually talk about. It's very luxe, though."

Hope was quiet, her earlier outburst having been just that. She sat with her back to the wall, where she had a perfect view of people coming and going. She focused her attention on two couples entering. The same man who had seated them took the couples to a table just three away from theirs.

A young woman appeared at the table to fill their water glasses. "Your server will be here momentarily with menus. We had to make changes, as we ran out of two of the nightly specials."

"No problem," Gracie said. "Could you bring us an iced tea?"

"Absolutely, I'll be just a moment."

"Do either of you think it strange they print, or whatever, the menus on demand?" Hope asked, still staring at the two couples.

"Not really. With fine dining, I think it's a matter of what they have available. Apparently, the Ale House serves different dishes nightly. I've been to a few restaurants in France. They have two or three main dishes on the menu. If they're out of anything, they reprint a small menu offering what they have left."

"Sounds like leftovers to me," Hope said.

Gracie focused her attention on her sister. "Why are you being so negative tonight?"

"It's the champagne," their mother answered for Hope.

"Does she drink often?"

"Stop talking about me," Hope said, her raised voice drawing the attention of the two couples at the other table. She lowered her voice. "And to answer your question, no, I rarely drink."

"Then be quiet. They're staring at you." Gracie tilted her head toward the two couples.

Hope glared at the table, a mixture of emotions dancing across her face. When she was angry, she always squinted and chewed her bottom lip. She was doing both now.

Without being too obvious, Gracie directed her eyes to the people who seemed to entrance Hope. She didn't recognize them, and nothing about them appeared out of the ordinary. Maybe Hope worked with them? She might have put one of them to sleep before surgery. Or maybe she had given one of the women an epidural. Not living here, Gracie didn't know what Hope's day-to-day life outside the hospital was like. They rarely talked about the men they were dating. Gracie hadn't had a real date in over a year. With the pandemic, she thought it likely Hope hadn't, either. Maybe she needed a bit of male attention, or possibly she had just been dumped by a long-time lover? She was clueless — and sad that she knew so little about her sister's life.

The girl delivered their iced tea along with menus. "I waited while they printed these out." She placed a small menu in front of each of them. While Gracie hadn't expected a piece of typing paper printed in Times

New Roman, she also hadn't expected such heavy paper, the burgundy script elegant yet easy to read. Of course, there were no prices on the menu, but she was sure her mother had taken care of that, as well, so it really wouldn't matter.

The specials were basic Texas cuisine with a flair. Brisket served with jalapeño chili and roasted potatoes. Honey-barbecue pork chops served with an apple and bean salad. For dessert, there was buttermilk pecan pie served with custard ice cream.

Though the offerings were simple, Gracie looked forward to trying foods she was familiar with but that had an added twist. Though she wasn't starving, after seeing the menu, she changed her mind about eating a light meal. In addition, most of the alcohol was out of her system. She took a sip of tea and pushed her menu aside.

Finally, their server came to the table. "I'm Helena. Sorry for the delay. Are you ladies ready to order drinks?"

"No," Gracie said, adamantly. "Sorry, we're having tea. Mom, Hope, have you all decided?"

They ordered the brisket and made small talk chitchatting about their spa experience. "It's been fun, doing all this girly stuff tonight, but why do I feel there's something more?" Gracie asked.

Her mother directed her attention to Hope. "Yes, there is more, but it's not my news to tell. It's your sister's."

Hope laughed, though she kept her voice low. "Mom, I've decided not to tell her just yet. Maybe when we're home. I'm not sure how she'll react."

"You can't do this to me! It's . . . mean. If I need to know whatever this is, just tell me now." Gracie was no longer in a good mood. She knew they had something to tell her, and now Hope was playing with her. She didn't like to be treated like an idiot, which Hope did more often than she admitted to herself. Almost a bully at times. Throwing her a branch, then yanking it back.

"Okay. There's a possibility I may be transferring to Dallas," Hope said.

Gracie felt let down. She had expected something much more exciting, even mind-boggling, the way her mother and Hope had been acting. They'd been all secretive earlier when she had overheard them talking; but now that the secret was out, she felt cheated.

"That's fantastic, Hope. We can see more of each other." She flew around the world, and Hope practically lived at the hospital. Gracie thought it wouldn't be a whole lot different from their visits to Amarillo.

"Gee, don't get all excited. It's not a sure thing yet, but I'll know soon. We have a new doctor from Dallas, and he's supposed to be brilliant. He's an internal medicine specialist, and get this, he's also a neurosurgeon. So I decided I wouldn't be needed as much and put in for a transfer. I need a change." Which was only partially true. She had other reasons she was not prepared to share with Gracie.

Gracie had never really considered that Hope might want a different life, one away from the town she had grown up in. Away from her ex-husband, who didn't bother her. Away from her mother, though they seemed to get along tremendously. Maybe things between Hope and their mom weren't as they appeared.

"Then I'll do whatever I can from my end, if you need me to," she offered, knowing that her sister was a control freak who wouldn't ask anyone for anything unless it was absolutely do-or-die necessary.

"Thanks, Gracie. I may need to stay at your place until I find one of my own, but again, it isn't a sure thing yet."

"Of course; we have an extra bedroom. Jessica and I use it to store odds and ends, but just say the word, and it's yours." She needed to check with Jessica, and should have before spitting out the first words that came to mind. She would send her an e-mail before she went to bed.

Their server interrupted further discussion when she arrived with their dinner. As soon as she left, they resumed small talk, all deciding the brisket was divine. When they finished, they declined dessert and coffee. Gracie was ready to call it a night.

CHAPTER NINE

As promised, José was waiting when they opened the door to leave the restaurant. "He is reliable," Hope said. "Unlike some men I've known."

Gracie rolled her eyes. Hope needed a boyfriend, and she would have a wider selection if she moved to Dallas. Of course, she would need a major attitude adjustment. She had always been bossy, controlling, and highly competitive. And, Gracie thought, Dallas might be too big and too sophisticated for Hope to navigate, though she wouldn't say that, as she did not want to hurt Hope's feelings.

"Did you ladies enjoy your dinner?" José asked, as he held the door for them.

"Yes, we had the brisket. Same as we had last night," Hope said without a trace of enthusiasm or appreciation.

"I'll make sure to tell Mercedes, my wife. We have an anniversary soon, and maybe

I'll bring her to the Ale House," he said, before gently closing the door.

"So he's married," Gracie said. "Very handsome, don't you think, Hope?" She wanted to weasel any info she could from Hope, ask if she was seeing anyone special.

"He is very easy on the eyes. The epitome of tall, dark, and handsome," Hope replied.

"So, is he your type?" Gracie asked.

Their mother didn't speak a word. She leaned against the plush backrest and was obviously relaxed and listening to them.

"I don't have a type, Gracie. People have common interests. I suppose I prefer a guy who is educated and has a sense of humor. Looks, well, they're important, but not *the* most important trait. So is that a type?" Hope asked, a slight grin on her face.

"Of course, you prefer smart men who can tell a good joke, and if he's good-looking, that's a bonus."

"Then call that my type," Hope said.

"Mom." Gracie raised her voice. "So tell us about this guy you're dating. What type of guy is he?"

Ella shook her head. "I swear, you two act like teenagers. But if you must know, he's someone I worked with. He's retired but has a part-time job to keep him occupied. He's very . . . elegant."

Gracie and Hope nodded.

"So, what about you, Gracie? I don't think you've ever had a serious relationship that I know of," her mother said, her tone serious.

"I dated a pilot for a while. I guess we were starting to get serious, but our schedules conflicted so much that we both knew the relationship couldn't survive being constantly separated. We're still friends, though."

"You are passionate about flying, pilots and all." Her mother stated the obvious. "I wonder where that comes from?" she mused. "I — well, never mind, you like what you do, as does Hope, so it doesn't matter how or why, as long as you're happy."

Just as the conversation was getting serious, José pulled the limo around to the back of the driveway. There was barely room, but he had once again skillfully managed to park without hitting their vehicles. He shut the engine off, then came around to open the door for them. He assisted each of them, closed the door, then grinned. "I hope you all enjoyed my services tonight. I don't usually drive, as I own the business, but I had a driver call out sick today. I enjoyed driving you ladies around our wonderful city." He shook each of their hands and said good night.

As soon as he pulled away, Gracie said, "Mother, did you give that man a tip?"

"What do you think?"

"Well, I don't know. It's what usually happens at the end of a service. These people are dependent on tips, Mom."

"I took care of that *before* José arrived. Remember, I planned this a few weeks ago; plus, he owns the limousine service and is quite well-off."

Once they were inside, they were all ready to call it a night.

"Mom, I might miss church because I'm really super tired," Gracie said, which was true, but she needed time to uncrate the painting, and who knew what time she would manage to get to bed? She sounded like a teenager.

"We've been having our services streamed, so you can watch them later. I always record them."

"Okay, girls, let's say our good nights," Hope said.

Once they were in their rooms, Ella called out, "Good night, Hope."

Hope followed suit. " 'Night, Mom."

" 'Night, Gracie," Ella called, to which Gracie replied, "Good night, Mother. 'Night, Hope. I'm going to sleep. I can't believe you still do this. We are not the Waltons."

"That's right, sweetie. We are the Wal*dens*."

Gracie waited a couple minutes to make sure her mom had finished the silly ritual they'd had as far back as she could remember.

While she waited for them to fall asleep, she sent an e-mail to Jessica, telling her that Hope might need to stay with them if her transfer went through, but only if Jessica was okay with it. She scrolled through her e-mails and saw nothing important. Then she turned her cell off for the night. It's not like she needed to make a call at this ungodly hour. She took her good shoes off, replaced them with her flip-flops, then switched to a pair of sandals. The flip-flops were too noisy. She was careful as she headed downstairs to go to the shed, where she would gather the tools she needed to uncrate the painting she had left there earlier. When she was in the kitchen, she paused. Hearing nothing from upstairs, she went out the back door to the shed. She entered it, carefully and silently closed the door, and turned on the light. It took her some time to locate the tools she needed and a satchel to put them in. She rejected the idea of uncrating the painting in the shed, afraid that someone would wake up to go to the bathroom and notice a light shining through the window.

If she woke her mom and Hope in the process of bringing the painting upstairs or uncrating it in her room, she thought it wouldn't be the end of the world. But no, she truly loved surprising people, so she opted for plan B.

If anyone were to see her walking at this hour, carrying the crate holding Callie's beautiful painting and a satchel of tools around her neck, they would probably think she was a thief. As she rounded the back of Clara's house, she realized that she didn't know whether or not they had an alarm. Again, hoping for the best, she carefully slid the lock to the gate aside with one hand, barely managing to keep a grip on her precious cargo with the other. In the backyard, she spotted Clara's shed. She knew that the painting would be safe there for a few hours after she uncrated it. As she hefted the wooden crate on her hip, her foot became tangled in wire.

Before she could brace herself, she fell forward, and she smashed her head on a large rock.

CHAPTER TEN

Ella had been an early riser for as long as she could remember. Mornings were her favorite time of day. The sunrise and the pastel-colored sky often drew her outside to drink her morning coffee. Sometimes she would go into her garden, check on a new bloom, or just take in the beauty she worked so hard to maintain. Gardening had been her therapy when Samuel was ill. The new growth, life, and beauty always gave her strength and hope.

It was cloudy the morning of Mother's Day, so she opted to stay inside. She was on her second cup of coffee when Hope came downstairs. Before she spoke, she brewed herself a cup of coffee in the Keurig. "Do you think this was a cheesy gift?" she asked her mom.

"Not hardly — I love it. I don't have to wait for my coffee to perk; plus, putting the percolator together and making sure not to

115

spill coffee grounds all over the counter was a bit of a pain. I love this. Pop in the coffee pod, and there you go."

Hope took her coffee to the island, pulling out a seat across from her mom. She took a few sips of coffee, needing it after such a late night. It had been after three in the morning before she had finally fallen asleep. Hope had much to think over after she had put in for a transfer. Then, of course, there was that other issue, for which she did not have an answer. But soon, she would have to get it figured out. Then, maybe she could live peacefully.

"Gracie still asleep?" Hope asked. "I thought I heard her sneaking downstairs last night, but I opened my door to check, and I didn't see her. I'm so used to my own place, it takes me a while before I get comfortable with the house at night."

"And I wouldn't know what to think if I lived somewhere else. This old place is the only home I've known, but I wouldn't have it any other way."

"I love it, too, especially the garden. If I had more acreage, I might've taken up gardening, too, but I don't. Though I do have my herb garden, and I enjoy the smells when it's cool in the morning. I try to do what you always do, check new growth, though I don't get any weeds in the planters. And before I forget — happy Mother's Day." She got up, went to the other side of the island, and gave her mother a hug. "I don't know what I would've done without you, Mom. I am humbled and ashamed, but we did what was best at the time. But now, I can't seem to find peace anymore. I thought a change might be in order. That's why I put in for the transfer to Dallas."

"I suspected as much," Ella said. "You will do what your heart tells you to do, and when that time comes along, you will know."

"I've thought about it for years, but so much time has passed, I wonder if I should just leave well enough alone?"

"It's your decision, Hope. I'll support whatever you decide."

"Thanks, Mother. You are the best, and you know it," Hope teased. "I think it's time Gracie got up. I'll run upstairs and give her the arctic wave." She headed upstairs to Gracie's room.

"She will not be happy," Ella said. But she knew that this was a thing between the two girls. One would jump on the bed whenever the other was sleeping, rip the covers off, and wave them up and down, hence the "arctic wave." Ella sighed. She missed the girls, and she was so lucky to have them here with her for Mother's Day.

Hope raced downstairs, sounding like an army. "Gracie isn't in her bed. Her purse is in her room and her cell phone. It doesn't look like she's slept in her bed."

"That's not like her. Maybe she's outside in the garden. Let's check." Ella slid her feet into the Crocs she reserved for gardening. Hope was barefoot.

They searched the two acres. "Mom, she isn't here."

Before Ella had a chance to answer, Jackie could he heard screaming in his backyard. They looked at each other, then ran over to Clara's to see what Jackie was screaming at. "Miss Ella, look at her. I think she's dead. Mama called an ambulance."

Ella almost fainted when she saw Gracie sprawled across the grass, facedown. "Hope, hurry," she called out to her daughter, knowing her medical experience would be of some use.

"Don't move her," Hope said. "Jackie, watch for the ambulance. Hurry!"

"Right away, Miss Hope."

Hope checked for a pulse. "Thank God, she's breathing. I can feel a pulse. Gracie, can you hear me? It's Hope." No response.

In shock, Ella watched as Hope administered to Gracie.

Hope lifted Gracie's hand, checking again to make sure she had heard a pulse. She checked her neck again, too, just to make sure. "She definitely has a pulse, Mom," Hope shouted.

In the distance, they heard the sirens wailing as the ambulance got closer and louder. As it pulled into the drive, Jackie and Clara ran out to the front so they could lead the EMTs to Gracie.

Ella couldn't believe this was happening. With expertise, the EMTs placed a neck brace around Gracie's neck, and then an oxygen mask on her face as soon as they had her on the gurney.

This sort of thing didn't happen here. It only happened to other people. It had to be a nightmare, and Ella prayed she would soon wake up and tell the girls how awful it was, but when she saw Gracie being lifted into the back of the ambulance, her face covered in crimson, her beautiful hair crusted with dried blood, she wanted to die right there on the spot. *Dear God, please save my baby,* she silently prayed. *Take me,* she thought, *not Gracie.* Her hands were shaking so badly, she couldn't use them to wipe the tears from her face.

"Mom," Hope shouted, "I'm following the ambulance to the hospital. Clara and Rob will drive you." Hope ran faster than she had in her entire life. Inside the house, in her room, she grabbed a pair of jeans and a T-shirt, slipped her Ugg slippers on, then raced out the door to her car. Never before had she had the desire to test the big engine in her Thunderbird. She slammed her foot on the accelerator, swerving as she rounded the drive; then, on the main road, she pushed the pedal to the floor, almost passing the ambulance. She stayed behind it, knowing it was headed to the nearest hospital, Amarillo General, where she worked. They were first class, with emergency and trauma units second to none, and if Gracie had to go to any hospital, Hope would've chosen AG. As soon as the ambulance pulled into the emergency parking area, Hope parked the Thunderbird in a doctor's spot nearby, not caring that it was against the rules. She had to find someone to tell this to as soon as she saw Gracie, knew what her condition was.

Inside, everything around her was a blur. All she wanted was to see Gracie, speak to the doctor, and pray her condition was stable and that this nightmare would end. Then it hit her. Last night, when she thought she had heard Gracie sneaking downstairs, she had been right. If something happened to her, she would never, ever forgive herself. She had made so many mistakes, and adding this to her list, Hope wasn't sure she could survive if Gracie didn't pull through.

Then Hope saw her friend working at the admissions desk and called out to her, "Joanne, the ambulance that just arrived — where is the patient? I'm her sister," Hope asked.

"Oh, Hope, I am so sorry. I think she's in station three. Go on," Joanne said.

"Watch for my mom; send her back when you can," Hope shouted over her shoulder, as she ran down the hall. People probably thought she had just escaped from a loony bin, given the way she looked. She couldn't care less. There was nothing more important than Gracie.

She entered station three, where she spotted two doctors from the trauma team and another doctor she didn't recognize surrounding Gracie, so she was unable to see her. She knew enough not to shout at them while they were doing their assessment. She chewed on her bottom lip so hard, she tasted blood. Two nurses came in with an array of supplies. She couldn't see what they had, so she was clueless. They were connecting Gracie to a heart monitor. When she saw her heartbeat, slow but still beating, she almost fell to the floor in relief.

"We need to get a CT scan, stat. Check her blood type; it looks like she's lost a lot of blood. I want red blood cells, just in case we need them." This was the doctor she didn't recognize, but there was something familiar about his voice. Maybe he was the new guy from Dallas, but he had an unusual accent. At that moment, she had to focus on Gracie and nothing else.

"Okay, let's get that CT, guys. Now," the new doctor said. "Victoria, go with them, check her pockets, see if she's got identification on her. And try to clean her face, I want to see her."

"Her name is Gracie. Gracie Lynn Walden," Hope shouted so she could be heard above all the commotion surrounding her.

"I'm her sister, Hope Walden," she said to the back of the tall doctor. He turned to look at her. Their eyes locked, and Hope knew.

"Ronan?" she asked, her voice not much more than a whisper.

"Hope Walden, from school," he said. "My Hope?"

Words she had longed to hear so many times since he had said them to her. Words she'd needed to hear so, so many years ago when she thought her world was going to end.

"Just Hope," she said. This wasn't the ideal situation for old lovers to have this conversation.

She didn't have to be a mind reader to know what he was thinking. "Gracie, right?"

She just nodded.

"How? When." He stumbled over his words, stunned by this wildly insane yet incredible news. He turned to Gracie again and smoothed the blood-caked hair from her face. Removing a penlight from his pocket, he gently lifted her eyelid to check her pupils. "Gracie belongs to me?"

"She does."

"Does she know? Why didn't you tell me?" He stepped away from the bed and whispered to her, "I don't know what to say."

The nurses continued executing orders given by Ronan, yet Hope felt like she was in a bubble where only she existed, with Ronan and Gracie.

"You don't have to say anything. Gracie doesn't know about you; I've never told her." She gave him a few seconds to soak up this information. More nodding. "There's more."

"Okay," Ronan said.

"Gracie believes I'm her" — she tried to swallow the lump in her throat — "sister." Before she completely fell apart, Hope slipped out of the room to absorb the enormity of Gracie and Ronan. Her entire world had flipped.

Dr. Laird, their family doctor with whom she had worked numerous times, stepped out of the room. "Hope, I'm so sorry, I didn't know. We will take the best care humanly possible of your sister." Dr. Laird questioned her. "Do you know what happened?"

Hope tried to focus, but all she could think of was Gracie, the blood covering her beautiful face, her thick hair matted with dried blood. "I don't know. We went out last night with Mom, celebrating early. It was around two in the morning when we got home. I thought I heard someone go downstairs around two-thirty, quarter to three. I looked out and saw no one, so I went back to bed. It must have been Gracie, but I don't know why she was at Clara's house. Mom's neighbor. She had a huge crate beside her. After mom and I were up for a while this morning, I went to check on Gracie, and it was obvious she hadn't slept in her bed. We searched the gardens, and that's when we heard our neighbor's son screaming. We rushed over, and that's when I saw Gracie. Jackie's mother had already called for an ambulance." Tears filled her eyes, but she didn't care. She would not let anything happen to Gracie.

"That's good. It gives us a timeline of sorts. She is unconscious now, but we will know more as soon as we see what the CT scan says. Her pulse is a bit shallow, but she's young, Hope. She's in good hands with Ronan. He's the best we have now, and he couldn't have arrived at a better time."

Hope thought she was going to faint, as his words were, to say the least, the understatement of the year, though of course he had no way of knowing that. She grabbed Dr. Laird's hand. "I need to sit," was all she could manage. It was all too much.

He led her to a chair a few steps down the hall from Gracie's room. "Stay here; I'll be right back." Dr. Laird returned with a bottle of Coke and a pill. She took the pill, swallowing it with the Coke. "Thanks."

He lowered himself so he could look at her. "Do I need to examine you?" Dr. Laird was in his early sixties, with thick white hair and wire-rimmed glasses that made his bright blue eyes a bit larger.

"No. What was that pill?" she asked.

"Ativan. It will help calm you."

"I am quite familiar with drugs," she said. "Not the bad kind, though."

He chuckled. "You're the best nurse anesthetist on staff. I know you know your drugs, kiddo. How many surgeries have we worked together?"

She shook her head. "Too many. Look, could you check Gracie? They should have had her in the CT room by now."

"Sure." He patted her shoulder and went back inside the room, then stepped out a few minutes later. "They're taking her now, but you might want to know she's mumbling, and that's a good sign."

"Thank God," Hope said. "Thank you, too."

"You need to thank Dr. O'Connor. He's the neurologist on duty tonight. He really is the best, Hope."

Ronan O'Connor. Now Dr. Ronan O'Connor, the new doctor, the neurosurgeon. Never in her wildest dreams could she have imagined this scenario. It made her feel as though she were losing her grip on reality. She and Ronan needed to discuss what to do when Gracie was able to speak, and she prayed that she would be able to come out of this without damage of any kind.

"Hope," her mother yelled when she saw

her. "How is Gracie? Is she going to be all right?"

"I pray that she will. They just took her down for a CT scan. Dr. Laird said she was mumbling, and that's a good sign. So we pray and wait," Hope said. "Let me get a chair for you." She needed a few minutes alone before she told her mother what she had just learned. This was crazy in so many ways.

Locating an extra chair in an empty cubicle down the hall, she carried it to the hallway outside the room. Her mother was seated in the chair she had left. She pulled her chair close to her mother's.

"Did Clara and Rob drive you?"

"Rob did. Jackie was so upset that Clara had to stay with him to calm him down. He's very sensitive."

"I'm grateful for Jackie. I'm sorry I said all those mean things. Maybe this is my punishment," Hope said. She deserved it, but not Gracie. She was kind and decent, always happy, loved everyone. Hope wished she could be more like her, but for now, all she cared about was her recovery.

Ella felt every one of her sixty-seven years. Other than losing Samuel at such a young age, she had had a happy life. A few bumps in the road, but nothing like this had ever happened before. Gracie was her baby, her sweet, sweet baby girl. Tears streamed down her face when she remembered the day they brought her home. She was a screamer, had a set of lungs an opera singer would envy. And all that hair. When she wasn't screaming, she was a perfect little angel.

Hope reached for her mother's hand and held onto it as though her life depended on it. Both were lost in their own thoughts. Hope felt the effects of the Ativan kick in. This must be how her patients felt when she gave them a shot of the stuff, knowing it was much stronger than the pill Dr. Laird gave her. Woozy and light-headed, she just let the medication do what it was meant to do. Leaning her head against the wall, she was hyperaware of the sounds of the hospital. Doctors being paged over the intercom, the clanking of metal, the swooshing sound of elevator doors opening and closing. Voices, people crying. She opened her eyes and looked at her mom beside her.

"Mom, will you be okay here for a few minutes? I need to speak to one of the doctors."

"You'll let me know as soon as you hear anything?"

"Of course I will. If you need anything, just ask Joanne — she's the admissions clerk; you remember her, right?"

"I do," Ella said. "Just do whatever you need to do, Hope. I'm not going anywhere."

"I'll be back. I'm finally going to do what I can to make things right. I may never get another chance."

CHAPTER ELEVEN

Four days later, Hope knew it was time.

"Hey, Poo," Hope said. "How's the head today?"

"Really? Poo? I'm in the hospital; someone might hear. My head hurts, if you must know. I feel like I've got the hangover from hell."

"You had a bad concussion, kiddo. You'll probably have a headache for a while longer, but we'll manage it with Tylenol. Dr. O'Connor gave specific instructions. You can't take strong pain meds now that you're fully awake. Sorry about the Poo, but who cares if they hear?" Hope replied. "I know *you* do, but trust me, that's not going to leave this room."

"It better not," Gracie said. Someone had cleaned the blood from her hair and taken the time to put it in a braid. "So what's going on? Is Mom okay? She's coming later this afternoon."

130

The door opened. "Mom, I just said you were coming this afternoon, but I'm glad you're here now," Gracie said, surprised. She scooted over, patted the bed. "Sit with me," she said.

Her mother spoke. "No, sweetie, I'll just sit in the chair. You need to be comfortable."

Gracie nodded. "You said you were coming this afternoon — not that I mind — so what's up? Have you heard from Clara? I feel horrible about Jackie, what I put him through, though I think he'll be okay. He's called three times, and I've assured him that I'll be okay. Did you find the painting?"

"Clara told me. He'll be fine, Gracie." Her mother looked at Hope. "The painting is perfect. We'll visit the gallery when you're up and about."

"Okay, I'll hold you to it. Is there something wrong, Mom? You look, well, kinda crappy," Gracie said. "Hope? What's going on?"

"Yes, there is something I need to tell you, but it's not bad," Ella said, a slight smile on her face, but her eyes were saying something else.

"Go on," Gracie encouraged. "I'm not going anywhere."

Hope walked over to her bedside and took her hand. "This isn't Mom's story to tell, so

131

I guess" — she swallowed — "it's mine."

"Okay, then spit it out," Gracie said.

Hope chewed her bottom lip, a bead of sweat forming above her lip. Gracie thought this might not be a good sign.

"There really is no other way to tell you what I'm about to, so . . ." Hope looked at her mother, who nodded. "When I was fifteen, remember I told you I was a bit of a party girl?"

Gracie laughed. "I do, but I don't care, you're a big girl now."

"I had a steady boyfriend in high school. We dated for two years. He moved away the summer before our senior year. I had just turned sixteen that May, so I had already planned what I was going to do when I graduated. You know what a planner I am?"

"I do, and I hope this is going somewhere, because you're not making sense," Gracie said. Taking the water glass from her side table, she took a sip. "And?" She put the cup down.

"Hope, you can tell her the details later," Ella said.

Now Gracie was concerned. This wasn't about some high-school prank. "For the second time, and . . . ?" she cajoled.

"I found out I was pregnant a few weeks into my senior year."

Gracie didn't move. Didn't say a word. This is not what she had been expecting to hear. "Okay," was all she could manage.

"As I said, my boyfriend had moved, and I had no way to stay in touch. This was before all the social-media rage. Later, I found out that he had moved back to Ireland with his family."

Gracie sat up in her bed so fast, a wave of dizziness forced her to lean back into the pillows.

"I am your mother, Gracie Lynn. Me. Mama thought it best, at the time. Dad was so sick, she truly didn't know what else to do. I was in a state of shock for a couple of months. Then, after we got used to the idea, it was decided that she would raise you as her daughter while I finished high school. Mom isn't your mom; she's your grand-mother, or Mimi, whatever. I am so sorry I didn't tell you. I should have years ago, but I didn't. I was, and am, a coward." Tears rivered down Hope's cheeks, but she didn't care. This might be the last time Gracie spoke to her. Or Mom.

Gracie took a deep breath to calm herself. She looked at her mother, who also had tears pouring from her dark brown eyes, so much like Hope's. This made sense. Kind of. She did look different. She had always known this, she had always assumed she looked like her father, whom she didn't remember. So this was the truth.

Another breath; she nodded, needed to think. No one said a word. Gracie appreciated the silence. She took another drink of water, then smoothed out the sheet. "Okay," she said. "I see. It actually makes sense. I am different, tall; you obviously had a convenient explanation for my appearance. Dad's dying so young was a bonus," she said, more to herself than to them.

"Gracie, it wasn't like that. This was not planned, and your father — grandfather — adored you. He agreed with me, for your sake and Hope's. She was young. As her mother, I felt this was my responsibility, too. Surely you can understand?" Ella pleaded.

"I suppose so." She nodded. If she had been in Hope's position, as a young girl, she would have agreed to this, too. But still, it shocked her. Yet it explained so many things. The missing pictures in that old album. Never any pictures of Ella when she was pregnant with her. Add the lack of physical likeness, and it all made sense. "So, do I get to know the unlucky guy, or what?" Gracie asked.

"He wasn't unlucky, Gracie; he didn't know about you. And I promise you that he does now, and he's" — she searched for the right word — "blown away."

"And what happened; how did he suddenly learn I existed thirty-two years later?" She looked at her mom, then Hope.

"Because he sort of saved your life," Hope said.

"Sort of? How did that come about?"

"Ronan O'Connor is your father. He's lived in Dallas since his college days. He transferred here just recently, but I didn't know until I saw him at the hospital," Hope said, utterly and completely filled with a sadness unlike any she had known.

"Really?" Gracie said, in a sort of perked-up tone.

"He is," Hope confirmed.

"Then I want to see him. Now, if that can be arranged," she said. Each word became more powerful, yet Hope detected a little bit of excitement in her sister. Her daughter. Hope stepped out of the room for a minute, returning with Dr. Ronan O'Connor.

"Hey, Gracie, how are you feeling, physically?" he asked.

This tall, handsome, brilliant man was her father! She offered a little smile. "Okay, I do have a headache, but I'll live with it. How about you? What about this parent thing?" she asked.

He sat down on the edge of her bed. "I think what happened to you is divine intervention. I think I have a purpose now. I didn't know about you, Gracie. If I had, I promise you I would have been in your life. I promise that I will be now." Tears filled his eyes. "You are my daughter, and I'm stunned, yes, but frankly, right now, I feel like I'm the luckiest man alive."

Gracie smiled at him through her tears. "Do you have a family?"

"I do now," he said. "I do now."

EPILOGUE

Gracie couldn't believe she had been in the hospital four days before waking up. Now she had spent four more days confined to her hospital bed, and she was going stir crazy. She ached to get up, take a shower, and go home, but the reasonable side of her knew this was where she needed to be. For the moment.

At first, she didn't remember why she was there, or how she had gotten there, until Hope, Mom, and her doctor came into the room to explain the situation. She was on day eight of her stay in the hospital and was beginning to come to terms with what she had learned. Three days ago, her entire life had changed, and it wasn't because of the accident. She could manage a broken ankle and a minor head injury, but the other news had shaken her to the core.

Recalling the conversation still gave her quite a shock, though she had come to believe that it was the best kind of shock to have.

Unsure of what she would do, how she could return to her old life as though nothing had happened. This afternoon, she would speak with a psychiatrist, who would help her figure out a way to cope with the shock of what she had just learned. It wasn't going to be easy; she knew that. But Gracie knew that she was tough, as tough as the doctor — her father — thought she was.

She also knew she was loved, more loved than she had ever known. With love, she would get through this. Maybe she would be an even better human after the newness of the many changes ahead soaked in, changes she would somehow come to terms with.

Suffering a mild traumatic brain injury hadn't been in her plans when she had taken Callie's painting to Clara's. Day by day, her memory of that night was becoming clearer. In the midst of the nightmare that she had, after worrying about surprising her mother on her special day with that painting, her sneaking around that night had changed all of their lives. A total one-eighty.

She touched the spot on her head where they had shaved part of her hair in order to stitch her wound. She had fifteen stitches, a broken ankle, and of course, the head injury, which she knew she was lucky to have survived. She had lost a lot of blood. Had Jackie not found her when he did, she might have died right there.

Thinking of that upset her, because it was her own fault. Gracie knew she didn't have to sneak and hide that painting. It was her own selfishness. She delighted in surprising others, in a good way. But this, well, it hadn't been a good surprise at all. Even though her mother loved the painting, trying to hide it hadn't been worth all the trouble she had caused, and it certainly wasn't worth sustaining all the injuries she had suffered.

Though her life was certainly going to be different, it wasn't a horrible kind of different. It would work if she allowed herself to come to terms with it, be as honest with herself as possible. If she hid her anger, she knew it could fester, become poisonous.

Her door opened, and a woman about Hope's age entered. "Hi, Gracie. I'm Dr. Keller. Do you feel up to a chat?"

"Sure," she said. "You're the psychiatrist?" she asked.

"I am."

"Then start asking me any question you

think will help me handle this life-changing event."

Dr. Keller replied, "I promise to do my best. Now, tell me how you felt the moment you learned what had happened, how it all came about."

Gracie spent the next hour telling Dr. Keller all of her innermost thoughts about the accident and the outcome, and that she really wasn't totally miserable with the changes. She agreed to a family therapy session. First with her mom — *grandmother* — and then Hope, and after that, she wanted them all together, including her father. This could work. The more she thought about it, the more she found she was truly okay with the changes coming in her life. It would be rocky at first, but weren't new beginnings always a little rocky at first?

Having made this decision, she took the cell phone that Hope had brought to the hospital on her last visit. She dialed Hope's cell number. She answered on the second ring. "Hey, girl, did I catch you at a bad time?"

"You can never catch me at a bad time," Hope said.

"Oh crap, act like yourself. If you start treating me like I'm a delicate little flower, I'll have to kick your butt when they let me out of this place."

"All right, smarty pants, I was about to meet one of your doctors for coffee in the cafeteria to discuss your case, but since I'm already here and he isn't, I suppose I can give you a few minutes of my time."

"I want to run an idea by you; then you promise you'll do whatever you can to make it happen?"

"Whoa, now that's a heck of way to ask a favor, but go ahead, shoot."

"As you know, they're releasing me tomorrow. I'm going to be a real pain at home, especially with the stairs at Mom's. So, how would you feel about my homecoming taking place at your house? No stairs, no main street for all the tourists to drive by the Walden house to get a glimpse of the nut job who tried to hide a gift and wound up in the hospital."

"Not what I was expecting to hear, but I would love to have you stay at my house. Mom" — Hope paused — "well, she might not be too keen with the idea, since at this very moment she's having one of those stair-lifts installed at the house. Just for you."

"Are you serious?"

"Yep. You know Mom. Once she gets an idea, she won't let it go. So she thought doing this would make the rest of your stay

141

easier, what with you hobbling around with crutches. Of course, she made perfect sense when she explained that she would need to use the lift herself one day when she was too old and crippled to walk upstairs. So, if you want to disappoint her, I don't have a problem with it. I would love for you to stay with me, Gracie. Truly."

"Then I'll just spend a night at your place, a night at Mom's, and maybe Dad's. It's all going to work out, Hope. I'm not angry, you know that, right?"

"So you say," Hope said, "but you should be."

"Says who?"

"Says your mother, your mom," Hope said. "Me."

"I'm an adult, remember. I know how I feel, Hope. I'm going to tell you a secret. Your birthday is next week, and Mother has planned a surprise party for you. In the garden. She's having it catered by the Ale House. And do you remember the older man who seated us the night we had dinner there? His name is Michael, and he was the principal at the elementary school where Mother taught. He's also the guy Mother has been seeing."

"Holy moly, girl. You can't keep a secret, can you."

"Yes, I can," Gracie said, "but you're a better keeper of secrets than I am. I wanted you to know that Ronan, *Dad,* is invited." She let her words soak in before she went on. "How do you feel about that?"

"I don't know."

Gracie's door opened just then. "Hope, listen, I need you to come to my room. Whatever that doctor has to say can wait. Please, it's kind of urgent."

"On my way," Hope said.

"She's on her way up," Gracie told her mother and Ronan, who had just walked into the room. "Act surprised when you see her, okay?"

Ronan O'Connor, Dr. Ronan O'Connor, all six-foot-six of him, smiled at her. He had the same gray-green eyes. The same reddish-brown hair. The same fair skin. The same as hers because Ronan O'Connor was her father. It still sounded crazy to her, but in a good way. The event that had led to this discovery, one that had almost cost her her life, was turning out to be the best news a woman could hope for. She still had trouble thinking of Hope as her mother and Mom as her grandmother. This was the secret they had spoken of that day when she had overheard them talking outside. They had always planned to tell her, but according to them, the timing had never been right.

Never in a zillion years had they expected this. When Dr. O'Connor saw Hope, he immediately remembered their relationship, the intimacy they had shared, and Hope had felt that given Gracie's medical condition, it was fate that had brought him back to Amarillo, back to a daughter he had never known he had, and back to the girl who had stolen his heart all those years ago. She had told Gracie this.

Hope pushed through the door, stopping when she saw her mother and Ronan in the room.

"I told you, Ronan, the woman is a sneak. She knew I was waiting for you in the cafeteria." Hope shook her head.

"She is a smart young lady. Smart parents," he said to Hope. "I'm proud of her, of you all, taking care of my girl." His Irish accent thickened with emotion. "I want us all together, as a family. Hope, we have a few things to work on, if you're willing?"

"Of course, whatever it takes," she said.

"Even if it means starting over? Dating, getting to know each other all over again?"

Hope grinned, her smile lighting up her beautiful brown eyes. "I'm game," she said.

Ella, who still referred to herself as Gracie's mother, and said she would always, sparkled like the brightest star in the sky. Her girl took this news better than they had expected, and now, they had Ronan in their lives.

He was forty-nine, never married — except to his work, he had said — and now, to discover he had a family, again he believed it was divine intervention that had sent him back to Amarillo.

Her father looked at her, a twinkle in his eyes. "You want to know what I think?" he asked his daughter.

She nodded.

"I think you're amazing, Gracie."

ELLA'S SWEET ICED TEA

3 family-size Luzianne tea bags (or brand
   of your choice)
6 cups water
3 cups ice
1 cup sugar
lemon slice (optional)
mint (optional)

Bring the 6 cups of water to a boil. Place
the tea bags in water; simmer for 10 minutes. Add sugar. Allow time to cool. Pour
tea and sugar mixture into a pitcher of
choice. Add 3 cups of ice. For weaker tea,
add water to desired strength.

Enjoy!

Ella

■ ■ ■ ■

MEANT TO BE

LORI FOSTER

■ ■ ■ ■

The Mother's Day party took place the week before the actual holiday, so that everyone living in the small town of Visitation, North Carolina, could take part without its disrupting their own, more private celebrations the next weekend. The townsfolk of the remote area loved having a reason to be on the large recreation lake owned by the Winston family.

It was one particular Winston, however, who occupied Cory Creed's thoughts. Without being *too* obvious, she glanced toward where he manned the refreshment shack. Because Austin Winston worked in construction, he had the very fit body of a manual laborer. When he moved, delicious muscles moved, too. Though he had a full-time job, whenever necessary, he also enjoyed lending his parents a hand at the lake.

It seemed to her that Austin was part fish, he was so often in the water. Between his job working outdoors, and his penchant for swimming, Austin's very fair hair was practically white, made more noticeable by his deep tan.

Today, he wore a loose T-shirt with board shorts, his hair typically mussed, dark sunglasses shielding his eyes.

He smiled at two kids, and Cory ached.

Unfortunately, his beautiful smiles were rarely for her.

Carrying her sandals in one hand, she made herself look away and finished crossing the sandy beach to where her mother was helping Austin's mom clear a few picnic tables. It wasn't right that the two very best mothers in the whole world were working during the party, but Cory knew them well enough to know there'd be no talking them into relaxing.

Just as she reached them, Luna, Austin's mom, said, "I think that's it for now," and after a quick friendly greeting to Cory, she hustled off toward the large house where she and Joe Winston lived, likely to grab a few more supplies.

Cory's mom smiled at her. "What a pretty dress." Teasing, she asked, "Did you wear it for anyone special?"

The yellow floral sundress did look nice with her dark hair and eyes, but she'd worn it to boost her morale, not to get attention. One, no matter what she wore, Austin wouldn't make a move. And two, she didn't care about any other guys noticing her.

"Actually . . ." Cory dropped to sit at the picnic table bench. "Do you have time to talk for a minute?"

Concern replacing her smile, her mother quickly sat. "Of course, honey. What's wrong?"

"Nothing is *wrong*, exactly."

"Baloney. I might not have your or Jamie's ability, but I have mother's intuition, and I can promise you it's stronger." Her mom put a hand to Cory's cheek. "I know you, and I know when something is bothering you."

Smile twitching into place, Cory repeated, "Mother's intuition?"

With lofty insistence, her mom stated, "All mothers have it." She considered that, then amended, "All *good* mothers, that is. Especially when they adore their children as much as I adore you."

Far too often, Cory felt like an outsider. Like her father, she had the uncanny ability to know things before they happened. Once upon a time, that gift had made her father's life a living hell — until her mom, Faith, had found him, loved him, accepted him, and in the process helped Jamie to accept everyone else.

For Cory, it had never been as bad, because she had Faith in her corner. From the time she'd been a baby, her mother had encouraged her ability, embraced it, and she'd helped Cory to understand and refine it. *Mother's intuition.* Yes, maybe it was a thing, because Faith had always known exactly what she needed and when.

Which was why Cory wanted to talk to her now. Rather than look morose — because by God, she wouldn't be — she forced a smile. "I made a decision today."

"Okay." In her typical, supportive way, Faith settled in beside her, close enough that their shoulders touched. "What kind of decision?"

Saying it out loud made it so final that the words stuck in her throat.

As she sensed Cory's uncertainty, Faith's gaze sharpened. "It has to do with Austin, doesn't it?"

See, *that.* That was why she needed her mom right now. Going for a teasing note, Cory said, "Wow, your mother's intuition is dead-on."

"Of course." Lightly, Faith tugged on one of Cory's long corkscrew curls.

"Well, I've decided it's past time that I

move on. I'm cutting Austin loose — not that I ever had him in the first place." Apparently, that had all been a figment of her imagination, or maybe wishful thinking. "I want to start over. New job, maybe new location for a while." She'd go where no one knew her, where she could be like everyone else. "Maybe a new guy, too, though I'm not in a hurry for that part of it."

At the mention of a new location, Faith's alarm showed. "You're talking about leaving Visitation?"

"Mom." Cory took her hand. "My job at the school is fun, and I love the kids, but there's no room for advancement." Just like her nonexistent relationship with Austin. "I'm twenty-three now. Past the age when I should be getting out on my own instead of living with you and Dad. But I promise I won't go far. I've been looking at jobs and apartments in the city. Only two hours away, which means we could visit often."

For long moments, Faith just stared at her before she seemed to come to a decision. "You know, it's not really your decision anymore."

"Of course it is."

Faith shook her head. "Years ago, when you were just a little girl, you knew you'd one day marry Austin. You announced it to your father and me as a foregone conclusion. Since Jamie didn't deny it, he must have recognized the statement as true."

As a remote viewer, her father had astounding ability, but his love for Cory had probably skewed his perception.

Or at least that's what Cory told herself.

Gently, Faith continued. "Regardless of how discouraged you might be right now, nothing has changed."

Maybe *she* had changed. Maybe she was no longer willing to wait for Austin to wise up.

Looking out over the lake, Cory reflected on that day so long ago. Austin had been spying on his older sister, Willow, and her boyfriend, Clay, while they swam. From the day Cory had met him, Austin had been protective of his older sister. They were extremely close.

He'd been almost fourteen at the time, and already so appealing to her ten-year-old heart. She'd surprised him, making him bonk his head on the boat trailer he hid under.

Knowing his concern for Willow, Cory had promised him that she and Clay would be fine — and they were. In fact, they'd be marrying in June.

154

Unfortunately, using a ten-year-old's candor and lack of discretion, she'd promised Austin something else, too. *One day, I'm going to marry you — and there's nothing you can do about it.*

In hindsight, she realized issuing that warning probably hadn't been the best move. For a long time after that, her nearness had freaked him out. Once he'd matured, he'd learned to just avoid her whenever possible. Now at twenty-seven, Austin watched her a lot, but whenever they spoke, he was merely polite.

In her heart, she still believed they were destined to marry — but at some point, she'd need Austin's cooperation, and she badly feared he'd fall in love with someone else first.

She'd put her life on hold long enough.

Turning in to her mother, Cory hugged her tight. In her current state of confusion, she needed her mother's understanding. "I'm sorry, Mom. I promise I'll still be around a lot. But I have to shake things up a bit."

Faith gave her a gentle smile. "Just because you know things, doesn't mean you can control them. Jamie learned that, you know. He could see problems unfolding, but he could rarely affect the outcomes. Let it be enough that you *know.* Do you think you can do that?"

"I can do it better from another place, without constantly bumping into Austin."

Faith actually laughed. "I can just imagine how he'll react to that."

"He'll be thrilled."

"That's bitterness talking." Straightening her shoulders in a familiar, stubborn way, Faith said, "You know I'll support you in any decision you make. But do you think you could try something else first? For me?"

Feeling a trap closing in — which was another thing her mother excelled at — Cory tried to change the topic. "Why don't we talk about it later? This is a Mother's Day celebration, and here I am —"

"Making me feel like the luckiest mom in the world," Faith finished for her. "You know that, don't you? You're a very special person, and having your trust, being your confidante, knowing you love me, makes me happier than you could ever imagine."

With a small laugh, Cory hugged her. "That's because you're the best mom ever. I'm so glad you took me in when you did."

"Cory," she reprimanded.

Yes, they rarely talked about the fact that Faith hadn't birthed her, had in fact accepted her from her real mother in order to keep her safe. The same unscrupulous people who'd considered her father a lab rat would have viewed Cory the same.

Only she'd been a defenseless baby instead of a grown, capable man.

"In all the ways that matter, you are my mom. One hundred percent. But I'll always be grateful that you were awesome enough to accept the challenge —"

"The honor," Faith countered.

"— and the expense —"

"The *fun,*" she insisted.

Cory's mouth twitched. "The responsibility of an infant —"

"The most wonderful gift ever."

Giving up, Cory grinned. "Okay, so I was a special, fun, pleasurable gift. Still —"

"There is no *still.* I'm incredibly proud of you. You're smart and beautiful, and I'm often in awe of your kindness."

Her kindness, not her ability. Somehow, her mother always knew what to say to cheer her up. "I love you, Mom."

"I love you, too. So very, very much."

Just then, Jamie cleared his throat. "Is it safe for me to intrude?"

Getting to her feet, Cory hugged him, too. "Dad, you never intrude, you know that. I just —"

"Needed a little time with your mother."

Of course he knew that. After all, she'd gotten her ability from him. Sometimes father and daughter could talk without words, but out of love and respect for Faith, they rarely did so in her presence.

Hands in the back pockets of his tattered jeans, dark eyes sharp with concern, Jamie held her gaze and said in that sage way of his, "You need to understand —"

"No, shush." Quickly, Cory put a finger to his mouth. "If it's about Austin, I'm done with that."

Taking her wrist, he lowered her hand. "No, you're not, and you know it."

"Jamie." Faith shooed him away. "A woman has to do things her own way."

"Mom has intuition," Cory said with a grin.

"*Mother's* intuition," Faith clarified. "That's the best, most powerful kind — and both of you, stop grinning."

Father and daughter quickly denied seeing any humor in the situation, but Cory knew her dad was just as amused as she.

"Now." Pretending to fuss, Faith smoothed Cory's untamable hair and then took her shoulders. "As your mother, I'm asking that you give it a few weeks before making any more decisions."

"It won't matter."

"And," Faith said, speaking over her, "as a woman, I'm telling you to stop being so accessible. In fact, you should leave the party. And don't look at Austin when you do."

"Leave?" No way. "It's a party for mothers. For *you*."

"We'll have our own get-together next Sunday. Besides, I don't think you'll be gone long. Just long enough for Austin to come looking for you."

Her gaze shot to Jamie's, and he nodded. Huh.

"You didn't know Austin would seek you out?" Faith asked.

"I'm blocking him." She no longer wanted to intrude on Austin's privacy. In her mind, he was free and clear, and that meant she had no rights.

"Oh, I like that," Faith said. "Keep on blocking him, okay?"

"Well . . . that's my plan."

"When he follows you, which he will, I want you to tell him all your concerns. Tell him you're giving up, okay?"

"I couldn't!" Cory figured it'd be better to simply . . . stop. Stop staring at him. Stop wanting him.

Stop loving him.

He'd get the message, and she wouldn't have to make any embarrassing confessions.

"Tell him why," Faith insisted, as if Cory hadn't refused. "You might also tell him how much you care, but you can decide that when you see how things are going."

Jamie frowned. "I don't think —"

"No, you don't. You *know,* and it's not at all the same thing. Look at it this way — falling in love is just as much fun as being in love. Let your daughter fall."

Cory choked on a laugh.

Smiling at Cory, her dad spread his arms wide and said, "Fall away — but it won't make any difference in the end."

"Don't listen to him. At least . . . not this time. Most of the time, yes, your father is brilliant. But this is the exception." Putting her arm around Cory, Faith turned her away from the table. "This time, just trust your mother."

She glanced over her shoulder, caught her dad's wink, and smiled in return. "Of course, I trust you. It's just —"

"Don't look," Faith whispered, "but Austin is watching you. He's confused, and that's a good thing. No, don't look!"

Cory froze. "Okay. Not looking." But man, the urge to verify her mom's claim was strong. *If* Austin watched her, it was probably out of wariness, because he was worried she'd approach him.

Again.

This time, he'd be relieved to find she did not give him a glance. "If you really think I should head out for a bit, I will." In her twenty-three years, her mother had never steered her wrong. "Actually, I wouldn't mind a little time just sitting on the mountain."

In a quick about-face, Faith said, "Don't go too far. Bobcats, bears, snakes, spiders —"

Again, her dad interrupted. "Solitude, nature, fresh air."

Faith narrowed her eyes. "You're assuring me she'll be fine?"

"Yes."

Since they both trusted Jamie's abilities without question, that settled that.

"Well, all right then." Faith smiled. "Besides, Austin will join you soon enough."

"And he's better at fighting bears than I am?"

"Safety in numbers," Faith insisted. "One more thing before you go."

"All right."

"There's a four year age difference between you and Austin. When you were fourteen and infatuated, he was an eighteen-year-old young man. By the time you turned eighteen, he was already twenty-two, working full time and ready to live on his own. I know you think you've been waiting forever, but I promise you, if he had approached you before you were of age, Jamie and I would have put a stop to it."

Cory didn't quite follow, but she nodded.

"My point," Faith said, "is that you think you've waited such a very long time, when really, it's only been a few years. Give Austin a chance to realize you're a woman now, not an underage girl who's merely smitten."

Wow. Realizing her mom was right, Cory smiled. "You're amazing."

Faith accepted that as her due. "Now go. And don't glance at him even once."

Nodding, Cory started away. "I won't be long. Maybe an hour or two."

With love in her eyes, Faith said, "Honey, you take all the time you need."

Austin Winston couldn't quite pull his gaze away from Cory. Somehow, he always sensed her nearness, so from the moment she'd shown up at the lake, he'd been aware of her — and braced himself for her impact. Usually, she'd make a beeline for him, and he had to be ready.

Today she didn't acknowledge him at all. In fact, she appeared lost in thought as she headed away from the party.

Tracking her, Austin took in the yellow sundress that drifted around her knees with her long stride. The proud set of her shoulders, the angle of her face in the sun.

The way those dark curls tumbled around her — and how she affected him.

Then he realized he wasn't the only guy looking. Hell, every single guy on the beach was watching her. A few even tried to engage her in conversation.

The bastards were flirting with her!

Why the hell hadn't he noticed that sooner? Volatile emotion put a cloud over his mood.

Cory had chased him forever, from the time she was just a girl. He'd come to think of her as *his*.

For years, she'd claimed they'd marry one day. Since she had uncanny abilities to know things like that, he'd believed her.

Still, he'd insisted they wouldn't. It was mostly her abilities that put him off. He wanted to be in charge of his own destiny, not have his fate decided by a gifted girl with strange insight.

Now, with him twenty-seven and her twenty-three, had she given up on the notion?

Had she given up on him?

There were three guys in particular whom

she spoke with. Austin knew them, liked them overall — but he didn't like them flirting with Cory.

Whatever they said made her smile, then laugh lightly. They'd amused her?

Finally, she moved on, and the minute she did, her smile faded to resolute determination. Without others watching, she looked far too . . . subdued.

Very unlike her.

"Two Cokes, please."

Blinking away the distraction, Austin realized a couple of girls in their late teens stood at the shack, eyeballing him with a little too much interest.

"Sure thing." He turned to dump ice in the cups, then used the dispenser to fill them. Handing the drinks over, he made sure his smile was only polite.

Yet even after they paid, the girls lingered. They tried to engage him in conversation. One of them boldly eyed him.

See, this was generally the moment when Cory would step up. She always seemed to know when he had unwanted attention, and she never minded running interference.

Even when the attention was *welcome,* Cory tried her best to put a stop to it. She was headstrong, determined, possessive where he was concerned . . . and leaving the party.

Why?

"Have fun," he said to the girls in obvious dismissal, turning his back as he fake-worked on organizing a shelf. The ploy was successful, and with relief, Austin watched them leave.

The usual refreshments were offered from the shack, along with special drink discounts for moms. A lot of young people had stopped by to get ice creams, colas, snacks . . . and many of them bought things for their mothers. All in all, it kept him busy.

The weather cooperated, with eighty-two degrees and a vibrant blue sky that reflected off the surface of the large lake. With the water still cold, adults were mostly watching from lounge chairs and picnic tables along the shoreline, or paddling in kayaks. The water temp didn't slow down the kids, though. They ran along the shore, jumped and splashed, and overall had a great time.

If he hadn't offered to help out today, Austin would have been in the lake already, too. He'd always loved the water.

At the moment, he enjoyed watching Cory more.

Every ten steps she took, someone stopped her to chat. Far too often, it was a group of guys.

He was scowling over that when Joe Winston, whom he now considered Dad in all meaningful ways, stopped by the snack shack with his arms loaded. Austin quickly opened the back door for him so Joe could carry in the supplies.

"How's it going?" Joe asked. "Need any help?"

"Not yet, no." He'd been manning the shack for over two hours already, but the time passed quickly. Or at least it had until he'd realized Cory was leaving.

"You need to enjoy the party, too."

"Willow's coming over with Clay any minute now, and they'll give me a couple of hours off."

With a shake of his head, Joe said, "Those two are never separated for more than a few minutes."

Austin grinned. "Clay doesn't want to take a chance on her getting away." His sister and her fiancé would officially tie the knot next month. Austin was surprised Clay had agreed to wait that long. Their relationship had started when Willow was only fourteen, and had gone through a few ups and downs, including time apart for college. But Willow was happy, Clay loved her like crazy, and Austin believed they'd have a good life together.

It helped that Cory had claimed his belief true. Really, that was all the reassurance he needed . . . because Cory was never wrong.

She'd also claimed he would marry her.

So why did it suddenly feel like everything was different?

Distracted by that thought, Austin took the most cumbersome box from Joe and set it on the counter to be unloaded. "Anything you want me to do once they take over here?"

Joe clapped him on the back. "Actually, I do have a favor to ask."

"Name it."

"Will you keep an eye on Cory?"

Given how she currently occupied his thoughts, Austin stalled. "Cory?"

"I don't know," Joe said. "She looks . . . down? It's not like her, and it worries your mom."

Austin adored Luna too much to let her worry, if he could do anything about it.

Yeah, that excuse works as well as any.

Was something bothering Cory? Was that why she'd ignored him? Wanting clarification, Austin asked, "Down how?"

"You know Cory."

Yeah, knew her well. Wanted her more often than he'd admit. Couldn't help but care about her.

But he was also in the long-standing habit of denying her.

"Sure," he said, keeping his reply innocuous. "She did seem lost in thought."

Austin considered the guys who'd chatted her up . . . but no, she'd laughed with them.

So what could it be? With her indomitable optimism about life, Cory was one of the most confident, upbeat women he'd ever known.

"Not sure what it is," Joe said, while breaking down an empty box. "I know she's chased you; I know you're not interested." Here, Joe glanced at him, waiting for confirmation.

Not interested? Of course he was, but he wouldn't admit that to Joe, so he only frowned.

Joe gave one small shake of his head and continued. "You're still friends, right? And I have a bad feeling."

Hell, a bad feeling from Joe was always alarming. He was a badass in the extreme, with sharply honed instincts that hadn't faded over time. He might not be a cop or bounty hunter anymore, and running a recreation lake wasn't dangerous, but Joe had never lost his edge.

"It can't be anything big, right? Cory knows" — Austin gestured — "things, right?

If it was anything serious, like a threat, she'd know about it in advance, and she'd tell someone." *Would she tell him?* Probably not — and that was his own damn fault.

"She's insightful," Joe agreed. "But just like gut instincts, what you feel isn't always easy to sort out."

Maybe for the average person, but for Cory? She'd inherited some unsettling talents from Jamie. Oddly, when it came to her dad, Austin didn't mind. Jamie was a fun character, mysterious, kind — and he'd been like a watchful guardian angel for the people of Visitation.

With Cory, it was a whole different matter.

For one thing, Cory claimed they would marry.

Frowning, Austin stepped to the front of the shack, found two people waiting in line, and with a quick apology, filled their orders while surreptitiously searching for Cory.

Finally, thanks to that bright yellow dress, he spotted her heading into the woods at the end of the property. Even from a distance, he saw that a frisky breeze molded the dress to her body.

Such a body it was. Though she never emphasized her curves, or dressed to draw attention, to him — probably to most guys

169

— it was impossible to miss. Somewhere along the way, Cory had gone from being a thin, long-legged girl, to a very soft, shapely woman. With her dark, silky curls unrestrained, she looked like a dream — the kind he had late at night, alone in his bed, when his thoughts got unruly.

The second he was hugged from behind, Austin recognized Luna's embrace. Comfort, that's what she brought to him. So many different levels of comfort.

Already smiling, he turned to face her, which made it easier for Luna to squeeze him tight. Over her head, Austin saw Joe grin.

"Hey." With a quick squeeze of his own, Austin set her back. "What brought that on?"

"I love you, that's what." Luna put a hand to his jaw. "It always amazes me how big you've gotten."

With a crooked grin, he said, "I couldn't stay a boy forever."

"I know. Now you're a handsome man, but to me, you'll always be that adorable nine-year-old rascal who stole my heart within minutes."

Chiming in, Joe said, "I still remember the black eye you sported the day we first met you." He grinned. "You were such a tough little nut."

"But such a cute nut," Luna qualified.

Austin choked on a laugh. At nine, he'd been contentious, covered in dirt, and full of attitude.

Remembering all that, he drew Luna back for yet another, longer hug, this time lifting her off her feet. He remembered meeting her for the first time, too, and being afraid to hope. Luna, being such an amazing person, had quickly reassured him. "I love you, too." He never minded telling her so. "I hope you're having fun?"

"I'm having a great time."

Joe moved up next to her. "Trying to get her to take the day off isn't easy. She keeps pitching in."

Sounded like Luna. She'd always been a whirlwind of activity. Pretending to be stern, Austin said, "The party is for moms, and you're the best mom, so you should be enjoying it."

The compliment put an *aww* expression on her face. "I enjoy making sure it's enjoyable for everyone."

Giving up with a laugh, Austin said, "I tried."

"I brought you something." Reaching back, Luna lifted a small bouquet of white carnations. "We're giving a flower to each of the mothers today. I thought of Chloe, of how much she loved you and Willow . . ." Letting the words trail off, she handed the bouquet to him. "I wanted you to have these for her."

It was just like Luna to make such an amazingly generous gesture.

In the background, there but not over-shadowing the emotions now touching his heart, Austin heard children playing, adults talking. The lake was a fun and busy hang-out . . . although there'd been a short time after he'd lost his mother, Chloe, when other relatives had shut it all down.

Back then, it seemed he and his sister Wil-low, as well as the lake, were too much trouble for anyone to deal with. Though their father had given the property to their mother as a way for her to support herself and them, he'd never acknowledged Austin or Willow as his own. When Chloe unexpect-edly died, they'd been alone, lost, and afraid, facing one uncaring relative after another, as well as the constant threat that they might be separated.

But that was before Luna had breezed in to take over. As a distant cousin, she'd claimed to know nothing about being a mother, yet that hadn't stopped her from loving them fiercely, understanding their grief, giving her unconditional support, and making them finally feel secure again.

They loved and missed their mom, but in every meaningful way, Luna had raised them. Even better, not once had she ever downplayed Austin's love of his real mom. He'd grown up knowing Luna didn't want to replace Chloe, just fill the empty spots left after her death.

There wasn't a day that Austin didn't give thanks for having her in his life. They'd talked a few times about him calling her "Mom," back when he'd been younger. With tears in her eyes, Luna had explained that she was happy with whatever he wanted to call her, as long as he knew that his mother had loved him, and that she loved him, too.

As a kid, he'd been astounded by her. As an adult, he marveled at how she'd changed her entire life for his sister and him.

In a million ways, he showed her how much she meant to him — and she showed him, too.

What he called her really didn't matter.

With her colorful hair and quirky fashion sense, Luna didn't look like a mother. To Austin, she looked better. Filled with kindness and a wealth of love.

Finally, the flowers held awkwardly in his

big hands, he said, "You are very, very special to me. Thank you."

A cagey look entered her golden eyes. "I'm also very observant, and I noticed you watching Cory."

Damn, nothing got by her. Trying to deflect, Austin downplayed his personal interest. "Joe said she was down?"

"Yes. Something is wrong. I feel it. Would you mind terribly checking on her?"

Surprise took him back a step. Sure, it was what he wanted to do, but he was so used to resisting . . . "I don't know where she went."

Patting his chest, Luna said, "I'm sure you'll figure it out," as if that were a foregone conclusion.

He looked at Joe, caught his shrug, and gave up. "I'll go once Willow and Clay get here to give me a break."

"Go now," Luna said softly. "Joe and I will watch things."

He almost groaned. "It's a *Mother's Day* party —"

"And Willow and Clay will be here any minute. Now go on, before she gets away."

Rubbing the back of his neck, Austin considered that.

. . . *before she gets away.*

"She will, you know." Luna moved closer

in a show of sympathy and understanding. "A woman will only wait so long."

"She's only twenty-three."

"And plenty of young men are interested. Pretty sure you noticed *that,* as well."

Yeah, he had.

"What would you do if Cory moved away?"

A terrible foreboding went up his spine. "Move away?"

"If she's not happy here, she just might, you know. Then what? Would you miss her?"

Scoffing, he said, "She's not going anywhere. Visitation is home." Wasn't it? "Jamie and Faith are here."

"Which only means she would always visit, not that she'd live here."

Did Luna know something?

"Go," she gently urged. "I have a feeling you have some things to work out, and it'll be best if you and Cory work them out together."

Never before had Luna involved herself in his personal relationships. But then, never before had he been serious about any girl. Cory *was* different — especially how he felt about her.

With new purpose, Austin said, "Right. Okay, sure. But I need to get Sully first."

As if he'd summoned them, his younger

sister, Raine, came to the refreshment counter, leading Sully with a leash. Since Luna and Joe were Raine's parents, her coloring was very different from his and Willow's. They had pale blond hair and dark brown eyes, but Raine, who'd recently turned sixteen, had hair as dark as Joe's, with golden brown eyes like Luna.

While they looked nothing alike, his sisters were both very pretty.

Sully, his adopted boxer stray, jumped up so he could see Austin over the service counter, then gave a friendly "woof" in greeting. After swimming in the lake, he looked happy but tuckered out.

Usually, when Austin wasn't working, Sully wouldn't let him out of his sight. But he loved the lake, and he adored Raine.

"Perfect timing," Austin said, giving Luna one last, quick hug, and Joe a shoulder clap. Something drove him, some vague urgency, spurred no doubt by Luna's concern, and it was telling him that he had to hurry.

After he'd rounded the shack and taken Sully's leash, Raine touched his arm. "She went across the road and up the mountain."

Did everyone know his freaking business? Playing dumb, Austin asked, "She who?"

Not at all fooled, Raine smirked. "Sully is wet, but you don't need your truck, anyway.

You'll catch up quicker on foot."

Blowing out a breath, Austin gave up all pretense of protesting. "Got it, thanks." He took off at a fast, determined stride.

Behind him, Raine laughed, Joe said something low, and Luna shushed them both. *She* didn't laugh. No, Luna had always taken his happiness very seriously, and apparently, she thought chasing after Cory would make him happy.

With the feeling she might be right, he glanced down at his dog. "You want to run, Sully?"

Given how the dog broke into a lope, the answer was *yes.*

CHAPTER TWO

"If I was ever going to be a mother," Cory said softly, "I'd want to be just like Mom and Luna."

Knowing he was busted, Austin looked down at Sully, who'd been very quiet as they approached. Didn't matter that they hadn't made a single sound. No twig had snapped. No dry leaves on the ground had rustled.

Nothing ever got by Cory.

Ever since they were kids, Cory had always known what he was doing, when he'd do it, and with whom he planned to do it.

She'd probably known he would follow her, too. Maybe that's why she'd taken off in the first place? To get him alone? Yeah, he liked that idea.

Stepping away from the trees, he and Sully approached.

They were high up on a slope overlooking the lake, but luckily, not deep into the mountain.

178

Like her father, Cory thought nothing of pushing through the thick brush and tackling the steep inclines. She never thought about wild animals, recluse spiders, or ticks.

Because Austin *did,* he preferred wide, well-worn trails . . . and luckily, Cory had used one this time, just as Raine had said. Usually, Sully had no respect for personal space and would jump right into Cory's lap. But the dog was wet and now had dirty paws, so Austin held him back.

It was cooler here in the shade of the evergreens. The spring rain two days ago had left the air fragrant, the ground loamy, and everything a vibrant green.

Austin waited for Cory to invite him over.

She didn't. In fact, other than that comment about the moms, she ignored him.

Something about her posture, the set of her narrow shoulders and the dip of her head, kept Austin alert. She looked . . . alone.

A horrible thought occurred to him: Maybe she'd left the party to *get away from him.*

As he stared at her, the wind moved those dark, corkscrew curls that couldn't be tamed.

Her hair had played into a few of his private fantasies. Dark, silky, free like

Cory . . . That wild hair framed an expressive face dominated by dark eyes that always saw too much.

With fair skin, a slender nose, and a lush mouth usually curved in a smile, Cory had matured from a cute kid into a stunning woman.

For years now, it seemed there'd been a spark between them, ever since she'd moved to Visitation as a little girl. She'd taken to him right off, dogging his heels, often in his head, and her mysterious eyes never failed to stare into his soul.

Before now, she'd never been reserved with him. It left him unsure how to greet her.

When she didn't say anything else, Austin stepped forward and sat beside her on one of the many jutting rocks. Her spine straightened, as if he'd surprised her.

Had she expected him to walk away?

Yeah, he sometimes had. Not because she wasn't appealing. Hell no. He couldn't think of a single woman with more sensual impact than Cory Creed.

But there'd been times when her perception made him uneasy; around her, it felt like he lost control, as if she called the shots. It was unnerving.

When he patted the space between them,

Sully came forward and snuffled against her elbow. Smiling, Cory lifted a hand and stroked his back. Satisfied that he, at least, was welcome, the dog stretched out and closed his eyes in contentment.

Silence fell between them.

From the spot she'd chosen, he could easily see the lake and beach below, as well as her mother, Faith, who stood talking with his mother, Luna.

Harking back to what she'd said, Austin frowned. "What do you mean *if* you were ever going to be a mom? Someday you'll have kids, right?" Over the years, she'd claimed that they would marry. Just because he hadn't taken the bait, that didn't mean she couldn't find someone else —

No, scratch that. Even the thought of her with another man burned his ass. But if she didn't marry him, she'd definitely choose someone else. He should have considered that sooner.

"No." Gently, she continued to stroke Sully.

Seeing her long lashes in profile, the dusky flush to her cheeks, kept him off kilter. "No what?"

"No, I won't ever be a mom."

Austin didn't like the way she said that with such finality. "Of course you will. You

181

being you, you'll make a terrific mother."

She slanted him a mean, speculative look. "Me being me?"

He'd meant with all her empathy, her ability to understand things. But the way she was looking at him . . . "You're a special person."

For only a second, she considered him; then she looked away. "I would never do this to another kid. Not ever."

Her conviction was different. Deeper. Cory wasn't teasing, wasn't trying to wheedle her way into his life.

She didn't look sad, so much as resigned, and it bothered him a lot. "You mean because of what you know? Your perception of things?"

One narrow shoulder lifted. "It wasn't easy being me, Austin. Not as a child." A slight hesitation, and then, "I scared people."

The unspoken words hung in the air between them: *I scared you.*

The urge to touch her swelled inside him. He curled his fingers tight to resist. "Not your mom."

Her expression softened. "No, not her. Not ever. She said she figured me out early, then learned to adapt." Her smile brightened a little more. "She changed her entire life for me. There's no one else in the world like her."

Everyone in Visitation now knew that Faith wasn't Cory's biological mother. As a remote viewer, Cory's father had abilities that few understood. He saw things that hadn't yet happened, knew things that no one else knew — just like his daughter.

But Jamie hadn't known about Cory. Emotion, Jamie said, skewed his perception.

He'd had one hell of a surprise when Faith brought them together. One look at Cory with her dad, and anyone could see they were related. She was a smaller, more delicate, definitely more feminine version of Jamie.

Cory twisted to face him, readjusting her position to sit yoga style despite the pretty dress, which she tucked in around her legs for modesty. "Different as we might be, you and I have that in common. Both of us love mothers who didn't give us life."

"True," he said, a little edgy whenever she turned that direct gaze on him, and maybe that's why he blundered in saying, "Though I had a mom who loved me before she died." He lifted the flowers Luna had given him. "I thank God for Luna all the time, but I haven't forgotten my mother, and neither has she."

Cory's smile faded. "I never knew my birth mother." Frowning a little, she looked down at her hands. "Mom says that my real mother cared enough about me to give me away so I'd stay safe. I guess that's something."

Damn, he should kick his own ass. Instead, he pulled a pretty white flower out of the bouquet and handed it to her.

Her brows twitched in confusion. "What's this?"

"I'm sure Faith is right. Your mother made the ultimate sacrifice. That had to be really hard for her." He trailed the petals over her knuckles. "She deserves a flower, too, right?"

Accepting it, Cory lifted it to her nose. "Thanks."

Austin rubbed the back of his neck, but the tension there continued to grow. He glanced at Sully, and the dog stared back in what looked like accusation.

This close to Cory, he breathed in the scent of warm skin and soft woman. His muscles tightened. "Why didn't you stay at the party?"

She countered with, "Why didn't you?"

Hoping to tease her into a more receptive mood, he asked, "You mean you don't already know?"

"I assume you followed me."

Austin's jaw loosened. "You *assume*?" Cory never had to assume. She always *knew* with rock-solid certainty.

Heaving a dramatic sigh, she said, "Actually, I blocked you," as if that wasn't momentous news. "So yeah, assuming is all I can do."

Rearing back, equal parts irate and disbelieving, Austin glared at her. "You blocked me *when*?"

"Few days ago." She twirled the flower, then teased it over Sully's nose. He started to eat it, making her smile. "No, you don't." Uncaring that his fur hadn't completely dried, she gave the dog a hug and went back to watching the party from a distance.

Ready for a nap, Sully licked his chops — something he did obsessively before he slept — then he got comfortable beside Cory, his head on his paws, his body leaning into her leg.

Austin wasn't sure what to say, so he only asked, "Why?"

"I'm twenty-three. You're twenty-seven. Nothing much has changed from that long-ago day when you said you'd never marry me. I figured it was time to let you off the hook."

An edgy sort of panic ignited in his gut. "You said it was already decided."

"Guess I don't know as much as I thought I did."

No, that wasn't right. Cory never second-guessed herself. Hell, he'd grown used to the idea of *them.* Used to her always being around.

Used to her wanting him.

Used to the idea that it was inevitable, that someday they'd be a couple — because she'd said so.

"It's my own fault," she responded, to a question he hadn't asked. "For years, I thought of you as mine. The thing is, when I was younger, I wasn't as adept at interpreting the jumble of emotions and images in my head. I liked you. I thought you were funny and cute. I enjoyed your company." She turned her face to the side. "You seemed so perfect to me, maybe I just daydreamed about marrying you, and then it felt so real . . ."

Heat went up his neck, turning his voice to a low grumble. "I'm far from perfect, and you know it."

"I guess. But you are gorgeous."

He had no idea what to say to that.

"Girls have always thought so," she went on. "And you're strong, with really solid shoulders, and muscular thighs —"

"Cory." The way she mentioned his thighs,

the intensity with which she looked at him there while speaking, felt like a special type of foreplay. "I work in construction. Being fit is just part of the job."

"You're also really nice. And everyone knows you're dedicated to your family."

"You're just seeing what you want to see."

Her mouth twitched. "Should I add modesty to that list of qualities?"

Snorting, Austin denied that claim. "I'm not modest."

"No reason to be." She laid the flower aside. "The thing is, I liked your imperfections as much as the rest of you. Mom always told me that no one was perfect, but that when I found the right person, I wouldn't mind the flaws too much."

His brain was still stuck on *when you meet the right person*. He thought *he* was the right person. Was Faith trying to talk her into other guys?

Cory's gaze met his. "I never minded your flaws."

Being accepted like that . . . it was far too appealing.

She looked away. "I've known for a while that you don't feel the same."

Though she didn't actually move, Austin felt her withdraw, if not physically, then surely emotionally. He wanted to get closer, to touch her. To bring her back to him.

Her smile went crooked. "I guess it just took me a little longer to accept it."

"And if I don't accept it?" Wait, what? Austin flattened his mouth, appalled that he'd said such a thing.

Not that Cory seemed to give any credence to his words. The look she sent him claimed *bullshit.*

And damned if that didn't fill him with new resolve.

"I'm planning to relocate," she said, knocking him off his feet again.

So Luna had been right about that? With air in short supply, he wheezed, "You're leaving Visitation?"

"I want to start over — new job, my own place." She glanced at him. "Dating."

What? Oh, hell no.

As if it didn't matter much, she said, "Everyone here knows me."

"Of course, they do." They knew her, liked and respected her.

"They know what I am, too. Now that I've decided to block people —"

So she wasn't just blocking him? She was completely denying her ability? He didn't want that. Cory's talents were an integral part of her. Like Luna's big heart and Joe's protectiveness.

"— I can start new," she said. "So far, I've looked at jobs and apartments in Raleigh."

Screw that. "Raleigh is too far away."

"A few hours." Negligently, as if it didn't matter, she stared off at nothing in particular. "Wherever I go, I promised Mom I'd visit a lot." Slanting him a look, she said, "But you wouldn't have to see me when I'm here. We could both get on with our lives."

Slowly straightening, Austin narrowed his eyes. "What if I want to see you?"

As if instructing a nitwit, she said slowly, "But . . . you don't."

No, he hadn't. Or at least he hadn't admitted it. But that was when he thought she'd still be around — and didn't that make him sound like a selfish ass?

Firmly, he said, "Yes, I do."

Her brows lifted. "You don't even like me."

"The hell I don't."

Both Cory and Sully gave him curious looks. Yeah, he'd just growled out that denial. *Way to win her over, idiot.*

"I like you, all right?" Unfortunately, for as long as they'd known each other, he'd been critical of her ability, seeing it as a liability instead of a valuable asset.

Damn, he'd been a total dick. Good thing Luna had convinced him to go after her, or she might have moved away without even telling him.

As if he'd surprised her, she continued to give him appraising looks. "Mom wanted me to give it a few more weeks. I sort of promised her I would."

Thank God. He released a tense breath — and immediately started figuring out how to convince her to stay. "You still have your job at the school?" Cory worked with kids who needed a little extra help in kindergarten and first grade. Her compassion and empathy made her ideal for the position.

"I won't quit until I've found something new."

So he still had a little time. "No big rush, right?"

"I already have a few feelers out for jobs. If one of those comes through —"

"I agree with your mom." *Growling again.* He really needed to get a handle on that. Sawing his teeth together, Austin struggled to sound more reasonable. "Give it a few weeks." There. That was better. For good measure, he added, "Promise me."

Obviously confused by his admittedly abrupt turnaround, she frowned. "I don't understand you."

He barely understood himself. All he knew was that he didn't want to lose her. *So why not tell her?*

Needing her to believe it, Austin stared into her spell-binding eyes. "I want you to stay."

In a barely there whisper, she asked, "Why?"

Damn, good question. Unfortunately, he didn't yet have a good answer.

He was saved when, with perfect timing, Sully began to snore. They both looked at the dog.

They both smiled, too.

Needing a minute to sort his thoughts, Austin put a hand on the dog's ruff. "He swam with Raine while I ran the shack. Guess he wore himself out."

"He's getting older."

"Ten," Austin agreed.

"Thirteen," she corrected — then winced. "Sorry. I didn't mean —"

"You know his age?" When she looked away, guilt burned through him. Had he done that to her? Made her ashamed of her gift? Without thinking it through, Austin touched her arm, and that quickly regained her attention.

Her skin was soft and warm. He wanted to curl his fingers around her, brush his thumb over her to absorb more of that softness.

He wanted to touch her everywhere. *Kiss* her everywhere.

He suddenly wanted that with consuming greed.

Fascinated, unmoving, Cory stared first at where he'd caressed her, then at his face. He saw her swallow.

Such a reaction. Maybe she liked the connection as much as he did. Hoping so, willing to build on that possibility, Austin retrenched enough to keep her at ease.

Sully seemed like a safe enough topic at the moment. "You remember when I found him sitting there in the middle of the road with a too-tight collar around his throat?"

"Yes." Her gentle voice soothed the awful memory. "You two were perfect for each other."

"I remember you telling me that." She'd told him a lot that day, including the information that Sully had escaped a neglectful owner and would be much happier with him.

It was one of his favorite revelations, because now he and Sully were best buds. "Did I ever thank you for that?"

"No."

He couldn't resist smoothing back one long, winding hank of hair. "Thank you."

Cory bit her lip. "You're welcome."

Seeing he'd unsettled her, Austin moved his hand back to the dog. "Thirteen, huh?" Older than he'd realized. No wonder the old guy was tired. "I'm glad you told me."

Watching him closely, she nodded.

"So." He looked her over. "What else did you see? About us, I mean?" Why had he never asked her before? Sitting here now, talking under the shade of tall trees with birds singing in the background, it seemed the most natural thing in the world.

Cory looked back down at the partygoers. "It was a mistake, telling you that we'd marry. It made you defensive and angry."

"We were both so young then." Dog hair now stuck to the skirt of her sundress, and perspiration put a sheen on her cheekbones. The heat enhanced her delicate scent, and he unconsciously breathed deeper to get more. He noticed every little thing about her, liking it all, and his voice went a little huskier. "We're not kids anymore."

He watched the slow rise and fall of her chest as she breathed, the hypnotic way she continued to pet Sully.

Crazily enough, he was a little jealous of his dog.

"Mom often warned me that I needed to temper what I revealed." Her lashes swept down, hiding her eyes. "So many times she's given me good advice. Unfortunately, I didn't always listen." She turned that dark, riveting gaze on him. "Now, I'm trying to be different."

Meaning she wouldn't give him any other details? Unable to accept that, Austin dropped his attention to her mouth, and that's where it stayed. "I don't want to be seen as a mistake."

"I didn't mean . . ."

Hoping to convince her, he said again, "Tell me what else you saw."

Instead, she dusted off her hands. "You don't really want to know, and I should be getting back."

When she started to rise, he wrapped his fingers around her slender forearm, not to restrain, but to entice. "Stay," he implored. "Just a little longer?"

Blinking in surprise, she settled back. "You really want to hear this?"

The smile took him by surprise, but he suddenly felt good, all because Cory would stay. "Yeah, I do."

As if she didn't quite believe him, she searched his expression. "I'm trying to let you go."

Knowing it was his own fault, he took that one on the chin. He'd taken her for granted. She had every right to walk away, but he'd do what he could to change her mind. "So did you see us getting married? Or did you only assume we would?"

She breathed a little harder.

Yeah, he knew he'd thrown her. The force of his emotions threw him, too, but Luna had made it clear what she thought, and he trusted her with all his heart.

It felt destined. Him and Cory.

The connection.

More.

So he stayed put and waited.

After an uncertain exhalation, Cory shook her head. "No, I didn't see a wedding, but I did see us on the lake with a small cottage built on the land your parents own, between where they live and where my parents live." She pointed. "Over in that wooded spot."

Incredulous, Austin stared at the plot of land she indicated. "I've been planning to build a house there. I've already talked to Joe about it. There's a natural clearing —"

"With a stream," she added. "And a lot of trees behind it."

Stunned, Austin stared at her. "I've never mentioned it." Not to anyone.

She gave a self-conscious shrug. "You didn't have to."

Because she'd seen it. Amazing, talented Cory.

Excited by the prospect of his plans becoming reality, he grinned. "Tell me more."

She hesitated, but not for long. "There's a giant boulder with a tree growing off the side. You'll build your house near it, because you like it."

"As a kid, I used to climb that rock, pretending it was a mountain."

A smile flickered over her mouth. "You figured one day your own kids would play on it."

"You've seen all that?" he asked, subtly shifting over a few inches.

She brought the flower to her nose. "Luna will insist on clearing a path between the houses, because she'll want you to visit often, and vice versa." She teased the flower over her lips — and teased him in the process. "You'll insist on a nice wraparound porch so you can sit out there in the evenings and enjoy all the wildlife."

"With a view of the lake?" That was his plan. Did she know it?

"Not the main lake, no, but you'll overlook the winding cove. Tall pines on the other side will give you privacy. The biggest fish loll there. Snappers, too. It's scenic, so you'll create a footpath to it, with a dock and a fishing boat, a couple of wooden chairs."

Expression guarded, she glanced at him and smiled. "It's pretty."

What she described was totally accurate to what he'd envisioned. "You said my kids would play on the big rock?"

Apprehension had her gaze skipping away.

When she said nothing else, Austin gave in to the urge to get nearer. Bracing one hand on the other side of Sully brought him near enough to take the edge off his need. "Will you tell me about them?"

"I shouldn't."

Because he wouldn't have those kids — unless he had them with her? With a nudge, he encouraged her. "C'mon. Tell me."

A little breathless, she asked, "You're sure you want to hear it?"

He might not have Cory's ability, but he was a man, and he felt the chemistry arcing hotly between them. Better yet, he knew she felt it, too. "I'm sure."

Tentative, she let a heartbeat of silence pass before giving in. "You'll have two sons, and like you, they'll love the water."

With the back of his knuckles, Austin brushed her jaw, over her neck, then her shoulder. Her softness drew him again and again.

Clearly puzzled, she watched him — but didn't move away.

197

I've got you now. She might not admit it, but she liked being touched as much as he enjoyed touching her. Each contact ratcheted the tension a little higher until he felt her anticipation of what would come next.

"No little girls?" With dark twisting curls and big soulful eyes. Why was he suddenly so sure there would also be a girl?

She looked away without replying.

"Cory." He trailed his fingers along her collarbone . . . and his voice went husky. "Who's their mother?"

"I don't know."

"Bull." Wanting to kiss her so badly made it difficult to think of anything else. "Tell me."

"No."

Fine; for now, he'd focus on the boys. "Do they have my blond hair, or is it dark like yours?"

A slight trembling gave away her emotional struggle. She stared straight ahead. "You don't want to do this, Austin. You've been clear on that."

Ignoring that weak protest, he moved his hand to the back of her neck. She was so physically delicate . . . and so emotionally strong. At least in most instances. Here, now, with him, she seemed incredibly fragile.

And he knew it was his fault. But he would fix things. Somehow. Honesty would be a good start. "I think one will look like me — and the other like you."

Denial tightened her features, and suddenly she blurted, "You've never even kissed me!" To emphasize his hold on her neck, she shrugged beneath his hand. "This is the first time you've really touched me. How the heck do you think we'd have kids when —"

Leaning in, he whispered, "I'm going to kiss you now."

"Now?"

That squeaky voice told him he'd surprised her yet again. Instead of denying him, though, she stared at his mouth . . . and wavered closer.

"You want me to." Unable to resist a second more, Austin lightly brushed his mouth over hers. Warm but fleeting. A tease.

A promise.

Against her lips, he growled, "Don't you?"

For an answer, she reached over Sully and grabbed his neck, smashing her mouth to his, giving a vibrating groan as she did so, almost making him laugh — and disrupting the dog's nap.

Grumbling, Sully sat up, forcing them apart.

After a glare of censure, the dog crawled out from between them, turned a tight circle, loudly licked his chops multiple times, and collapsed again with a huff.

Through it all, Austin stared into her eyes. Neither of them blinked.

Breathing harder, Cory licked her lips. "That was —"

"A start." Without the dog as a barrier, he lifted Cory over and onto his lap. "Let's try this again."

"I don't understand —"

Taking control of the kiss this time, he started light and easy. His lips to hers. Pressing, holding. Her warm breath accelerated. Her fingers contracted on his shoulders.

His Cory was a powder keg of volatile need.

One arm around her back, the other over her waist, he kept her close and lightly touched his tongue to her parted lips.

It wasn't enough.

Turning his head for a better fit, he nudged her mouth wider, licked in, explored.

And finally, he tasted her the way he really wanted.

Lord, she was hot.

For a second or two, Cory went still, just absorbing the kiss, accepting it. But that didn't last. She wasn't a passive woman who didn't take part in life. Not his Cory.

Making a small sound of hunger, she fisted her hands in his shirt and pressed herself tighter to him. As she opened for him, her tongue dueled with his and turned the kiss scorching.

Her eagerness was contagious, pushing him closer to the edge — or maybe it was her addictive taste, the fresh, stirring scent of her, and how it felt to have her rounded backside snuggled in so close.

That backside . . . yeah, he'd been admiring her body for years, maybe more years than he should have. Though the two-piece swimsuit she often favored when swimming was tame compared to what most women wore to the lake, no one else affected him like she did.

Bending over her, he deepened the kiss, constantly readjusting, deeper, hotter. Her hair hung over his forearm, and her breasts pressed to his chest.

Everything combined to weaken his control.

The surge of lust, mixed with tenderness, left him a little lost. He had to ease up before he completely forgot himself. They were in the woods, on a damned hill, with the whole of Visitation not far below.

As she'd said, it was their first kiss, and he had no business taking it so far, so fast.

Leaving her with little pecks along her stubborn jaw and light nuzzles against her fragrant neck, Austin straightened to see her expression.

Eyes heavy, lips wet, she regarded him with what looked like awe.

Christ, she was beautiful. No one had ever looked at him the way Cory did. Like a man with an addiction, he craved more.

Her breath shuddered in. "That was . . ." At a loss for words, she exhaled shakily. "Wow."

"Yeah. For me, too." Smiling from the inside out, Austin murmured, "Are you still blocking me?"

Her attention went to his mouth. "Mmm?"

"Cory?" Her dazed confusion warmed him. "Are you in my head?"

"No." Then, with a little more alertness, "I told you I don't do that anymore."

That was something he'd have to clear up later, but for now, his carnal thoughts weren't fit to be shared at this moment — their first real moment together. If she knew everything he wanted, it might scare her off.

Emotions flitted across her face. Without moving from her draped position over his lap, she asked, "Why?"

"I got carried away, that's all."

"And now you regret it?"

"I regret that it took me so long to wise up." Why had he waited? She'd passed eighteen years ago. So what if she sometimes spooked him? What a wuss he'd been. "What about you?"

"No." Her fingers toyed with the now-wrinkled material of his shirt. "I've imagined kissing you a million times. It never happened, so I decided it wouldn't. I figured I'd never know what it was like." She leveled a frown on him. "And I decided to move on."

Skipping past that last part, he said, "I'm glad you weren't disappointed."

"When I left, I didn't know you'd follow me, but Mom thought you might." She looked up at him. "Now I'm glad you did."

So Faith had him pegged? Not surprising, really. It figured that she'd have to be extra sharp to maneuver through the combined talents of Jamie and Cory.

Smile curving, Austin admitted, "Luna told me to follow you."

While she considered that, her fingers trailed over the back of his neck, almost as if she couldn't resist touching him. "Why?"

The simple stroke fired his blood all over

again. His imagination put those soft, warm fingers in places she hadn't yet touched. "I think she sensed something was wrong. Between us, I mean."

"Impossible — since there is no *us*."

Apparently, he needed to remind her of the here and now. "You don't think so? So that wasn't your tongue in my mouth?" He tugged her hand away from his neck, kissed her palm, and placed it over his chest. "That's not you touching me right now?"

Mocking him, she asked, "Are you involved with every woman you kiss in the woods?"

He wasn't, damn it, and she knew it. "Luna was right, wasn't she? You've given up on me."

Rather than answer, Cory looked at her nails. "How come when Luna knows something, you just listen, but when I know something, you get all freaked out?"

He noticed she didn't deny giving up on him. "I don't *freak out*."

Her bold gaze called him a liar, but her mouth taunted, "Do, too."

Maybe when he'd been younger, he'd freaked a little. Now, he wasn't sure how he felt about her ability. "Look, there's no comparison between you and . . . ." Realization smacked him upside the head. He stared at her — and saw her with new eyes.

"Between me and Luna?" she prompted, all huffy and indignant. "I would hope not." Then, with more seriousness, "I don't want to *mother* you, Austin."

Heart thundering, he shook his head and admitted the stunning truth. "Between you and other women." He'd dated plenty of times. As she'd said, he'd been kissing girls in these woods since he was just a boy. But none of them had felt right, not like this did. With her.

Cory was unlike anyone he knew, and her effect on him was just as exceptional.

If he lost that connection . . . no, he couldn't.

He had a few weeks to fix things, and by God, he'd figure out a way.

She eyed him with suspicion. "What exactly does that mean?"

Only one thing seemed really clear at the moment. "I don't want you giving up on me."

"But you're the one —"

"Let's start fresh, right here, right now." He curved his fingers around her neck, moved his thumb over her jaw. "Forget the past and just go forward from this moment." From that awesome kiss. "What do you think?"

"I don't know. I'm already making plans."

To leave him. To hook up with other guys. "But you promised your mother to wait, right?"

"Yes."

He forged on, determined to win her over. "I work tomorrow, but how about dinner after? Say six o'clock? We can talk about . . . things." Important things. Like her staying in Visitation. Like the future. And their lives. *Together.*

She stared at him, confounded. "Dinner?" Before he could answer, she tacked on, "You're asking me on a date?"

"Yes." When he put his mind to it, he could be charming. Plenty of women had told him so, and this woman mattered more than any other. He'd screwed up. He'd own it.

And he'd make it right.

Knowing what he had on the line, Austin brought her closer. Voice low and convincing, he urged, "Say yes."

That rough voice put her mysterious gaze on high alert. Finally, she gave a slow, albeit reluctant nod. "All right."

Feeling that he'd just scaled the biggest hurdle, Austin let out a breath. "Great. So you won't leave town?"

"Not yet."

Not *ever,* if he had his way. "And you won't date anyone else until we've worked things out?"

As if he was nuts, she pulled back. "Like who?"

Maybe she didn't realize how many guys would jump on the opportunity. "Anyone other than me."

She thought about it for far too long. "Will you still be seeing other women?"

"No."

His quick reply sent her brows up.

"That'd be fair, right?" Calling a halt before he screwed up again, he said, "Now how about we get back to the party?"

Looking down the hill, she warned, "People will know something's up if we go back together. Especially our moms." She gave him a sideways glance. "Nothing gets by either of them."

He didn't care. He had a feeling Luna already knew, and she'd definitely acted in his best interests. And Faith, who'd won over the mysterious Jamie, saw more than she ever let on. The mothers were smart, on point, and very aware of anything that had to do with their kids.

Meaning it, Austin said, "So? I don't mind." In fact, knowing the dudes who'd stopped her to talk would still be around, he wanted everyone to notice them together. "Do you?"

Another long, unblinking stare.

Encouraging the answer he wanted, Austin took her mouth in a firm but fast kiss. "Say you don't mind."

Her smile came slowly and looked oh-so-sweet. "No, I don't, but then I was never the one who —"

Another far-from-satisfying smooch cut off that unnecessary reminder. He'd come very close to losing her. Knew it, would have to live with it, and now just wanted to get beyond it.

He put a lot of possessiveness into that brief kiss; a lot of promise, too.

If only she'd notice.

Eyes flaring, she asked, "Are you planning to kiss me every time I —"

He said against her lips, "Yeah, I think I am. Kissing you is nicer than I ever suspected, so any excuse will do."

She held silent while considering that. "You know . . . I don't think I'll mind."

Happy to take any win he could get, he brought them both to their feet. "I'll pick you up tomorrow, okay?"

Cory stared up at him. "Okay. But if you're just messing with me, I'll make you sorry."

She probably would, too. He'd learned as a kid that Cory had diabolical ways of getting even. Always, he'd considered her ballsy beyond belief. Now he recognized her vulnerability, too. It was a heart-tugging combo, and he wasn't immune.

Putting his forehead to hers, he whispered, "Give me a chance, and I'll convince you of my sincerity."

Her hands opened on his chest, her sigh teased his lips . . . and she nodded.

Cory in an agreeable mood? Yeah, he could get used to that.

"C'mon, Sully, we're ready to go." Grumbling, the dog lumbered to his feet, stretched elaborately, yawned, and finally joined them. Austin took Cory's hand, and they headed back down the trail.

The three of them together. Just as it should be.

CHAPTER THREE

Faith saw her daughter and Austin approaching, hand in hand, Austin wearing a triumphant smile and Cory looking bemused. If only Cory saw what she saw. As a mother, she knew her daughter was special in so many wonderful ways, beautiful inside and out. Any man would be lucky to have her, but Austin was the one she wanted, and so Faith wanted him for her.

Though Jamie had already zeroed in on what was happening, she elbowed him. "He has her off kilter."

"Cory knows what she's doing."

Rolling her eyes, Faith elbowed him again. "Being in love is a whole different thing. It confuses everyone."

He smiled at her. "I remember."

Yes, she'd turned Jamie's life upside down before she'd won him over. Would Cory do the same to Austin? Biting her lip, she glanced at Jamie again.

He opened his mouth —

And Faith quickly said, "No, don't tell me. In my heart, I know they'll work it out. Cory is a catch, right? And Austin isn't a slacker, so he has to realize it."

"You're very sure of yourself."

Putting on her loftiest expression, she said, "I'm a mother. We understand these things."

His smile turned indulgent. "I can't argue that."

Suddenly, Luna was there, ready to collude. "Did you see?"

Faith nodded fast. "What do you think it means?"

Because she'd refused to let Jamie weigh in, he shook his head. "I'll find Joe and keep him company."

Neither woman paid him any attention.

Luna said, "I strongly suggested that Austin follow her today."

"Good for you. I suggested Cory leave without once acknowledging him."

"Oh, that was perfect. We all noticed something was going on — including Austin." Luna glanced back at the kids. "In so many ways, he's just like Joe, avoiding marriage simply out of habit."

"Marriage?" Faith laughed. "They haven't even had a date, yet."

Luna waved that off. "I know my boy. He's loyal to a fault, and he cares a lot about Cory. That's why he knew he couldn't date her."

"I don't follow."

"It wouldn't *just* be dating. Deep down, Austin's always known she was right for him, that as soon as he got close with her, it'd lead straight to forever. He just needed to be ready first."

"You could be right. The problem is that he held her off for so long, she was starting to second-guess herself."

"Well, I hope she realizes the truth now." Luna watched as Austin steered Cory to the snack shack, probably to give his sister and Clay a break. "You see? Already he's keeping her close. Now that he's figured out how he feels, he doesn't want to give anyone else a chance to sneak in."

"Let's get a better look." Trying to appear nonchalant, Faith led the way to the shack.

Willow, who was just leaving when they got there, sent Luna a conspiratorial smile. "Romance," she whispered, "is afoot."

With his arm over Willow's shoulders and Sully's leash held in his other hand, Clay added, "About time."

Faith grinned with them. She wasn't surprised that Clay would take that attitude, since he'd been openly in love with Willow forever. "Where are you two headed?"

Clay ran a hand over Sully's back. "Taking this old guy to the house so he can eat and rest. He's already had a busy day."

"Give him a treat, too," Luna said. "I keep them in the pantry for when he visits."

With that done, they stopped by the shack. People came and went in a steady flow, keeping Austin and Cory busy.

Faith and Luna hung around for a few minutes, just observing and sharing small talk — and maybe hoping to overhear something important. Both kids were too involved with customers to talk much, though, so they were just about to leave.

Then a group of young men approached. They purchased colas, but it was clear that they mostly wanted to talk with Cory.

Faith glanced at Luna, who suppressed a grin, and they settled in to watch.

Cory didn't seem to think anything of the guys' chattiness, but Austin immediately put his arm over her shoulders. That made Cory go still . . . then glance at him in inquiry.

Luna whispered, "I've got my money on Austin."

"Me, too," Faith replied. "At least she's aware of him. More often than not with other men, Cory barely notices their attention."

It was hilarious how Austin subtly tried to make it clear she was taken, all without Cory's participation. Austin even hugged her once, then pressed a kiss to her temple.

With Austin being so demonstrative, and Cory paying them no mind, the young men gradually gave up.

But not Chad. Faith knew the handsome young man was Cory's age, and that he'd asked her out before.

Ignoring Austin, Chad said, "Would you like to swim later?"

"I didn't bring my suit," Cory said.

"We could go out in the kayak, then." Determined, he leaned on the counter. "It's a nice day to be on the water."

"Thanks, but I'll be helping out here."

Stymied, Chad said, "Maybe when you're done —"

"I'll be driving her home," Austin said.

As if only then realizing the tension between them, Cory blinked at both men. "Actually, I came here in my car, so I'll be driving myself."

Austin made a show of hugging her again. "Then I'll walk you to your car."

Chad's gaze bounced back and forth between them. "Maybe tomorrow —"

"We have a date," Austin stated.

Rounding on him, Cory whispered, "You're being rude."

"Just upfront." He stared at Chad. "You and I have an agreement, remember?"

"Don't make me regret it by insulting my friends."

"No problem — if he's *only* a friend."

Grinning, Chad put up both hands. "Can't blame a guy for trying."

Flushed, Cory turned back to him. "Thank you, Chad. I'm sorry that *some people* are deliberately misunderstanding the situation."

Chad's grin turned into a laugh. "Actually . . . Austin understands perfectly. But no worries. I get it."

While Cory looked stymied, Austin said, "Good."

As Chad left, Cory slowly pivoted to face Austin, no doubt ready to blast him.

Faith interceded. "Have either of you eaten?"

"Actually, I haven't." Austin turned to Cory. "You?"

She shook her head. "Thanks, Mom, but I'm not hungry."

"I made that pasta salad you like so much."

Smiling, Cory said, "Maybe a little, then."

Luna patted Cory's arm. "I'll put together two plates." Without waiting for a reply, she hurried off.

"She'll bring you enough to feed an army," Austin warned.

Cory gave him a sharp glance. "She's nice — always."

"Meaning I'm not?"

"You," she said in clear warning, "are —"

"Trying to make it clear we're working things out now." To Faith, he added, "We are, you know."

With Cory's disgruntlement so plain, Faith wasn't sure what to say, so she just smiled.

Softening, Austin took Cory's shoulders. "Maybe you didn't realize it, but Chad was totally coming on to you, right in front of me, by the way."

"He was being friendly."

"He wanted to be friendly alone. In a boat."

With a roll of her eyes, Cory looked to Faith for backup.

She'd never seen her daughter so flustered, and it sort of amused her. "Sorry, honey, but Austin's right. He was."

"Thank you, Faith." He planted a kiss on Cory's mulish mouth, leaving her befuddled. "I need to grab a few more snack bags.

Be right back." With alacrity, he disappeared behind the shelves of chips.

"A strategic retreat," Faith noted with a grin.

It was a small building, and Austin wasn't far enough away not to hear, so as she sorted the cash drawer, Cory lowered her voice to a whisper. "I have no idea what's gotten into him."

"I do."

Cory's hands stilled over the money. She hesitated, glanced toward where Austin had disappeared, then turned to Faith. "Feel free to share, because I'm lost."

"You two fell into a rut, with you waiting and him resisting. Soon as you stopped waiting, he realized he'd screwed up."

She chewed her lip. "That's pretty much what he said, too."

"You don't believe him?"

"I do." She glanced at the shelves of chips again. "It's just that things happened too quickly."

"And you don't trust it?"

After closing the cash drawer, Cory laced her fingers together. "I'm not sure what to think. I guess I'm hopeful, but that scares me, because it's almost like he was coerced."

Uh-oh. Had she and Luna manipulated the situation? Maybe a little. "Men can be fickle. He thought he had you wrapped up for far too long, and now he knows he doesn't."

"But he does. He always has."

If only her daughter had a little more guile. Rolling her eyes, Faith said, "Honey, don't make it so easy for him."

With another quick glance, Cory lowered her voice. "He's taking me to dinner tomorrow. On a date."

"I heard him tell Chad that."

"He asked, I agreed, but I still don't understand it."

"I think it was meant to be." Faith touched her cheek. "More importantly, *you* think it was meant to be."

"Yeah, well, now I'm not so sure."

Yes, love did that to a person. "I'm confident enough for both of us. You'll see."

Austin rejoined them. "If you want to take a break with your mom, I can cover here."

"That's okay." Faith stepped back. She wanted them together, not apart. "I need to find Jamie now, anyway."

Before she stepped away, she saw Austin gaze at Cory, then touch her hair, her cheek, before leaning in for a very sweet kiss.

Whatever reservations Cory had, Austin didn't seem to share them. How ironic would it be to get him on board . . . just as

Cory changed her mind?

No. Faith wouldn't believe it. They were meant to be together. Somehow, they'd figure it out. She *would* see her daughter happy, one way or another.

When Austin got home from work the next day, Sully greeted him with his usual exhilaration. Regardless of the weather, or how tired or sweaty he might be, Austin's first priority was always a quick trip outside for Sully to do his business.

He grabbed the dog's leash, and they walked their usual route around the complex. The small, rustic cabin he rented was convenient to his construction job, and . . . it felt nothing like home.

Other than the proximity to a bed, he had no interest in bringing Cory there.

As he and Sully strolled, a few neighbors waved, and kids ran by playing.

All in all, a usual day — except that he'd be seeing Cory shortly, under very unusual circumstances. He'd thought about her all day long while pouring concrete under the hot sun. He'd thought about her while devouring his lunch in the shade under a tree.

Actually, he'd thought about her last

night, too, when he should have been sleeping.

He'd take Sully, of course. The dog already spent too much of his day alone during the week, and Austin felt certain that Cory wouldn't mind. She loved Sully.

Did she love him, too? Sure, she wanted to marry him. At least, he thought she still did. But love? She'd never really said.

And suddenly, that mattered a lot.

When Sully stopped to sniff the grass, Austin looked away. He had to. Sully wouldn't answer nature's call with anyone watching him.

Fighting a smile, aware of his dog giving him the side-eye, Austin again thought about Cory, about being with her soon.

Kissing her.

Sorting out the tangle of their past.

He kept picturing the kids she'd described, kids they would have together. And the house where they'd all live as a family.

Contentment filled a void he hadn't noticed before.

Yesterday at the shack, he'd sensed Cory's reservations. Hadn't let it slow him down, though. Even with her mom analyzing his every move, he'd done his best to remind her they had something between them, something she claimed would lead to marriage.

Because Cory was blocking him so she wouldn't automatically know his intent, he'd had to resort to old-fashioned flirting. Little touches, intimate smiles, deliberate nearness.

Not a hardship. In fact, not doing those things would have been a lot tougher. He wanted her. *Her,* not anyone else.

When Sully finished up his business, Austin started moving again.

After a quick shower and a change of clothes, he made his plans for the evening. He wanted uninterrupted time alone with her, but not at this impersonal cabin, and not at one of the limited restaurants nearby.

Going to the bedroom, Austin got the extra quilt from the top of the closet and stored it behind the seat of his truck. He strode back into the house and found Sully sitting at attention, hopeful of an invite.

Knowing the dog watched him, Austin got a water dish and bottle of water from the kitchen, a few treats, a long lead that he could tie to a tree . . . and a cushy dog bed.

Ears perked, Sully waited.

Finally, Austin asked, "You wanna go?"

Shooting forward as if launched, the dog raced an eager circle around him. Laughing, Austin hooked the leash to the dog's collar. "Yeah, I'm looking forward to it, too."

When he opened the passenger door, Sully leapt in. Tongue out, body jiggling, he showed his happiness. He didn't care where they were going, as long as he got to be with Austin.

Moved by that realization, Austin said, "I love you too, bud." He got everything stowed, checked the time, and headed to the nearest take-out restaurant. At the drive-through, he ordered chicken, biscuits, mac and cheese, and a chocolate cake. All of Cory's favorites. When he explained he was headed for a picnic, the guy ringing him up added napkins, plates, and plasticware.

He got to Jamie and Faith's home ten minutes early. Their families were close, so Austin had been there before plenty of times.

But never specifically to pick up Cory.

Feeling unaccountably awkward, he led Sully up to the front porch, but before he could knock, the door opened, and Faith stood there expectantly.

Cory's mom lacked her ability, but she was far from obtuse. She knew this was a momentous occasion — one Cory had predicted. Likely, she also knew everything Austin hoped would occur, and that made the back of his neck warm.

Smile knowing, Faith stepped back. "Come on in."

He gestured at Sully. "I have my dog —"

"So I see." She held the door wide, and Sully, quick to accept the invitation, trotted in.

Following, Austin said, "If you're sure . . . ?" He glanced beyond Faith to see Jamie standing in the kitchen doorway, arms crossed, one shoulder against the wall, those dark eyes so much like Cory's boring into him.

Austin stalled. Cory might be blocking him, but Jamie wasn't. Doing his best to clear his thoughts, he said, "Hey, Jamie."

Without a smile, Jamie nodded.

Yup, he definitely knew that Austin wanted to get her alone, and why.

Before he could dwell on it, Faith latched onto his arm and led him to the sofa. "Cory will be right out. Can I get you something to drink?"

"I'm good, thanks." He'd be better if Jamie would blink. He glanced at Cory's father, but no, that dead stare remained in place, almost like a warning.

What could he say? Cory was a grown woman with a mind of her own and a will of iron. Never would Austin pressure her, and if he tried, Cory would level him.

As if realizing the truth of that, Jamie finally relaxed. He knelt down and called Sully to him. Leaning back on the couch, Austin drew a breath, only to strangle again as Cory stepped out of the hall.

Without realizing it, he got back to his feet, his gaze devouring her.

In little cutoff shorts and a skimpy halter, her hair in a high ponytail that exposed her neck, back, and shoulders, she looked better than good. Hotter, too. It was an unusual look for a woman who was generally a conservative dresser and gave him hope they were on the same page.

Because with every second that passed, he wanted her more.

Cory went straight to his dog, kneeling down to cup Sully's furry face. "Sully, hello. How are you, baby?"

After giving her a quick licking kiss, Sully rolled to his back, legs in the air to demand stomach rubs. Laughing, Cory sat down and obliged the dog.

Wishing he could read her as easily as she read him, Austin explained, "I didn't want to leave him alone."

"Of course you wouldn't," Cory said in approval. "I wouldn't have liked it if you had."

Faith smiled. Jamie just eyed him with suspicion.

Uneasy under the combined scrutiny, Austin decided the sooner they left, the better. "You ready?"

"Take your bug repellent," Jamie suggested. Because yeah, he probably knew they'd be outside, in a clearing in the woods.

"Oh." Cory glanced at Austin, then away. "Okay, sure." She disappeared back down the hall.

Damn. Austin avoided eye contact. Having his every thought dissected was one reason he'd avoided Cory.

But no longer, he reminded himself.

He brought his gaze up to meet Jamie's. "I packed everything for a picnic, but yeah, I forgot the bug spray, so thanks for the reminder."

Jamie cocked one brow.

Faith, moving right past that awkward moment, just smiled. "A picnic sounds wonderful."

When Cory returned, Austin held out a hand.

With only a brief hesitation, Cory stepped forward and entwined her smaller, cooler fingers with his. Her beaming smile made him smile, too.

He couldn't wait to get her alone — and at the moment, he didn't care who knew it.

While Austin let Sully visit with nature, Cory spread out the quilt on the exact spot she knew would be the front porch of his future house. It was such a beautiful area, with redbud trees and dogwoods mixing with pine and oak trees. Moss-covered boulders ran the perimeter of the rushing creek, with little wildflowers poking up around them. The air smelled so fresh, and dappled sunlight filtered through branches overhead.

This was the life she was meant to have.

With Austin.

His low voice drew her gaze. In cargo shorts, a faded logo T-shirt, and unlaced sneakers, he looked incredibly good to her. Casual in the way of a man who worked hard and enjoyed his time off. The soft cotton of his shirt hugged impressively wide shoulders. When he patted Sully, his biceps flexed.

From a scruffy boy to a lanky teen, to a man filled out with muscle, he'd always appealed to her.

She'd wanted him forever. She wanted him now. Today.

The sooner, the better.

Who knew if things would work out between them? If they didn't, she at least wanted a memory to hold before she moved away.

While getting ready earlier, she'd settled on a plan, a plan she kept all to herself. Though her dad hadn't said anything, she'd sensed he had reservations about her and Austin getting together. On the other hand, her mother exuded extreme optimism.

Since Cory had blocked Austin, she'd have to rely on different truths — the truth of what she wanted, the truth that Austin was a good man.

The truth that, in her heart, she knew they were meant to be.

Getting busy, she set out the food containers, placed Sully's bed to the side of the quilt, filled his water dish, and put his chew treat close by.

"You didn't have to do all this." Tying Sully's long lead to a tree, Austin secured the dog so he couldn't run off if a critter — or a leaf — taunted him.

Did that mean Austin planned to be distracted?

Given the way he watched her . . . maybe.

Sitting cross-legged on the quilt, Cory stared up at him. "You like what I'm wearing?"

Surprised by the bold question, Austin paused, then slowly grinned. "Sure got my attention." He seated himself beside her. "This is all new, right? But if you want to go straight at it, then yes, I like what you're wearing."

Trying to reconcile what he said with the way he was looking at her, she tipped her head. "Why?"

With his smile going warmer, Austin sent his gaze over her shoulders, her throat . . . the top of her chest. "I guess I've always known you were hot, you know? It's hard to miss, even though I was actively trying not to notice. But in this outfit? I'm glad other guys aren't seeing you right now."

Cory chewed that over but didn't want to make assumptions. "Because . . . ?"

"Because they'd do whatever they could to steal you away from me, and I don't want the competition." He frowned as he said it. "There isn't, is there? Competition, I mean?"

God, he could be so frustrating. She adored Austin, but she wouldn't let him get away with that. Pinning him with a stern look, she whispered, "Are you talking about Chad again?"

He did a double take at her darkening mood. "Chad . . . or anyone else."

"Let me make something clear."

Though his mouth didn't smile, his eyes sure did. "Gonna give me hell, huh?"

"You embarrassed me yesterday at the shack."

That took care of his humor and gentled his tone. "I'm sorry."

"We made a deal."

Nodding, he said, "You, me, and no one else."

"I can stick to it, and I trust that you will, as well."

"Hundred percent."

More reasonable than she'd expected. Cory relaxed. "Good. So if any other guys talk to me —"

"I'll try to tamp down the jealousy." Before she could get over that telling admission, he added, "But honey, you were seriously missing the message. Chad wants you, and he's not the only one. If you gave any of them even a tiny bit of encouragement, they'd be all over it."

"It?"

"An opportunity to move in on you. So here's the deal. I'll try not to be a possessive ass, if you'll open those innocent eyes and see what's right in front of you."

Unable to help it, she laughed.

Blowing out a breath, Austin grumbled, "I

229

tried." Using more energy than needed, he started dishing up the food.

Cory watched, amused by the heaping servings. "I hope both those plates are for you, because that's twice what I can eat."

He hesitated with a large scoop of mac and cheese suspended over the plate, as if he'd only just realized what he was doing. "Right. Sorry."

He put back two pieces of chicken, leaving her with a single plump wing on her plate. She took the spoon from him and returned it to the little tub of mac and cheese, too. "I don't suppose you got honey for my biscuit?"

"Of course I did." Austin dug in the bag and produced a little packet. "I know you like it."

"You do?" She'd never mentioned it to him.

Leaning in, he touched his mouth to hers. Lightly. Sparingly.

And still, he stole her breath. "I know a lot about you, Cory Creed. Never think I wasn't paying attention."

Well, that was news to her!

Smug, he pressed her plate toward her. "Let's eat."

Probably not a bad idea. At least it'd give her a minute to reflect on everything he'd already said.

With only the sounds of the woods around them, they spent the next few minutes enjoying the meal. Austin finished off the massive portions on his plate, and she got another piece of chicken to nibble on.

Stretched out on his side in a ray of sunshine, Sully snored.

Somewhere nearby, a woodpecker hammered on a tree.

Fluffy white clouds drifted over the sky.

And her heart felt too big for her chest.

The moment felt right. This very special spot felt right.

But she didn't want to rush him.

After they'd each finished off a piece of cake, he said, "Now, about those guys." Cleaning his hands on a napkin, he explained, "The ones at the party yesterday. I saw them talking to you." He busied himself clearing the quilt, putting the trash together. "They asked you out?"

"Not really."

He continued to watch her. "How does a guy *not really* ask you out?"

It was hard to explain something she'd always lived with. Embarrassing, too, because she didn't want him to see her as others did.

Appearing suspicious at her quiet mood,

he scooted closer. "Did they say something to upset you?"

Worse and worse. "I'm not that fragile, so no, they don't upset me." Seeing that he wouldn't relent, she huffed. "You know how the people around here are. They're curious about what I know, so they joke with me and ask silly questions. None of them are really interested."

His expression seemed to grow more intent. "What silly questions?"

"Mack wanted to know if I could see him in my future. Randy asked if I'd like to show him around the mountain."

"Those dicks."

Surprised that *he* seemed bothered by it, Cory shrugged. "Ted asked me to suggest a good time for us to go out when no one would interrupt us. I laughed, because I knew they weren't serious —"

"Why do you think they weren't serious?"

The reality wasn't pretty. "To them, I'm like a carnival act." Facing the truth was something she'd had to do her entire life. She knew people liked her, but she also made them wary.

Reaching out, Austin lifted one long curl that had escaped her ponytail. He wrapped it around his finger. "For such an insightful person, you sure are blind about this." His warm gaze held her captive. "The thing is, I want you all to myself, but more than that, I want you to see yourself the way others see you."

"You're saying they weren't teasing?"

"To get your attention, sure. Not because of what you know, but because of who you are."

Curiosity ripe, Cory breathed, "And who am I?"

His hand, warm and firm, his fingertips a little rough from labor, curved around her cheek, cradling her face gently. "You're dark, mysterious eyes that see everything. A pretty face framed by all these fantasy-inspiring curls." He lightly stroked her bare shoulder. "You're baby-soft skin and a secret smile that feels like foreplay." His gaze dropped to her mouth — and stayed there. "You're a smokin' hot body hidden in sweet clothes."

Warmth rose in her face, then spread out everywhere. No one had ever given her compliments like that. Both flattered and embarrassed, she wasn't sure what to do, but she couldn't look away.

His thumb moved over her shoulder in a stirring caress, and his gaze came back to hers. "The real kicker, though, is your easy sense of humor, your interest in other people, how much you care, and the ways you try to help. You're genuinely *nice,* Cory. Everyone I know likes you."

Her lips parted. Did he like her? If so, then how much?

Everywhere he touched her — heck, everywhere he looked — she tingled in an electric way. She knew she wanted Austin, had wanted him for a long time. Knowing it and experiencing it were two very different things.

She'd watched him with other women before, and he usually seemed . . . intent? Yeah, that word fit the absorbed way he focused on her now. More often than not, when she'd seen Austin with women, he'd had an end goal in mind and had worked toward it.

Sex. Shared pleasure.

But he hadn't been committed to anyone, not the way Cory wanted him committed to her.

So did his attention now mean he wanted to have sex? Or was it more?

Hoping for more, she considered how to react.

Of course, she could read him, to see what he had planned . . . but no. Too many times doing that had gotten her into trouble. From now on, she wanted to be like everyone else. She wanted to figure things out the way normal people did.

The way Austin did.

"You're too quiet," he said. "Tell me you believe me."

"Actually . . . I don't know." Then she admitted, "I was concentrating."

"Yeah?" As his gaze traveled over her, a smile tugged at his mouth. "Me, too."

Now what did that mean? "Concentrating on what?"

His grin widened. "You first."

Why not? She wanted him to know that she understood his reservations, and that she'd try to alleviate them. Not looking into his eyes, not seeing his expression, made it a little easier.

Or so she thought.

But everything about Austin fascinated her, including the tanned color of his skin, how his neck was stronger than hers, the cords leading to his collarbone.

Not touching him proved impossible, so she let her fingertips tease just above the neckline of his shirt. "Reading people is second nature for me. More often than not, it just happens without me thinking about it."

As if he really got it, he asked, "Like breathing?"

235

"Yes." The base of his throat was warm and smooth, but toward his jaw, whiskers rasped against the sensitive pads of her fingers. "Since I don't want to do that anymore —"

"Ever?"

Why did he sound so appalled? "It's what you'd prefer, right?"

As his troubled gaze met hers, he visibly searched for words.

"You've made it clear before," she insisted. "You don't like it that I . . . know things."

"I didn't, no." He took her plate and moved it away, so that nothing was between them. "When I was younger, I admit it spooked me."

It'd spook him again if she jumped into his head. "It sent you running away from me."

"Cory." He laced their fingers together. "We were kids. I was annoying, I know, and you teased back in return." That crooked grin came again. "Do you remember telling me a snail would crawl into my room at night? That it'd sleep in my mouth and leave behind a lot of slime?"

She bit her lip, but it didn't stifle the snicker. "You deserved that."

"I almost smothered myself, sleeping with a pillow over my head." Quieter, he asked,

"Was it any wonder we butted heads? I was an obnoxious boy, and you had a wicked mean streak."

She huffed out a breath. "That wasn't the problem, and you know it."

Speaking over her, he said, "Then, when I was just starting to get interested in girls —"

"You started that *really* young!"

"— there you were, heckling me again."

Feeling silly, she hid her grin. "I didn't."

"Cory," he chided. "I was almost fourteen, full of curiosity and testosterone, and Penny Wilkerson was willing and able to —"

"I know what she was willing to do." Mumbling, she added, "And I still think she was too old for you."

"Only by a few years." He went back to teasing. "You told me Joe would find out, and that made me nervous."

"Not nervous enough, because I knew you'd still go to her."

He frowned. "You saw me with her?" He touched her forehead. "Up here, I mean?"

"Part of it — then I blocked the rest." Even as a kid, she'd been possessive of Austin, and knowing he was with someone else, *experimenting,* had crushed her.

"I'm sorry." He added, "Boys that age have sex on the brain."

"So do girls."

His mouth opened . . . but then closed. "Right. Of course." He frowned. "You're saying you —"

"Not as young as you, no." But she wasn't about to go into details with him. Nothing she'd done with anyone else had been satisfying, because she was meant to be with Austin. "All that experimenting and curiosity of yours . . ." She flapped a hand. "It's one reason I told you we'd marry."

"So you didn't know it for sure back then?" Tilting his head, he considered that. "You just said it to get even — like the story about the snail?"

Well, she'd talked herself into that corner, hadn't she? Evading him, she looked over at Sully. His lips moved as he snored. She couldn't help smiling over that.

"Don't want to talk about it, huh?"

No, not really. But again, trying to figure out the right thing to say —

"Don't do that." He tugged her closer, then bent to press his mouth to hers in a long, hot kiss. "You don't have to hold back, not with me, okay? And if you decide to read me, well, just know that I have a one-track mind right now, but it's because this feels right. With you, I mean."

She so badly wanted to believe that. "You

realize I'm not a mind reader, right? I can't know your every thought. I just see things that have happened —"

"Or will happen."

No use in denying it. The problem was that she didn't always see things clearly enough to completely understand them. "I'm blocking all that, remember?"

"Just with me, or with everyone?"

"Everyone." She hesitated.

"Ah, now it makes sense. If you weren't blocking those guys who flirted with you —"

Rolling her eyes, she corrected, "They *teased.*"

"— then you'd have understood what they really want is a chance with you."

Could Austin be right? Had she been so focused on him that she'd missed other things, other guys? Her dad always said that emotion clouded his perception.

"When you go quiet, it worries me."

Her gaze skipped up to his. A slight smile showed he wasn't worried at all, and that particular look in his eyes sent a warm thrill spiraling through her.

To get him back on track, she gave a verbal nudge. "You said you were concentrating, too?"

"Yeah." Catching her upper arms, he drew

her across his lap, but didn't stop there. Still turning with her, he lowered her to her back on the quilt and came down over her. Balanced on his forearms, he let his gaze caress her face and settle on her mouth. "I was trying not to do this — but I think I just lost that battle."

CHAPTER FOUR

Cory didn't protest their more intimate position, but still, he tried to hold back. Rushing her wasn't fair, especially when they had so much to discuss.

She wanted to be someone else with him.

Denying her abilities wouldn't remove them. Asking her not to use her talents would be like asking her to pretend, all the time. There had to be another answer.

For the first time, he wondered how her parents worked it out. Did Jamie temper his talent around Faith, or had Faith learned to deal with it?

He knew that Joe and Luna had gone through many adjustments. When Luna had first come to Visitation to care for him and Willow, she'd brought Joe strictly as backup. She'd tried to deny, especially to herself, that she and Joe had a future. Being older and wiser now, Austin understood her reservations back then.

And yet, they'd turned out to be the perfect couple, supportive of each other, attentive, and dedicated.

Awesome parents.

Luna had accepted Joe as an overprotective alpha, and he'd accepted that Luna viewed the world in a different way.

Cory's soft, cool palm touched his face. "Got to admit, you've confused me again. I was all set for you to kiss me, and instead, you're just staring at me."

"Because you're so pretty."

Her doubtful smile proved she didn't believe him. How could she not know her own appeal? Was that his fault, too?

"Austin? What are we doing?"

"Getting comfortable together?" Yeah, that sounded reasonable. "You don't like it?"

"I like it," she whispered. "Being this close to you, feeling you." Her hands moved over his shoulders, down his spine, to the small of his back. "You're so hard."

Ducking his face to her neck kept her from seeing his grin. Hard? Yeah, he was getting there fast.

He nuzzled the sensitive skin where her neck met her shoulder. "You're so soft." Thanks to the skimpy halter, she had a lot of skin exposed.

"I've wanted to touch you for a long time."

Damn, much more of that and he'd forget this was their first official date. Still, he heard himself say, "Touch me however and wherever you want." Before she could question that, he put his mouth to hers in a gentle press, back and forth, a little deeper, a better fit . . . a lick.

Her lips parted in invitation, and as he explored her teeth, her tongue, she gave a small sound of need — and the kiss went wild.

As if they'd suffered years of abstinence, they both ignited.

It felt . . . absolutely perfect.

Because it was Cory.

As if in sync, each adjustment brought them closer until her small body cushioned his, and he surrounded her, and they moved together in an ever-increasing intimacy.

Change? Hell no, he didn't want her to change.

The Cory he knew, *this* Cory, was incredibly exciting. He'd always had fun sparring with her. Resisting her.

Now kissing her — this was the best of all.

She surprised him by hooking one leg around his, her fingertips digging into his shoulders, her own tongue busy in a fevered exploration.

He never knew for sure what Cory would do or say, but her boldness surprised and pleased him.

If she wasn't herself, would their relationship even be real?

Then again, if she was herself, she'd already know where this was going. Since he didn't yet know, they wouldn't be on equal ground.

Easing up from her mouth, Austin studied each of her features. The long lashes on her closed eyes. The fullness of her parted lips. The dusky color of her flushed cheeks.

He'd been falling in love with her over the years, but somehow, he hadn't known. Sneaky, that's what she was, coming in to steal his heart — and then trying to give it back.

It was hers; had been hers for a very long time.

As he smiled down at her, her eyes slowly opened. She licked her already damp lips, and he felt it everywhere.

"What?" she whispered.

"You are just so sweet."

"How so?"

He kissed her again, a slow, devouring kiss that went on longer than he meant it to before he summoned the control to pull back. "Your scent, your taste, but mostly who you are."

Confusion tweaked her brows together. "I think I'd rather be exciting than sweet."

"You're that, too." Austin couldn't stop touching her, grazing his fingers over her downy cheek, toying with a few wild curls that came free. "I don't want you to change, Cory."

"You don't?"

He shook his head. "Definitely not. Who you are, what you can do, is special."

Her expression softened. "That's what Mom said."

"Your mother is a very smart person." Shifting to lie at her side, he rested his hand on her midriff, beneath the halter, above the low waistband of her shorts. She was so slight, he could span her waist by opening his fingers.

His gaze lifted to her breasts. She'd be a handful. And those hips . . . but he'd known other women built just as nicely, and they didn't level him with this odd mix of possessiveness, tenderness, and scorching lust.

Aware of her holding her breath, he let his fingers drift — but not too much. "No changing, okay? But there's something to be said for spontaneity. Like this." He bent to kiss a path from her stomach to one hipbone.

245

Her fingers threaded lightly into his hair.

This close to her, he breathed in the scent of her skin, warmed from the sunshine and humidity of the day. Near her hipbone, he opened his mouth for a gentle love bite, followed by a soothing stroke of his tongue.

"Austin?" she breathed.

Damp, nibbling kisses carried him up her midriff and lifted her halter along the way.

"We're going to have sex?"

Yup, there was that boldness. Sliding a hand up her side, he said, "How about we wait and see?"

"You don't know?"

Impossible to suppress his chuckle. "Well, I wasn't expecting to so soon, but now I'm hopeful." When she didn't grin, his humor faded. "What about you?"

All too seriously, she whispered, "I vote yes."

That did it for him. Closing in for another kiss, Austin stopped holding back. Now he kissed her with absorbed determination, needing her there with him, every bit as hot, just as anxious. While he feasted on her mouth, he let his hands learn the dips and hollows of her body, the firm curves, the soft swells.

When she reached up, fumbling with something, he was so focused on teasing the frayed hem of her shorts that he barely noticed what she was doing — that is, until she pressed him back. Breathing hard, he levered up to his forearms again — and she lowered her halter.

Breasts exposed, her gaze holding his, she tugged, shifted, and removed the halter completely. Dropping it off to the side, lying there bathed in spring sunshine, she smiled at him.

His mouth went dry. Hard? Hell yeah, he was hard. Painfully so.

Her breasts were pale, round, with dark rose nipples already pebbled tight. Unable to resist, he curved a hand around her, then released a breath at the feel of her like this, bare, warm.

For him.

"Kiss me again."

He thrummed her nipple. "Here?"

"Not yet." She pulled him down to her and took his mouth in a kiss meant to devastate.

Totally worked.

Long minutes later, when he knew he couldn't take much more, he kissed her cheek, her throat, and asked, "Want to lose the shorts, too?"

"Your shirt first."

No problem with that at all. In a rush, he

moved to the side and stripped it away. He had the forethought to glance at Sully.

And found the dog looking back.

Breath held, Austin waited, but with a snuffle and a wiggle to get comfortable again, Sully closed his eyes. *Whew.*

He turned back to Cory. If someone had painted a personal fantasy for him, Cory, like this, would be it.

In a barely-there whisper, she asked, "He's sleeping again?"

"For now." Resting on one elbow, he freed his other hand to stroke all over her. "We'll have to be quiet."

Her mouth twitched. "I didn't plan to be loud."

"No? Well, damn." As he traced a fingertip around one nipple, he murmured, "Maybe next time."

She said, "Or the time after?"

Austin nodded. "And probably the one after that."

It was sexy as hell the way she watched him, the way her eyes got heavy and her breathing deepened. "Sounds like we'll be doing this a lot."

"God, I hope so."

With a contented sigh, she said, "Me, too."

After that, there were no more words between them, because none were needed.

Instead, as he touched her in all the ways he'd thought about, she gave him low sounds of pleasure, high gasps of excitement, and the occasional soft moan.

Her breasts were extremely sensitive, her nipples more so, especially when he drew her in for a soft, wet suckle.

She tricked him again, shimmying around until she'd opened her shorts and unzipped them. Primed, he helped her to take them down her legs, and removed her panties at the same time. Sunshine kissed her everywhere, adding a golden glow to her fair skin.

All mine, he thought.

That was, if he could convince her. No, he pushed the uncertainty away. Cory cared for him. He'd build on that to fulfill her prophecy of their marriage. Whatever it took, he was up for the challenge. In more ways than one.

Rolling to his back, he shoved down his shorts and boxers, and kicked off his worn, unlaced sneakers. In rapid order, he pulled a wallet from his pocket, found the single condom he carried, and rolled it on.

When he turned back to Cory, he found her riveted on his cock. Had she expected him to skip the condom?

Yes, they'd have kids. He believed that, because he believed her.

But marriage first.

They'd do things right, and they'd have those kids when she was ready, not before.

"Okay?" he asked in a whisper.

When she got her attention back to his face, he found a wealth of emotion in her eyes. "Thank you. I hadn't thought . . . didn't even consider . . ."

"I'll take care of you."

Her smile bloomed. "And I'll take care of you."

A man couldn't ask for more than that.

She ran her fingertips over his erection, making him go still.

"You're not tanned down here."

He almost choked. "Did you expect me to work my job naked?"

One shoulder lifted . . . and she clasped him in her small hand. "I know you've sunbathed before."

"In trunks," he strangled out. Damn, much more of that, and it'd be over for him. For whatever reason, she fired his blood like no one ever had.

"Have you ever skinny-dipped?"

He had, with other women, but that wasn't something he'd discuss right now. "Let's just say nothing before you, before right now, matters anymore."

Her fathomless gaze lifted to his face. "We

could say that — if it was true."

Austin caught her wrist, regretfully removing her hand and mildly bearing it down to rest beside her head as he settled over her. "The truth is that this feels incredibly new and special, yet somehow familiar, too. It feels right. At least to me."

Searching for the truth, she took her time studying him while he waited in an agony of suspense for her verdict.

No, he didn't think she'd call a halt, but this wasn't just about sex.

It was sex with Cory.

A starting point for their future.

And though she might not realize it, a commitment. After he'd shown her how good it could be between them, then they could talk.

Finally, she smiled. "It's that way for me, too."

Mingled relief, lust, and promise had him devouring her mouth again. Just as involved, Cory touched him everywhere. Remembering to be quiet wasn't easy. Minutes later, as he parted her thighs, he whispered, "Shh . . ."

And got her snicker in return.

Silly Cory. *Sexy* Cory. He held her face, looking into her beautiful eyes, and thrust deep.

Perfection.

Not just how they fit together, how incredible it felt to be with her like this, but also how she reacted, holding him tight, biting her lip to stifle a groan. It wasn't easy, but he waited, remaining still within her until she caught her breath. Giving him a look so sultry that he felt scorched, she subtly shifted, bringing one leg up high and around him.

They both went for a kiss at the same time, their mouths mating as he rolled his hips, pulling away from her, then sinking in again, faster and faster. She met his rhythm, even accelerated the pace with her own urgency.

Good thing no one came upon them, and that Sully preferred to sleep in the sun, because Austin lost track of everything but her. Her taste, the scent of her excitement, the softness of her body, and the escalating sounds of her pleasure.

Putting her head back, her neck beautifully arched, she tightened. Liquid heat surrounded him, her heels pressed into the small of his back, and she gave a low, vibrating groan as she came.

His own release forgotten as he enjoyed hers, he couldn't look away. As the tension faded and her body softened, he hugged her close, his face in her neck, and let go.

She hadn't been prepared. Yes, she'd known that sex with Austin would be special, but this was more. So much more.

They should be doing this for the rest of their lives. For her, no other man existed. Never had and, although she'd fooled herself for a while there, never would. He was it for her. Now and forever.

She loved the feel of his weight on her, how their activity had left his broad shoulders damp from exertion. How his hot breath pelted her throat. How he possessively cupped her breast even now, so gentle but also sure.

Will you marry me? The words burned in her throat, but she'd resolved to give him space, so she swallowed them back and instead moved her foot along his hairy calf.

When he didn't stir, she asked, "Are you okay?"

That got her a soft laugh. "Yeah." Struggling up to his forearms, he smiled down at her, mellow and lethargic after his release. "I feel awesome, in fact. You?"

"Very awesome." Everything about him fascinated her. His eyes were brown, dark like hers, but more unusual because of the

253

contrast with his fair hair. Here with the sunshine all around them, she detected golden flecks. She could get lost staring into his eyes.

"I like how you look at me, Cory." The kiss that he gave her now was different, sweet, comfortable, an expression of affection instead of banked need.

He toyed with her hair, tucking back a curl here, easing one forward there, lifting a lock to his nose to breathe her in. "Next time, I'd love it if you left it free." He brushed the tip of the curl over her lips, then followed it with a kiss and a huskily murmured, "It's a personal fantasy of mine."

Already on board, Cory asked, "When?"

Lazily, he looked over her shoulders and upper chest. "If we don't get you covered up, it might be happening any minute now, but I'm afraid we're already risking things by being out in the open like this, and I only have the one condom." His palm settled against her cheek. "I would never want to embarrass you, or take chances on things you might not yet want."

His thoughtfulness was a good starting point. When he rolled to the side, she sat up and reached for her panties. After removing the condom and putting it with their trash, he snagged his boxers.

He was so matter-of-fact about things she'd never before considered. Sex outside, the disposal of a rubber, dressing again. It might have been awkward, except this was Austin, and she wanted to share everything with him.

Sully eyed them both, decided they were done, and sat up with a jaw-breaking yawn.

"Perfect timing," Austin said, suddenly very engrossed in watching her dress.

"So this next time." She lifted her hips to pull up her shorts and saw his chest expand on a deeper breath. Being openly admired by him was a nice change of pace. However, she wanted more. A lot more. "Where would we go, if not here?"

He reached for his shirt, shook it out, and stuck his arms through the sleeves before pulling it over his head. "I have a rental cabin in town. You already know that, right?"

Since she knew everything about him, she merely shrugged and tied the halter strings behind her head. "That's where we'd go?"

"Even if I get started tomorrow, and I'm thinking I might, it'll still take time to build the house here. You live with your folks, so that's out. My cabin is all that's left."

There were the mountains, and she wouldn't mind finding a nice quiet spot up there for them to be together, but she knew she was more comfortable there than most people. "Your cabin is fine by me."

Moving behind her, he found the halter strings that tied at her waist and, after dropping a warm kiss on her bare shoulder, took care of tying them for her.

Urging her to lean against him, he folded his arms around her and propped his chin atop her head. "I didn't take you to my cabin today, because it feels impersonal. Just a place I stay, but not really home. Definitely not right for our first time together."

Aha. Twisting to peer back at him, Cory asked with great interest, "So you were planning all along for us to have sex today?"

"Actually, I was planning to wait, to give you time. I didn't want to rush you." Wearing a rascal's grin, he admitted, "I'd hoped to make out a little, though." In a now-familiar move, he drew her up and into his lap. "If I'd thought about the way you've always affected me, I should have realized that wouldn't work."

It proved impossible to keep the disgruntlement from her face. If she'd affected him at all, he wouldn't have held out for so long.

"You're wrong, you know." As if he'd read her mind, he kissed the end of her nose, her lips, then the frown between her brows. "I never knew how you did it, but you always managed to show up where I was. Even before I saw you, I knew you were near. I *felt* it. Everywhere." He watched his hand as he stretched out one long curl, then released it to bounce back. "I'd try, but I couldn't resist looking for you. Or watching you. When you smiled, I smiled. If you frowned, it worried me." As if that idea bothered him, his mouth flattened. "The more I tried to pretend you weren't there, the worse it got."

Now that she'd seen every inch of him, his body fascinated her even more. She wished he'd left off his shirt so she could feel the muscles in his chest, see his flat brown nipples, maybe trace that sexy line of hair that led from his navel downward.

Renewed need restricted her lungs. Her breasts felt heavy all over again. "I'm glad we came here. It's peaceful and private."

"And special." Holding her now-loosened ponytail, he urged her face up to his. "We'll have a home here, Cory."

Knowing he waited for her to acknowledge that, she whispered, "It's . . . a problem for me, that your attitude changed so quickly, I mean. You went from avoiding me to —"

"Wising up. To recognizing that I'd never be as happy without you as I would with you." He traced lazy circles on her shoulder, along the top of her halter, and then to her lips. "Give me a chance to make up for lost time."

"More sex?"

His hold tightened as he laughed. "Anytime you're willing. But I meant dates. Dinners together. Just hanging out, watching TV in the evening. Being a part of things around here so everyone realizes we're together."

Considering that, Cory offered a concession. "We could also look at house plans." She peeked at him and found him watching her. "I mean, I know you already have an idea of what you want —"

"You have an idea of what I want, too, but it's not just about me. It's about us." Sully moseyed over to plop down beside them. Automatically, Austin put a hand on the dog's scruff and stroked him. "I have a book of house plans that I bought. I already marked a few that I like, but I'd love your input. Maybe tomorrow, after I get off work, I could grill dinner for us at my place, and then we could look them over."

On a rush of happiness, Cory nodded. "I'd love that."

Sully's *woof* interrupted the kiss he gave her, and they both laughed. Austin patted the dog while talking, imagining, and planning a future.

With her.

Faith couldn't have been happier. Austin and Cory had just left on yet another date, and her daughter positively glowed with happiness.

Every single night for the entire week, they'd been together. They each worked during the day, then got together immediately after. Cory got home from school smiling and left smiling. She obviously relished her time with Austin.

One of those nights, at Faith's insistence, Austin had joined them for dinner. Even Jamie had behaved, though he'd still given Austin several long, perceptive looks. Usually, Austin was gazing at Cory with such bold emotion in his eyes, Faith didn't need Jamie's gifts to understand the young man's feelings.

He loved her daughter. And Cory loved him.

Now, standing at the window with the curtain lifted aside, Faith watched them drive away, feeling very content with their progress.

Jamie put his arms around her. "Things aren't settled yet."

"You hush it," she told him, dropping the

curtain and turning to face him. "None of your cryptic predictions."

"It's fact, not a prediction."

"All relationships go through trials," she insisted. "That's just a part of being in love."

With a small, tolerant smile, he asked, "Have I been a trial?"

"You've been the most wonderful husband and father ever . . . who is occasionally a bit much, sometimes overbearing, and so very, very astute."

Jamie grinned at that. "Should I tell you what you've been?"

"No." She tried to sidle away.

Jamie held her to him, his strong arms gentle, his tone teasing. "You've been a wild bull who stampeded my heart —"

"Jamie!"

"— and I wouldn't have it any other way."

Leave it to Jamie to make her laugh. There was a time when he'd lacked any sense of humor. But she'd changed that, and together, they'd raised a most amazing daughter.

Sobering, Faith snuggled close, her cheek to his chest so she could feel his heartbeat. Her voice dropped to a whisper. "Tell me she'll be fine."

"She'll be loved every bit as much as you are." He ruined that reassurance by adding,

"And when Austin is at his most desperate, Cory will be exactly what he needs."

Shoving herself back, Faith glared at him. "Desperate?"

Slowly, he nodded — and tightened his hold on her. "Desperate, terrified, and panicked."

"Jamie?" she whispered, her heart threatening to punch right out of her body. "What are you saying?"

"I'm saying it'll be all right. You trust me, Faith. Now trust our daughter, too."

God, it wasn't easy. "Cory won't be hurt?"

"Cory will be set free."

She did trust Jamie, with all her heart, but still, she bounced her small fist off his rock-hard shoulder. "Damn it, I need answers."

"What happened to your mother's intuition?"

"You're about to be bludgeoned over the head with it!" That he would tease told her all she needed to know. Everything would be okay.

His smile came slowly. "You're the most incredible mother, doing everything you can to make our daughter happy. Even trying to tackle things not in your power." Smile widening, Jamie kissed her forehead and gave her the words she needed. "All will be well. You'll see."

Sometimes, being married to a man like Jamie could be incredibly trying. She hoped Austin knew what he was getting into.

"He'll love her anyway," Jamie said, already knowing her thoughts. "Just as you love me."

"I do," she vowed. "Very, very much."

"You're my miracle, Faith. Now let's go have dinner before we need to leave."

Since she'd thought they were staying in for the night, she asked, "Where are we going?"

"Later, we'll meet them at the hospital — and *yes,* everyone will be fine. You have my word."

Jamie revealed things in his own way, in his own time. She had his word, and his love. For her, that was always enough.

Resting in the bed with Cory half-sprawled over his chest, Austin thought about how happy she seemed. For a week, he'd done his utmost to win her over completely. Not a hardship. He'd enjoyed every second of her company.

They shared everything, and they burned up the sheets.

He thought he knew sex, but sex with Cory was in a whole different league of pleasure. She was adventurous and traditional, sexy and sweet, generous and sometimes greedy. Whatever he wanted or needed to give, she seemed to be in agreement.

He enjoyed their time out of bed, too. Lounging with her on the couch to watch a movie, bumping hips while cleaning the kitchen together after dinner, quiet conversation while walking Sully around the complex . . . and this, holding her after sex, feeling the uncommon closeness to her.

It all made him yearn for more.

Sully had adapted to having her there, and when she went home each night, the dog missed her.

But not as much as Austin did.

Though it was fast, he knew he wanted her with him in a permanent way. No doubts at all. If they married now, they could build memories as they built their home.

He couldn't imagine anything more perfect.

Cory seemed at peace with the current arrangement, but Austin kept thinking of how close he'd come to losing her. It drove him to secure their future.

Idly stroking her bare spine, down to that delectable behind and up again, he thought of how satisfying it would be to hold her like this all through the night, and to wake with her each morning. One thought led to another, and though he didn't mean to spring it on her, the words came out before he could censor them. "I love you."

Rearing up, her eyes wide in shock, Cory gaped at him. "What?"

Since he'd already said it, he saw no reason not to say it again. Maybe a hundred times. "I love you. So damn much." When she breathed a little harder but didn't say anything in return, he felt compelled to explain. "Pretty sure I've always loved you. I know I've always considered you mine. It's why no other woman could get close. You'd already taken everything I had to give. I just had to get used to the idea."

Showing no signs of believing him, Cory shook her head. "I scare you."

"No," he gently denied, feeling a smile tug at his mouth. And his heart. "Not since I was a kid. Not for a long time."

Still, she stayed silent, and it bothered him. "Do you love me, Cory?"

Tension built, one heartbeat, then two. Leaning down, she put a firm, lingering kiss on his mouth, and said, *"Yes,"* with enough feeling to convince him.

Immediately after that, she tucked her face under his chin and snuggled in, her hold bordering on desperate.

Because she didn't believe he returned her love?

If so, she had to still be blocking him, trying to give him what she thought he wanted. Otherwise, she'd *know.*

So he had his work cut out for him. Considering how long she'd waited for him, it seemed fair.

Trying not to pressure her, Austin charted a path down her spine again, then cuddled her lush backside. "Are you hiding because you aren't sure?"

Jolting up, she glared at him. "I've never been more certain of anything in my life."

Knotted muscles loosened in his neck and shoulders. "Good. Because I love every part of you."

She started to shake her head.

"Everything," he reiterated. "Including your special talents."

When Sully scratched at the door, she dodged the topic by leaving the bed. "I'll get him."

It would take him a lifetime to get used to seeing her like this, beautifully naked and at ease.

With him.

Damn it, they belonged together. She knew it, too, but because he'd dragged his feet too long, she didn't trust him, and he

265

wasn't sure how to fix that.

Watching her pull on his T-shirt and her own shorts, Austin tried to think of a way to convince her.

Instead of coming in, Sully led her back down the hall, which likely meant he needed to do his business.

Realizing she wouldn't come back to bed, Austin quickly pulled on his own shorts to follow her. "Hold up, Cory."

She didn't slow down. Talking nonstop with the dog, she all but raced for the back door, where Sully had a lead that kept him in the small yard.

Hot on her heels, Austin waited until she had Sully hooked and the dog had loped out to the yard before he pulled her into the doorway and put his mouth to hers in a heated kiss.

Apparently liking that more than conversation, Cory pressed against him in encouragement.

Not that he needed any.

Only a few hours ago, he'd picked her up, and they'd gone straight to his cabin. They'd played with Sully for a bit, but once the dog had stretched out for another nap, they'd headed straight to the bed — and that's where they'd stayed.

He should have been sated at least until

after dinner, but instead, he burned for her again.

Austin had to remind himself of his priorities, and the top priority was convincing Cory that he accepted every part of her.

Framing her face in his hands, he touched his forehead to hers. "I love you, Cory."

Again, she hid from him. "I love you, too."

"But?"

"I don't know. I'm trying to sort it out."

His heart ached. "There's nothing to sort out. We're meant to be, remember?"

"You never thought so before." He heard the hurt she tried to hide when she whispered, "Not until I shut down my abilities."

Claiming that to be a coincidence wouldn't sway her. But applying the truth to their future might. "I was an ass, and I know it. When I think of anyone shortchanging our kids, belittling their talents" — as he'd belittled hers — "I want to rage." He didn't have those kids yet, but he already loved them, and he badly wanted to protect them. Had Jamie felt that way? If so, it explained a lot of those dark frowns he'd sent Austin's way.

As if the honesty of his admission struck a chord, Cory tipped her head back to study him. "It's only our daughter who will have the gift."

267

He moved his thumbs over her cheeks, wanting to cherish her. Wanting her to understand how incredibly precious she was to him. "Then she'll be as special as her mother, and her brothers will defend her to the end of time."

Expression changing, she teased, "In the same way you always defended Willow?"

"At the time, I was all Willow had." He'd done the best he could, but being a young boy had kept him at a disadvantage. "Our kids will never be in that position." Luna and Joe had shown him what family should be. Now that he knew, he'd insist on nothing less. "We'll be together, we'll protect them, and they'll always know they're loved and accepted."

"That sounds really nice."

"It will be. I promise."

At that moment, they both heard kids laughing. Austin looked up first and found three boys peeking around the privacy fence that divided the small yards behind each unit.

Apparently, the kids were playing kickball, and the ball had gotten away from them. When they spotted Sully, they stopped to give him a few pets.

Luckily, his dog loved kids and was always gentle with them.

Austin waved at the boys.

After waving back, they grabbed the ball and rushed off.

"Thank God I grabbed my shorts," Cory said, laughing quietly against his chest.

"My shirt covers you."

Smiling up at him, she said, "How about we get started with dinner? I'm hungry."

Clearly, she didn't want to continue the conversation yet. She'd been patient with him, so he could do no less for her. Kissing her temple, he asked, "How do steaks off the grill sound?"

"Perfect."

"Then I'll get started. Sully will want to stay out for a while, anyway."

"If you didn't insist on picking me up, you could spend more time with him."

"Are you kidding? He loves to ride in my truck. Besides, if we didn't pick you up, we couldn't drive you back home. Sully and I would rather spend those last minutes with you each night."

Speaking of Sully . . . the dog trotted up with a stick in his mouth and a challenge in his eyes. Cory laughed. "Go play fetch for a bit, and I'll get the food ready."

He would have protested, except that's how they did things. Working together, sharing responsibilities. There'd been a time or

269

two when Sully was napping against her, so he'd prepped the dinner. Another time when Sully wouldn't go to the bathroom until he'd examined every blade of grass, so she'd done the cleanup.

Austin wanted that happy coexistence for a lifetime, but for now, he merely said, "I'll fire up the grill first, then play with Sully."

It was a little over an hour before they'd finished eating at his small picnic table out back. After plenty of time spent chasing sticks, Sully had settled under the table near Austin's bare feet. The sun still lit the yard, but it was cooler, with a slight breeze stirring the air.

He felt mellow. He felt horny.

He was madly in love.

Unable to resist, Austin reached over the table for Cory's hand. "You're too far away."

At his urging, she switched sides to sit beside him. Bracing one arm on the table, he half-faced her. "Wouldn't it be nice to spend the whole evening together?"

"Actually . . ." She covered his hand with her own. "Yes." Her gaze flickered up to his, but mostly she concentrated on outlining his fingers, measuring his larger hand against her own, and ramping up his need. "I was thinking about that earlier."

Perfect. Trying not to overreact, he said

casually, "Yeah?"

"I should get my own place."

What? Not what he'd been suggesting at all. He wanted her with him, not in another apartment.

"If I'm going to stay in Visitation —"

He locked his fingers with hers. "You are, right?" He'd thought their relationship was moving right along, and instead, she still considered leaving?

"I am," she said, putting him at ease.

Relieved, Austin let out a breath. "Good to know."

"I made up my mind yesterday. Being here with you like this . . ."

Her words tapered off, so Austin filled in for her. "It feels right, doesn't it?"

Without looking at him, she said, "I never doubted it would."

Turning her face up to his, Austin kissed her chin, over her cheek to her ear, and damn his impatience, he couldn't resist suggesting, "Then don't block me." Her relaxed posture grew a little more rigid, but he couldn't pull back. "Honey, use your gifts to see how much I love you. *All* of you. Will you do that for me?"

For far too long, she resisted. He understood why. He also knew that if she read him, she'd know exactly how he felt, and

271

there'd be no more reason to doubt him.

Finally, when his patience neared the breaking point, she drew in a shaky breath, closed her eyes — and a sort of horror fell over her face.

Whatever she'd just picked up on, it wasn't good. Warily, Austin asked, "What's wrong?"

Sensing a problem, Sully crawled out to look at them. "It's all right, boy." Whatever it was, he'd make it okay.

Then to Cory, he said, "Come on, babe, don't leave me in suspense." He saw her breathing harder, and it scared him. "Talk to me."

Her eyes opened, and all he saw was sympathy.

"Cory?" Just then, his cell phone rang. Cory scooted closer, her hand on his shoulder. Unsure what to think, Austin glanced at the screen, saw it was Raine, and answered with a quick, "What's up, hon?"

"Austin." Raine swallowed heavily. "We need you."

His stomach bottomed out. Still staring at Cory, at the worry she expressed, he asked with dread, "What's happened?"

In a broken whisper, Raine said, "Mom was on her way home from the grocery when another driver drifted into her lane.

They collided. We . . . we're at the hospital annex."

His heart shot into his throat, and before he'd even thought about moving, he was on his feet. "How bad?"

"I don't know." Voice dropping, Raine whispered, "I passed the accident on my way here. There was blood everywhere."

Urgency galvanized him. On autopilot, Austin headed inside, his stride long and hurried. "Where's Willow?"

"She's here with Clay."

Good. At least Raine wasn't alone. "And Joe?"

"Dad was at home, but he's on his way."

God, poor Joe. He loved Luna so much that the time it took him to arrive would feel like a year of hell. "I'll be there in fifteen minutes, okay?"

"Just drive safely, please." Raine disconnected.

Returning the phone to his pocket, Austin turned — and Cory was there.

She'd followed him in, and she had Sully with her. The poor dog looked confused.

"Hey." He gave Sully a few quick pats. "It'll be okay, bud." It had to be.

He'd lost one mother long ago. He couldn't lose another.

In short order, Cory deposited the dirty

dishes in the sink, refilled Sully's water dish, and gave him a chew treat to keep him busy. "We'll be back soon, Sully. You just rest."

The dog sent Austin one more look of concern, then sat down on his bed.

"Good boy." With a final hug for Sully, Cory stood and snagged his hand. "I need thirty seconds to put on real clothes, and you need a shirt and shoes."

Right. Glad for the direction, Austin hurried ahead of her and grabbed the first shirt he found. By the time he'd shoved his feet into his sneakers, Cory was more or less dressed, too. Braless, her hair wild, she said, "I'm going with you."

Honestly, he hadn't considered that she might not. "Thanks." Within seconds, he had the truck on the road again.

The town was small, and since the hospital was quite a distance away, an annex had been built closer to town. Doctors of all sorts rotated to the building to care for patients and to deal with emergency issues. He'd been there before, once when he injured himself on the job, and again when Raine was younger and had fallen out of a tree, spraining her wrist.

But not for anything like this.

During the short drive, his thoughts churned in a dozen different directions.

For her part, Cory stayed quiet. When he glanced at her, she appeared to be concentrating. It struck him that right before the call, she'd already known. "Cory?" He needed to know what he was walking into, but at the same time, he was half-afraid to find out.

She stared straight ahead at nothing in particular. Her eyebrows twitched, her mouth firmed — and then relief overshadowed everything else.

Animated, she reached for his forearm. "She's going to be okay."

Though he kept his attention on the road, Austin grabbed that promise like a lifeline. "You think, or you know?"

"I *know.*"

A quick glance showed him her blinding smile. The confidence that was such a part of Cory allowed Austin to believe, too. "You see something?"

"Yes, and it's a wonderful scene."

He still needed to find out what had happened, but optimism lifted the heavy weight from his chest, allowing him to drink in a cleansing breath. "You can give me the details in a minute." For now, he wanted to hurry inside to his sisters. Rapidly, he parked and rounded the hood.

Her smile still in place, Cory hopped out

before he reached her and fell into step beside him. "She'll be fine," she murmured. "She'll be fine."

Amazing Cory. *She was his life.*

"I love you, Cory. So damn much." He pushed open the entry doors, and they stepped inside. "Thank you for being you."

Chapter Five

They almost collided with Joe on the way to the ER, each of them hurrying, coming from different directions. Seeing Austin, Joe said, "Stay with your sisters," and continued his ground-eating stride.

"Wait." Austin snagged his arm. "Have you seen her yet?"

"Just got here." Looking tortured, Joe pulled free, anxious to get to his wife.

"Cory says she'll be okay."

The words stalled Joe. Slowly, he turned, his gaze first on Austin, then shooting past him to land on Cory. With near savage intensity, he stepped closer and demanded, "Tell me you're sure."

Amazing. So Joe would believe Cory without question?

Cory didn't balk at Joe's intensity. "I see her a few years from now with my daughter — *our* daughter," she clarified, smiling at Austin. "Though she's too young to understand, Luna is holding her and telling her about the special gifts she inherited from Dad and me." Cory touched his arm. "I don't know how badly she's injured right now, but I do know she *will* be fine. I swear it to you."

Some of the volatile emotion left Joe's expression, making him look less dangerous. With one sharp nod, he drew her in for a quick hug. "Thanks, hon." Then he was off again.

Keeping Cory close, Austin looked toward the seating area, where his sisters waited. Raine, who stood in the open doorway, had one fisted hand pressed to her stomach, the other to her mouth. Her eyes were wide and swimming with tears.

Behind her fist, she smiled.

So she'd overheard? Then those must be tears of relief.

He had that confirmed when she charged out and threw herself against Cory. "I'm so glad you're here and that you know Mom will be all right."

"I'm glad I'm here, too," Cory said, looking over her head at Austin. "It's where I belong."

With him. In good times and bad. Austin's throat went thick. Cory didn't just have a gift. She *was* a gift.

And she was his.

"Will you tell me everything?" Raine asked. "I don't want to be afraid."

"Of course." Cory led her to where two cushioned chairs sat together. Heads close, they spoke in quiet conversation.

Willow hadn't been near enough to hear, and Austin could see she was still scared. Clay held her against his chest, rocking her slightly, kissing her temple. Consoling her and caring for her. Neither of them had yet noticed his arrival.

In their darkest times, after their mother's death when they'd been left alone, in that void before Luna had arrived, Willow had looked out for him. She'd protected him and done her best to care for him.

As a little boy, he couldn't do much in return except be disgruntled at his helplessness — and show his gratitude in how fiercely he defended her against anyone who dared to insult her. Now, thanks to Cory, he could finally give his sister something substantive, something more than his love and loyalty.

Walking into the room, he said softly, "Willow?"

Her head lifted. *"Austin."* She rushed over, dragging Clay in her wake.

Before she could say a word, Austin spoke.

"Cory says she'll be fine, and you know Cory is never wrong."

Coming to a jarring halt, Willow stared at him. Her dark eyes, so much like his own, filled with hope. "She was wrong about you two marrying."

"No," he whispered. "She wasn't."

Willow's expression brightened. "You believe Cory?"

"I do. About everything."

Smile tremulous, Willow swiped at her wet cheeks. "Good. Me, too." She gave Austin an approving hug, then stepped back to Clay. "I'm so relieved, but I still want to see her."

"Of course you do." Cory rejoined them, a smiling Raine beside her. "And you will, very shortly, in fact."

Awed, Raine whispered, "Is this something else you know?"

"Actually, I just heard her." Cory tilted her head. "You didn't?"

They all paused . . . and Luna's strident voice carried to them, insisting she was fine and demanding that Joe reassure her children.

Together, they all laughed, the sounds varying from amusement and joy to a release of bone-deep fear.

That was Luna, always caring for her kids

first and foremost. She'd made them into a close-knit family of which she was the heart and soul.

She wasn't his mother, but she was his Mom, and that was far more important.

Opening his arms to his sisters, Austin embraced them tightly — and relished the way they hugged him back. Willow snagged Cory and brought her into the group hug, too. Clay stood back smiling, until Raine grabbed him. They ended up in a big cluster, laughing a little, overwhelmed with relief.

Beleaguered, Joe stuck his head around the corner. "She's fine," he said first, drawing everyone's attention and breaking them apart. "It looks bad, but I swear it isn't. A few bruises on her cheek and forehead. Before she was found, she was helping the idiot driver who veered into her lane, and he had a head wound that got blood everywhere." Half under his breath, Joe muttered, "Damn near stopped my heart."

Jamie and Faith came onto the scene just then. In his sage way, so unlike his daughter and her blurted insights, Jamie said, "The other driver has a broken arm, but is otherwise fine, as well." He held out a bag. "We brought one of Faith's shirts for Luna to change into."

Without missing a beat, Joe not only accepted the proffered shirt, but thanked Jamie with a one-arm hug and a firm clap to the back that left the other man staggering.

Joe didn't seem to notice as he turned to Austin, Willow, and Raine. "Give them a few minutes to finish checking her over and cleaning her up. Then you can see her. Oh, and she said to tell you she loves you all — that includes Clay and Cory — and she's sorry for the fuss." His gaze rolled over to Jamie. "Anything I'm missing?"

Jamie shrugged. "We'll celebrate Mother's Day on Sunday together, at our house, so Faith can pamper Luna."

"She won't like that," Faith said cheerfully. "But I'll insist."

"Got it. Luna can return the shirt then."

Austin took in the group of them and couldn't help chuckling. There may have been a time when Joe didn't trust Jamie's insight, but he certainly did now. He hadn't even questioned how Jamie knew about the blood or the other driver.

Not only that, Joe trusted Cory, too. They were all wonderfully unique, all part of his life, and knowing that filled him with satisfaction.

"Someone hit your funny bone?" Joe asked.

"I'm going to love tying our families together through marriage. That is, if Cory will —"

"She will," Jamie said, which earned him a slug in the shoulder from Faith.

"Let her answer, will you?" Faith turned to Cory with a wide smile. "Go on, honey."

"Yes." Cory stepped close to Austin, squeezing him tight. "Definitely *yes.*"

Grinning, Joe made an about-face. "If I don't tell Luna the news right away, I'll catch hell." He headed back to his wife with a quickened step.

Seconds later, they all heard Luna's triumphant, "Yes!"

And then they heard Joe insisting that she couldn't yet get out of the bed, and he couldn't parade them all through.

It was another ten minutes before Luna was allowed visitors.

Only one person was allowed back at a time, and by silent agreement, Willow and Austin let Raine go first — not because Luna was *more* her mother; that wasn't possible — but because Raine was the youngest.

When Raine returned a few minutes later, crying happy tears, Willow didn't give

Austin a vote, she just shot to her feet and jogged to the curtained alcove.

Austin didn't mind. He was with Cory and her parents, and for once, Jamie wasn't watching him with dark intent.

Faith started making plans for Mother's Day at their house, but Cory recruited Austin, and together, they took over. Raine joined in, as did Clay, to insist that they'd handle the food prep, serving, and cleanup, so that the moms, for once, could take it easy.

When Faith started to argue, Jamie confided, "They're going to win," so she gave up gracefully.

Why put in the effort when she knew how it would end?

Finally, it was Austin's turn to see Luna. Cory said, "Give her a hug from me."

"She'll like that." With a little trepidation and a lot of love, Austin headed to the curtained-off alcove. He found Luna sitting up on the side of the bed, her hair wrecked, since an attendant had obviously washed parts of it to remove blood. Her makeup was smeared, her cheek and forehead bruised, but she wore a beautiful smile.

Gently, aware that she'd been hurt and he could so easily have lost her, Austin enfolded her in his arms. "That hug was from Cory.

This one is from me." Again, he cradled her close, relishing the fact that she was with him, alive and as effervescent as ever.

"I do love that girl."

"Me, too." Emotion crowded his throat, making his voice thick. His life might have started out a little rough, without a father, with a mother who died too soon, but thanks to Luna, he now had more blessings than he could count.

"Congratulations." Luna pressed him back. "I am so, so happy for you."

"Thanks, Mom." He saw her eyes flare, and a second later, her face softened with the love she so freely gave.

Typical of Luna, she didn't make a big deal of it. She didn't have to. From day one, she'd always understood him to the point that sometimes, words weren't necessary.

Austin took a seat beside her on the flat mattress, her hand cradled in his. "Do you remember when you first moved in, and I wouldn't stay in my bed?"

"You broke my heart," she admitted, leaning her head on his shoulder. "Such a little guy, so young, but you didn't want anyone to know about the nightmares you had when you tried to sleep."

"I used to dream that I lost Willow, too." The memories flooded back, some bad, others incredibly good. "You didn't tell me I had to go to bed. You didn't demand I stay in my room. You didn't even get upset with me."

"Of course not, but neither could I let you wander around outside alone, no matter how many times you'd done that."

Before Luna. The previous string of relatives who'd stayed with them hadn't really cared what he did, as long as he didn't bother them. He'd gotten really good at sneaking out.

But not good enough.

Once Luna had arrived, she'd curbed his nocturnal activities in the kindest way.

"You walked with me, night after night. Down the stairs, around the living room and through the kitchen, along the hall and up the stairs again . . ."

"Sometimes for hours." Grinning, she nudged him with her shoulder. "You had boundless energy, it seemed."

"But you didn't, and still you kept our nightly routine. For me."

"I loved you on sight. You know that."

Yes, he did. "You've been loving me for years." Many years more than his own mother had lived. "You're my mom, and eventually, you'll be grandma to my kids."

Her eyes went damp. "You're my son, and

I love you with all my heart."

Same as she did Willow and Raine.

Suddenly, she twisted to face him. "Wait! You said grandkids?" Eyes rounding, she warned, "Don't you dare tease me, Austin. You know how much I'll love being a grandma."

He couldn't suppress a grin. "Bet you said the same thing to Willow."

"I did, but she and Clay want to wait a bit, and that's okay, too."

"Well." Austin gave her a slanted look. "I don't know how soon it's happening, but Cory did mention that we'd have two sons and a daughter."

"Oh my. *Three*?" Putting a hand to her heart, Luna said, "I wonder if Faith already knows? Jamie probably told her, and she hasn't said a word."

"I'm not sure Cory wanted anyone to know, so she might have kept it locked away."

"Such wonderful news." With her smile so big, the bruises were barely noticeable. "Tell me everything quick, before the nurse returns with my discharge papers, and don't leave out a single detail."

Out in the waiting room, Cory watched as Luna's laughter drew Joe's heated gaze. No special talents were needed to know he loved Luna more than life.

Much as Cory loved Austin.

And now that she'd opened up to him, she knew Austin felt the same. The level of his love stunned her.

Today, as she'd shared what she knew about Luna, she'd felt his pride. He loved her, all of her, and though she knew they'd have their conflicts, as all couples did, she also knew they'd grow old together.

She hoped he didn't want a big wedding, because something small would suit her perfectly. Just their family, maybe at the courthouse.

Soon.

Her dad said, "Next weekend will work. Mother's Day is this weekend, and you don't want to step on that."

Accepting that she and her dad communicated on a different level, Cory agreed without surprise.

Faith said, "Wait, what's happening next weekend?"

"Austin and I will marry." She looked toward Willow and Clay, cozied up together. They'd marry in June. Would they mind if she and Austin married before them?

"No, they won't. Willow will be happy for Austin."

Faith grumbled, "Damn it, include me in this conversation."

"You'll be included," Cory promised. "We have so much to discuss."

"You're fretting for no reason — and you know it." Jamie smiled at Faith. "But even so, sometimes a daughter wants to share with her mom."

Coming up behind Cory, Austin said, "She shouldn't be fretting at all." He bent to kiss her forehead. "I love you, you love me, we'll get married as soon as I can convince you, and we'll have a wonderful life together."

"Wise man," Jamie said.

Cory came quickly to her feet. "How's Luna?"

"Thrilled that she'll be a grandma." He pulled her in close. "When does that happen, by the way? Mom wanted to know."

She didn't miss the way he'd referred to Luna, and it pleased her. Not because he'd ever shortchanged Luna, but because it was a sign they were moving forward, instead of looking back.

Jamie opened his mouth, but Cory replied before he could. "How does a year from now sound for the first?"

Startled, Faith said, "I'll be a grandma in a year?"

"A boy," Jamie and Cory said at the same time, prompting Austin to laugh.

Faith swatted at Jamie. "You knew and didn't tell me?"

"Someone" — his look made it clear that he meant her — "told me to let the romance unfold naturally."

Dissatisfied by that answer, Faith narrowed her eyes in speculation. "What else do you know, Jamie Creed?"

Dark eyes filled with affection, he tucked back her red hair. "I know you'd rather be celebrating our daughter's engagement than giving me hell."

"Well . . ." Begrudgingly, she agreed. "You're right about that."

Leading Austin a few feet away, Cory smoothed a hand over his chest. "Just so you know, Sully will be around to meet our kids."

A little boggled by that news, he put a hand to his head. "They'll all be born soon?"

"Yes, like stair steps."

Slowly, the shock eased away, and he smiled, accepting, happy. In love with her.

"I was worrying about him being home alone," he admitted. "I was distracted when we left."

"Sully's fine, but he's waiting for you."

"For us," Austin corrected. "Now that we know we'll be married, there's no reason for you to leave me."

That sounded like both a plea and a demand, but it was what she wanted, so she agreed. "I'm glad to stay." Her future with Austin was secure. No, it hadn't quite rolled out the way she'd figured, but this, family, fun, and laughter, was even better. "We'll be together for the rest of our lives."

Mother's Day was overcast and gray, but it didn't put a damper on the gathering. With two upcoming weddings to celebrate, Luna recovered, and all of them together, nothing could really do that.

Sitting with Luna at one end of the table, Faith watched as Austin and Cory carried in platters of grilled meat and vegetables. Willow and Clay had set up everything inside, and Raine made sure everyone had iced tea. Sully sat between Joe and Jamie while they looked over the house plans Cory and Austin had settled on.

The kids had all refused to let the moms do a single thing.

That suited Faith, since it also made Luna kick back and relax. In the last couple of days, Luna was getting out more, though she still wore a few fading bruises.

"Thank you for having us over." Luna glanced at Joe. "This is the first break I've had from his hovering."

"He's still worried." Faith let her gaze move over those visible bruises. They'd settled into a ghastly green ringed by mustard yellow. "You're sure you don't have any aches and pains?"

"Shh." Low, so no one else would hear, Luna confided, "If I so much as wince, they'll all start pampering me again."

"And you'd rather do the pampering?"

Luna grinned. "You know me too well." She fluffed her hair, now colored a vibrant strawberry blond. "I had to dye my hair just to get some alone time."

Faith laughed. Even now, Willow, Austin, and Raine kept glancing at Luna to make certain she had everything she needed. Faith wouldn't have been surprised if one of them had tried to prop Luna's feet on a cushion. "It's beautiful. I love how you change it so often."

"I bore easily."

"But not with me," Joe said, proving he'd been listening in.

After a roll of her eyes, Luna smiled. "No, never with you."

Once all the food was served and everyone was seated at the table, Willow raised her

292

tea glass in a toast. "To the most amazing moms ever."

Raine said, "Hear, hear!"

"To the wise advice that finally brought Austin and me together," Cory added, and got another round of effusive agreement.

Austin said, "To being Mom, when you didn't have to."

Faith and Luna both protested that.

"Thank you," Cory said, her tone solemn and sincere, "for being the very best examples of what a mother should be."

Willow and Raine cheered.

Tears stinging her eyes, Faith reached for Jamie's hand and felt his warm fingers close around hers. When Luna turned to Joe, he blew her a kiss.

"We're not perfect," Faith said, and Luna agreed.

"You're better." Austin lifted his glass higher. "You're both overprotective, opinionated, watchful, and caring."

"Meaning you're the absolute best," Cory said.

Austin smiled. "Anyone can be a mother, but it takes a very special woman to be a mom. Happy Mother's Day."

■ ■ ■ ■

THE MOTHER'S DAY CROWN

CAROLYN BROWN

■ ■ ■ ■

CHAPTER ONE

"I feel as free as a bird." Dotty held up a hand to high-five her best friend, Winnie.

The crack when they slapped hands could be heard all up and down the halls of the Pecan Valley Retirement Center. A smile deepened the wrinkles around Dotty's mouth and bright blue eyes. "It's liberating, not to think about mowing the lawn and making sure the plants are watered this summer, ain't it? But I thought Monica was going to cry when I handed her the keys and the paperwork."

"She'll settle into the change, and didn't I tell you how good it would feel to be free of all that stuff?" Winnie eased down on the brown and orange plaid sofa. "It's like making peace with the fact that we're both happy as baby piglets in a fresh mudhole right here in this retirement home. We should've done this five years ago. You are welcome."

"For what?" Dotty asked.

"Putting our names on the list to live here," Winnie answered.

"I suppose you're going to lord it over me like you do that trophy for the best afghan, aren't you?" Dotty sighed.

"Yep, I am," Winnie said, nodding. "If you'd have agreed to come with me, you wouldn't have had to wait three months for an apartment, but oh, no, you weren't leaving your home. They gave your place to someone else, and you had to be lonely for all those weeks. So, you are welcome for me putting both our names on the list, and for me begging the supervisor here to put your name back at the top when this place came open. If it hadn't been for that, you wouldn't live here, and you wouldn't even have a chance to be Mother of the Year."

"I want that Mother's Day crown so bad." Dotty sat down in the recliner she'd brought from her house three months ago and hit the button on the side to raise the footrest. "I'm going to wear the fancy blue dress that I bought for Monica's wedding at the Mother's Day party. Promise me you'll take a picture of Gladys's face when they put the crown on me." She reached up with both hands and set an imaginary crown on her thick, curly hair.

"Pshh!" Winnie cut her brown eyes over at Dotty. "I told you not to buy that dress. The way your granddaughter is dragging her feet when it comes to commitment, that dress will be old, faded, and out of date by the time she gets around to walkin' down the aisle. She might even end up being an old maid, and you'll never have them great-grandkids you want so bad."

Dotty shook a bony finger at Winnie. "You can blame your grandson for the way my granddaughter shies away from relationships. Tyler broke her heart, and she's never gotten over it."

"Hmmph," Winnie snorted. "That was ten years ago. She needs to grow up, and you're not going to need to wear that dress anyway, because I'm going to win the crown. I was here a week before you finally made up your mind to join me, so I'm the senior resident of the two of us, and besides, I'm prettier and nicer than you."

"You are not," Dotty argued. "And them combs that hold the crown on need someone with enough hair to keep the thing from fallin' off. You ain't got enough hair left to even hold the dang thing in place."

"I'll superglue it to my head and sleep in it if I win," Winnie told her, "and I'm wearing the pink dress that I wore on Easter.

Your blue dress is way too fancy for the Mother's Day party. Didn't you see the pictures on the bulletin board in the dining room? The women were all dressed semi-casual, kind of like they were fixin' to go to Sunday school."

"Then *I'll* bring some class to the party," Dotty said, "and I'm going to get more votes than you do."

"Like you did when I won the blue ribbon at the fair for my afghan." Winnie shot a dirty look at her best friend.

"It's my turn to win, since you got the prize for the best afghan," Dotty argued.

"You goin' to stuff the ballot box," Winnie countered.

"Every resident only gets one vote — period," Dotty reminded her. "I'll vote for you if you vote for me. That way, maybe we can beat out Gladys with our joined forces. She's got five crowns lined up on the shelf in her room, already."

"She's been here ten years, so everyone knows her, and they say she's" — Winnie's voice went an octave higher — " 'just the sweetest thing ever,' or something like that. I'm going to prove that I'm just as lovable as she is."

"I'll just sit back and watch y'all try to outdo me." Dotty narrowed her eyes and thought about ways to garner more votes. "We could get Monica and Tyler to vote every time they come to see us, because visitors get a vote a day."

"Great idea." Winnie nodded. "But remember, the staff gets two votes each a day. Gladys has a bowl of hard candy in her apartment that she offers the nurses and aides, and even the cleaning staff, when they come in to see her."

"Is there anything in the rules that say we can't bribe votes with candy and food?" Dotty asked.

"Not that I ever read in the booklet they gave me when I checked into this place, and Gladys can have her old hard candy." Winnie giggled. "I've got one of them two-pound bags of miniature candy bars in my room. I bet the folks like chocolate better than peppermints."

Dotty shot a dirty look toward Winnie. Some best friend she was.

"What's that for?" Winnie asked.

"You didn't tell me that you had candy bars," Dotty answered. "I'm going to call Monica and tell her to bring mini-cupcakes tomorrow."

"I'm not stupid. You've always been competitive, so I got a head start on you," Winnie declared. "I even give the cleaning folks chocolate, 'cause they get two votes a day, too, just like the doctors and nurses. And since my grandson Tyler is the resident PA here at the center, he can vote three times a day. I'm going back across the hall to my place. Come on over, and we'll watch our soap opera after lunch."

"You'd like that, wouldn't you? That way, if anyone comes in, you can give them a candy bar, and they'll vote for you. I'll just watch our soap at my place until after Mother's Day, thank you very much." Dotty had no doubt that she would miss Winnie. They'd watched their program together for the past twenty years. But the game was on, and Dotty had her heart set on that crown, which was way prettier than the blue ribbon and trophy Winnie got for her afghan.

"You aren't nice even to me, and I'm your best friend, so I don't think you'll need to wear that blue dress." Winnie got up slowly and left the room.

Dotty pulled her phone out of her pocket and called Monica.

"Hello, Nana," her granddaughter answered. "Is everything all right? Have you changed your mind?"

"Hell, no!" Dotty said. "I'm at peace with my decision. Where are you right now?"

"At the grocery store, buying supplies for

a couple of weeks," Monica answered. "Do you need something?"

"Yep, I want a dozen of those miniature cupcakes brought to me every day for the next two weeks. You can bring the first dozen tomorrow, and if they don't have nice ones there, then you can make some for me. There's a mini-cupcake pan in the cabinet to the right of the stove," Dotty answered. "I'm going to win that Mother's Day crown just to prove to Winnie that I'm nicer than she is."

"Good grief!" Monica sighed. "Are you two competing, again?"

"Yes, we are," Dotty answered, "and this time, I'm going to win. I intend to wear that crown on Mother's Day here at Pecan Valley and get my picture on the bulletin board in the lobby. That way, she can't hold that trophy she got for her afghan at the county fair over my head any longer."

"Nana, you two have been best friends for most of your lives," Monica reminded her. "Why can't you stop this competition?"

"Because we have so much fun, and it makes things exciting. I won five bucks last week when I bet her that Gladys and Harry were in a relationship," Dotty bragged.

Monica gasped. "Nana! Those two old people have to be at least ninety."

"Both of them are eighty years old," Dotty corrected her. "They're the same age me and Winnie are. They ain't lived a righteous life like me and Winnie, so God aged them worse than He did us."

"Are you jealous? Do you have a little crush on Harry? And with all this arguing you and Winnie do, how can you say you're closer to God than Gladys?" Monica teased.

"Hell, no!" Dotty's voice went up to the screeching she made when she saw a mouse dart across the floor. "I'm not jealous, and me and Winnie is like sisters. We argue and bicker, but God help anyone who tries to get between us. We'll join forces and take them down. And honey, I'm not falling in love, and if I did, it would be with a guy who doesn't need a walker, and who has his own teeth. I'd need a little more from a man if I was going to let him bounce my bed springs."

"Nana!" Monica gasped again. "What has got over you? You and Winnie cleaned the church and never missed a Sunday. I've never heard you talk about sex or what goes on in the bedroom."

Dotty laughed so hard that she snorted. "Honey" — she wiped her eyes with her shirt sleeve — "you should've been a fly on the wall and listened to some of those conversations while we were cleaning the church. It's a wonder lightning bolts didn't come out of the sky, shoot through the rafters, and turn us both into a pile of ashes right there between the pews. I've got to go now. My game show is coming on television. Don't forget to bring those cupcakes."

"Will do," Monica said. "See you in the morning."

"Bye now." Dotty ended the call, picked up the remote, and turned on the TV.

"She's still alive and just as sassy as ever," Monica said, sighing as she parked her car in the driveway of her Nana's house between Bells and Luella, Texas. "Then why does this feel so final?"

She didn't have an answer, so she slung open the car door and marched across the yard. The roses were in desperate need of some tender loving care. There were cat prints in the dust on the porch, and next week, she would have to either mow the lawn or pay someone to do it for her. If Nana had been there, the roses would have looked like they were ready to be photographed for a magazine, and the porch would have been shiny clean.

She fished around in her purse for the key ring her grandmother had given her when she went by the assisted living center located in Bells that morning. Just having the keys in her hand meant that Nana had decided to "try" the facility with her friend Winnie, and she wasn't coming back home. Nana was going to stay at the Pecan Valley Retirement Center for the rest of her days.

Tears flowed down Monica's cheeks and dripped onto her T-shirt. Change was one of the few things she hated, and inheriting Nana's house and what was left in it would be a huge change in Monica's world. She opened the old wooden screen door, and memories of all the times she had slammed that door flashed through her mind.

Monica Joanne, how many times have I told you not to slam the door? Nana's voice was clear in her head.

"But, Nana, we didn't have a door like this at our house, and it's so much fun to slam it and then see if I can jump off the porch before I hear the noise." More tears dammed up behind her eyes as she looked down at the keys. The whole place now belonged to her — *kit and kaboodle,* as Nana had said. She'd be responsible for keeping the lawn, taking care of the roses, and making sure to wash the cat prints off the front porch. THE BEST GRANDMA IN THE WORLD fob on the key ring was telling the absolute truth. Dorothy Allen, aka Dotty or Nana, was the best and always would be, but Monica didn't think she should be in an assisted living center, even if she was eighty years old.

"Hey! Are you going to live here or rent the place out?" Tyler Magee yelled from the other side of the picket yard fence.

"That would be none of your business," Monica said through clenched teeth. Winnie had deeded her place over to Tyler, and Monica had prayed the whole way from Sherman to Luella that he had already sold it and moved to Siberia or maybe somewhere in the middle of Africa.

"I heard that Dotty gave you her house this morning?" Tyler pressured. "I've been sorting through things that Granny left behind and haven't even made a dent. I've been going through stuff over here a little at a time. I couldn't decide whether to rent the place out or live here, but this past week, I made up my mind to move in. They won't let me have pets in the house I'm renting, and I promised to take care of Granny's cat, so . . ." He shrugged. "Besides, I like the peace and quiet out here in the country."

Evidently, God had better things to do today than listen to her prayers, or maybe He felt kind of sorry for Siberia and Africa

and didn't want to inflict a two-timing —
she blushed at the name she was about to
call him — on either place.

"So do I," Monica said as she unlocked
the door and disappeared into the house.
She stopped inside the door and took a deep
breath. The scent of lavender, Nana's favorite fragrance, still lingered. The living room
looked empty now that the outdated orange
and brown plaid sofa and Nana's recliner
were gone. The only piece of furniture left
in the room was an old, wooden rocker with
wide arms. Monica slumped down into it
and sighed. "Why, Lord, would you do this
to me?"

*Don't be blamin' God for Tyler and Raylene
Carter's mistakes,* scolded Nana's voice in
her head.

"But God could have struck Raylene's
conscience," she grumbled, "or maybe set
just a little fire under her butt to let her
know where she was headed if she did
something so mean."

She glanced around at the bare walls.
Light spots and lots and lots of nail holes
dotted them where Nana had taken pictures
down. Monica hated to paint, but before
she moved in, she would have to either do it
herself or hire it done, and she was way too
tight with her money to pay someone to do

what she was capable of doing herself.

She pushed up out of the rocking chair and went to the kitchen. She ran her hand over the yellow-topped chrome table with its four matching chairs. One of her earliest memories was sitting on a big thick phone book on one of those chairs. The first decision she made that morning was to leave the antique set right where it was. The second was to move out of her apartment in Denison and into this house.

Tyler knew that he should be in the house figuring out what to donate to the women's shelter in Sherman and what to keep, but after seeing Monica, he needed a moment. He sat down on the porch swing and let his mind wander back to the biggest mistake he had ever made in his entire life.

That would have been ten years ago, when he let Raylene Carter talk him into going into Nana Allen's garage with her during their early graduation party. That started a mess that was like a small snowball rolling down a hill. By the time it got to the bottom, it was as big as a boulder.

Raylene backed him up against the wall and kissed him with lots and lots of tongue. He didn't even realize that she was unbuttoning his shirt until she pulled it over his shoulders. She had his belt undone, his pants unzipped, and her hand inside his underwear when Monica flipped on the light.

"Busted!" Raylene giggled.

Monica's face turned scarlet. Tears sprang from her eyes and ran down her cheeks. Then she simply flipped the light back off and closed the door.

"I guess that means you're needing a date to the prom now." Raylene removed her hand. "Pick me up at six. I'm wearing red, and I don't like roses, so get me a white orchid for my corsage."

He had tried to talk to Monica, but she wouldn't even speak to him, and being the stupid young guy he was at that time, he had taken Raylene to the prom. He had been miserable all night, especially when he found out that Raylene had deliberately caused the problem because Monica had beat her out for the valedictorian honor.

"If I couldn't be number one, then she deserved to suffer, so I broke y'all up," Raylene had told him when they got to the prom.

"That was downright mean," he told her.

"I worked hard to be valedictorian. I'm going to a private after-party, and you're not invited, so I'll be ready to go home at eleven o'clock. You can drop me at my house, but don't expect a goodnight kiss," she'd said bluntly.

Granny's calico cat, Sheba, hopped up onto his lap, turned around a few times, then curled up and closed her eyes. Winnie had given him specific instructions about what to feed her and how to take care of her when she'd given him the house.

"She's a good cat, and a wonderful mouser, so you take care of her. That's the only thing I'm asking you to do. I don't care what you keep or what you give away, whether you live in the house all the time, part of the time, or sell it. Just don't give Sheba away or take her to a shelter," Granny had said.

"You missin' her?" Tyler rubbed the sleeping cat's fur. "Me, too, but I miss Monica even more. I can go visit with Granny, but Monica won't even talk to me — not even after ten years."

She's not ever going to talk to you if you don't make an effort, the pesky voice in his head said. *You were the one who messed up, so you should be the one to try to make it right.*

"I *did* try for a whole summer," he muttered.

Sheba opened one eye and growled.

"So, you're not on my side, either," he said, and sighed. "Okay, I get the message."

He set the cat on the porch swing, took a deep breath, and slowly walked down the steps and across the yard. Just as he opened the gate separating the Magee and the Allen properties, Monica came out of the house and headed to her car. She popped open the trunk and picked up two bags of groceries.

Tyler sucked in another lungful of air and let it out slowly as he unfastened the gate and headed toward her car. She was on the porch when he picked up the last three bags and started toward the house with them.

"What are you doing?" she asked.

"Being a good neighbor," he said, smiling. "We're going to live next door to each other. We might as well be civil, for our grandmothers' sakes if nothing else. It would break both of their hearts if we wouldn't even speak to each other or help each other out when we get in a bind."

"I suppose it would." She nodded. "Just put the bags on the kitchen table, and thank you."

Tyler chuckled.

"What's so funny?" Monica asked.

"I was just wondering if you're going to keep this kitchen table and chairs. Granny has a red one just like it, and I can't give it up. I'm going to sell the one in my rental house and keep hers because of the memories. Do you remember how many times we rolled homemade play dough out on either table when we were little kids? Or had milk and cookies, or came in from playing in the snow and had hot chocolate and popcorn at one or the other of these tables?" he asked as he set the bags down.

Monica whipped around, and her brown eyes locked with his. "Tyler, I remember everything — even the things that I wish I could forget."

"I apologized dozens of times." He blinked and looked out the window at a couple of squirrels playing in a pecan tree.

"Sometimes, it's too late for an apology." She unloaded one of the bags into the cabinet.

"Even after ten years?" he asked.

"*Especially* after that long! I still have trouble with commitment and trust," she told him. "We were best friends, and then you were my boyfriend, and then . . ."

"And then we were more, and I let Raylene ruin it, but I can't blame her totally. I was stupid enough to let her entice me into that garage, so part of it's my fault," he finished for her. "Can we, at least, be neighbors and maybe friends?"

"Let's start with neighbors and see how that goes," she answered.

"Fair enough." He motioned toward the walls with a flick of his hand. "Since we're neighbors, do you want some help painting before you move in? We could swap off evenings. I'll help you until we get this place done, and then you can help me."

Monica hesitated so long that he figured she was going to refuse, but she finally said, "I hate to paint, so I'll take you up on that offer."

Tyler could hardly contain his excitement, but he just nodded. This was a step in the right direction, but he sure didn't want to spook her or do anything that might make her change her mind.

Second chances, even minor ones, didn't come along very often, and he wasn't about to jeopardize anything.

Chapter Two

Monica punched in the code at the door of the assisted living center and was passing the nurse's desk when a lady called out to her. "Miss Allen, our manager wants to talk to you. Follow me, please."

Sweet Jesus in heaven, Monica thought. *Has Nana already been kicked out of this place?*

The woman led her down a hallway and knocked on a door. A brass plate said GLORIA CALDWELL, SUPERVISOR.

"Miss Allen." Gloria stood up and rounded her cluttered desk with an outstretched hand. "I'm so glad to meet you. Dotty and Winnie are fitting in so well here, and they are such fun to have around. They bring the morale up for everyone in the center."

Monica breathed a heavy sigh of relief and shook hands with the tall, thin woman. "Thank you so much."

"Dotty tells me you're a registered nurse and that you are going to be living in Luella." Gloria smiled and went back to sit in her chair. "Please have a seat." She motioned to the wing-back chairs in front of her desk.

Monica set her tote bag on the floor and eased down into one of the chairs. "Thank you again, and yes, ma'am, I'm an RN. I work in Denison at a nursing home, but I've taken my two-week vacation to get Nana's place ready for me to move into."

"I'm going to have a position for an RN opening in a month. I'd sure like for you to think about applying for the job," Gloria said. "Leona, our day shift RN, is retiring on June first, and I'd like to hire someone young to take her place. We don't have a big turnover in staff. Most of our employees have been here for years. Leona was here when I took this job, and I've been at Pecan Valley twenty years. Would you think about it? Of course, there's the usual vetting business. Background checks and references, but you've already done all that, so you know the ropes."

Monica's mind ran in circles. The commute would be less than ten minutes, and she would have a day shift, as opposed to her current job working from three to eleven, getting home just before midnight.

"It's surely something to think about, but what about the fact that my grandmother is a resident here?" Monica asked. "Will that pose a problem?"

"Not really," Gloria answered. "Your job description wouldn't put you in daily contact with the residents. Their primary care is handled by LPNs and aides. You would oversee those staff members and do a lot of paperwork. You'd have your own office and be on hand if Dr. Magee needed assistance with an emergency."

"Dr. Magee?" Monica asked.

"Tyler Magee is our day shift physician's assistant. He works closely with the staff at the hospital and routinely gives each resident a physical. He's a very nice person, and we've been so pleased with his work here at Pecan Valley," Gloria told her.

There's the kicker! Monica thought. "Can I have some time to think about it?" she asked.

"I'm going to stop taking applications next week so that I'll have a week for interviews and then some time for the vetting process," Gloria told her.

Monica stood up. "I'll let you know by the end of the week, and thank you for telling me about the opening."

317

"Fair enough, and you are welcome." Gloria smiled again. "Before you leave today, go by Leona's office and visit with her. She's right across the hall."

"I'll do that." Monica left the room and closed the door behind her. Her head still spinning with the pros and cons, she had started toward her grandmother's wing when the door across the hall opened.

"Can I help you?" a short lady with gray hair asked.

"You must be Leona. I'm Monica Allen, and Gloria was just telling me that you're retiring soon," Monica answered.

"Come on into my office." Leona motioned her inside the room.

It wasn't as big as the room across the hall, but it had a nice view of a flower garden that had been created in the center's U-shape.

"Have a seat," Leona said. "I have to admit something. I've gotten very attached to my patients, including Dotty and Winnie, even though they haven't been here long. I asked Dr. Magee if he could recommend someone to take my place; someone that would be gentle with the family here. That's the way I look at these folks. They deserve respect and dignity, not someone who might snap at them and not listen to what they

318

have to say. He told me about you, and Dotty talks about you constantly, so I've got some idea of your character."

"Nana is a whole lot biased," Monica admitted with a smile.

"Maybe so, but we've got a dozen or so residents here that used to live in Luella. I don't think they are all biased." Leona said with a smile. "Think about it, and if you have any questions, just call me." She passed a business card over to Monica.

"Thank you," Monica said and took the card.

She was halfway down the hall when another door opened, and Tyler stepped out with a tablet in his hands. With his dark hair and light blue eyes, he was even more handsome than he'd been in high school. She had managed through the years to avoid him, but it looked as if their paths would cross pretty often, whether she applied for the job at Pecan Valley or not.

He flashed a brilliant smile her way. "Good morning. I understand that Gloria and Leona have talked to you about applying for a job here."

"How . . . what . . . I just," she stammered.

"This place is like a tiny village," Tyler said, chuckling. "Everyone knows everything. Besides, this is exciting news for the residents. A new young RN on day shift is a big thing. So, are you considering applying for the job?"

"I haven't even had time to wrap my head around the idea," she admitted.

"It's a fantastic place to work, if my opinion means anything," he said, and waved over his shoulder as he hurried off to the next room.

Monica heard music coming from behind one door and laughter from the one across the hall. She didn't hear a single moan from elderly folks who were bedfast and in pain. "That's a plus," she muttered.

A little way down the hall, Dotty stepped out of her room. "What are you just standing there for? Did you bring my cupcakes, and what did you tell Gloria?"

Monica could hardly believe her eyes. Her grandmother was wearing a royal blue party dress, a crown made of aluminum foil, and mismatched socks. She hurried the rest of the way down the hall and into Nana's room. "Halloween is over," she said as she unloaded cupcakes and her grandmother's favorite cookies into the cabinet in the tiny kitchen.

"I know that, silly girl." Nana opened the package of chocolate cookies, picked up one, and popped the whole thing into her mouth. "I'm practicing my walk down the red carpet for when I'm crowned Mother of the Year in a couple of weeks."

Monica tilted her head to one side. "Is that the crown?"

"Of course not. The real one is beautiful and has shiny rhinestones. I just needed something on my head to practice with." Dotty smiled and reached for another cookie.

Monica hoped that if Nana did win the tiara, she didn't have chocolate between her teeth when she smiled for the bulletin board picture. "Who won the title last year?"

"Gladys Garber," Dotty answered through gritted teeth. "She flirted with your grandpa and tried to break us up when we were in high school. I intend to end her winning streak."

"Oh?" Monica raised an eyebrow. "Tell me more."

"We'd been together since we were thirteen, and it was our senior year. We were getting married that fall after we graduated. Then Gladys got between us, and we almost didn't make it. Sorry old witch just had her eye on Eddie's money, not on him," Dotty said as she paced back and forth across the living room floor. "Walk slow and remember to smile at all the people who'll be at the celebration," she coached herself and did a perfect royal wave at all the imaginary people in her apartment.

"Grandpa had money?" Monica was almost as amazed by that fact as she was by how much Nana's story paralleled hers. Evidently, every generation had its share of mean women.

"He didn't, but his folks were a notch above comfortable. His mama had passed away when he was in elementary school, and then his dad died about ten years after we married, leaving the ranch to us. By the time you were born, your grandpa had come down with cancer, so we sold the place and built the little house I gave you," she said. "But Gladys was mad at me because I got homecoming queen that year, and she wanted to get back at me. Sound familiar?"

"Little bit," Monica answered.

"Difference is, I fought for my man, and you walked away from yours." Dotty made a turn at the door and started back to the other side of the room. "If you'd blacked Raylene's eye or yanked part of that blond hair out by the roots, you would have felt so much better."

"Did you do that?" Monica asked.

Dotty nodded and then had to straighten her crown. "I got off the school bus with her that afternoon and whupped her all the way to her house. We both landed in a mud puddle before it was over. Mama was so mad at me for ruining my dress that she threatened to ground me until she heard what happened. You might have got a little mud in your hair, but I think you could have taken her."

"Nana, I don't want to have this conversation today," Monica said.

"My theory is that you might as well settle whatever comes up on the day it happens, not ten years down the road." Dotty went to the refrigerator and poured a glass of milk, picked up the package of cookies, and set them on the coffee table. Then she sat down in her recliner. "But since you don't want to talk about Raylene, let's talk about the job that you're going to apply for."

"I haven't decided whether I'm going to do that or not." Monica wondered, if she had lit into Raylene in the garage that night instead of running away, would things have been totally different?

"Why not?" Dotty asked. "Please hand me my milk. I'm afraid to try to sit down with it in my hands for fear I'll slosh it out when I kick my footrest up. I don't want to ruin my pretty dress."

Monica picked up the glass and put it in

Dotty's hand, and then took a seat on the sofa.

"Thank you," Dotty said, and took a sip. "And exactly why wouldn't you apply for the job? It's a day job, and the patients are all mobile to some degree." She tucked her chin and looked out over the top of her bifocals. "Is it because Tyler works here?"

"No, of course not!" Monica crossed her fingers and tucked them under her leg. "I'm an adult, and I've moved past that time in my life."

"Bull crap!" Dotty said. "If you had gotten over Tyler Magee, you'd be married now, and my pretty dress" — she sighed and sniffled a little — "wouldn't still be hanging in the closet going to waste."

"Nana, if and when I get married, I'm going to the courthouse. There won't be a big wedding, so you just wear that pretty dress any day you want. Don't save it for a wedding." Monica said the words, but guilt settled over her shoulders like a heavy blanket. Her grandmother wanted a great-grandchild so badly, and she was already well into her eighties.

"I'm calling bull crap on that, too." Dotty laughed out loud. "Your mama has been planning your wedding for years, and I know my son well enough to know that there's no way Kent will let you disappoint Ginger."

"Are you serious?" Monica asked. "Mama has already started planning my wedding? Why would she do that?"

"Yep," Dotty said. "She even showed me the book she has. Pictures of dresses, venues, and even flowers and the different cakes. Honey, you're the only chicken in the nest, and she wants your special day to be a memory that you'll always hold dear to your heart."

"But aren't all those things supposed to be *my* decisions?" Even more guilt jumped onto Monica's shoulders.

"I gave birth to your father when I was twenty-seven. He and your mother were both twenty-five when you were born. You're twenty-eight, girl. We just want to have things ready, like my pretty dress here," she said, smoothing the bodice with her free hand, "when you do make up your mind."

"I won't be rushed," Monica declared, "and I intend to live with a guy for at least a year before I consent to marry him, anyway. That way, I can be sure we are compatible, and that I can trust him."

Dotty laid a hand over her heart. "Thank God we live in a world where the towns-folks won't stone you for that. Just pick one out and live with him, but don't keep us waiting forever. And honey, if you'll listen to your heart, you'll know who to trust and who to kick out to the curb after the first couple of dates."

"I'll get right on that," Monica said. "Now, let's talk about those mini-cupcakes. Why do you need a dozen every day?"

"To give to the staff and visitors, so they'll think I'm as nice as Winnie and Gladys," Dotty answered, "and don't you forget to vote on the way out, either."

"Wouldn't dream of it," Monica muttered.

Dotty and Winnie always sat at the same table in the dining room, whether they were competing for the crown or gossiping about one of the other residents. Their table sat against the wall, leaving only room for three people, and most often, the third chair wasn't even used.

But that day, Tyler made it to the dining room about halfway through the meal and waved at them to save him the extra chair. Dotty hung her unused napkin over it and just dared anyone to even look cross-eyed at the seat.

Several residents waved at him and motioned for him to join them when he headed back, but he just nodded toward his grandmother's table.

"What's going on today?" he asked as he set his tray down.

Monica came to see me," Dotty said.

Winnie turned to focus on Tyler. "Have you talked to her?"

"Little bit last night, and just in passing this morning," Tyler answered. "She agreed to let me help her paint the walls of her house before she moves in."

"That's a start," Winnie said. "How did you feel when you saw her again?"

Dotty didn't give him time to answer. "How long has it been since you kids have talked?"

"We hadn't had a conversation since that night," he admitted. "Five years ago, we said hello to each other, but that was just because we ran into each other at Walmart," Tyler answered. "And if you're asking whether I still have feelings for her, the answer is yes. I've dated other women, but I can't forget Monica. Maybe it's something that guys don't talk about or know how to explain, but there's still that old chemistry between us. I can feel it strongly, whether she does or not."

"She was your first love," Winnie said. "People never forget their first love."

"I believe it, and I'm hoping that someday

she'll forgive me so that we can make a new start." Tyler took a bite of his meat loaf.

"Paging Dr. Magee," a voice announced over the PA system. "Room forty-five, please."

"That's my call. What I got of the meat loaf was good," he said as he pushed the chair back and hurried down the hall.

"We need to join forces," Winnie whispered.

Dotty's head bobbed up and down in agreement. "I agree, and on more than just our grandkids. I hate watching our show by myself, so let's agree to share the Mother's Day crown. If I win, I'll wear it for the first half of the party. If you win, you can wear it for the first half. The loser takes the last half."

"Sounds fair, but who gets to keep it in their room?" Winnie asked.

"We'll share custody." Dotty finished off her meat loaf and took a bite of chocolate pie.

Winnie waggled her forefinger close to Dotty's face. "You didn't eat all your vegetables. You can't have pie until you do."

Dotty slapped her finger away. "I'm past eighty years old. I'm going to eat what I want, and die when I'm supposed to, and I do not waste desserts."

Winnie pushed back what was left of her meat loaf and green beans and dived into her slab of pumpkin cake with brown sugar icing. "I guess it would be a sin not to eat our dessert."

"That's right," Dotty agreed. "And we do not want to grieve the holy spirit."

"What's that got to do with dessert?" Winnie asked.

"Sinnin' makes Jesus cry," Dotty answered her. "But this ain't Sunday, so we don't need to talk religion."

"But we do need to think about how we can join forces for our grandkids," Winnie said between bites. "How are we going to go about that?"

"We're going to put our heads together and come up with a plan," Dotty whispered. "What if Monica and Tyler don't like each other? Should we try to fix him up with someone else?"

"Oh, hell no!" Winnie shook her head. "We aren't going to fail at putting our grandkids together, so we aren't even going to think about another person for either of them."

Dotty finished the last bite of her pie. "Then we'll just have to work hard at our mission. We've planned that those two would be together since they were toddlers,

329

so that we can share great-grandkids. Tyler has said that he can't forget Monica, and I know she feels the same way about him."

"Did she say so?" Winnie's eyes grew wide.

"Nope, but I can read my granddaughter like a book. If she didn't still have feelings for him, she would have found someone else years ago. Now, let's go watch our show," Dotty said. "We're goin' to make all the staff members love us."

"Gladys ain't got a snowball's chance in hell of beating us." Winnie grinned.

"That's the gospel truth." Dotty nodded and led the way to her apartment.

Monica went by the hardware store and picked up a fistful of paint samples and then headed home. Sheba was waiting on the porch for her, so she stopped to pet the cat for a few minutes. "How did you get out of the house? Winnie doesn't let you go roaming around."

Sheba meowed and went to the door.

Monica fished the key out of her purse, unlocked the door, and threw it open. Sheba beat her inside and curled up on the rocking chair. "How are you with paint colors?" she asked as she began to tape about a dozen swatches to the walls.

Sheba sighed once and closed her eyes.

"I guess that means you don't care if I use off-white, or pale yellow, or any of these other colors," Monica said. "I bet you don't care if I apply for that job, either." She sat down in the middle of the hardwood floor and stared at all the colors. Finally, she got up and went back to her grandmother's old bedroom with another handful of paint colors. She taped them to the wall and sat down on the floor in that room. "Should I do the whole house the same, or . . ."

A hard knock on the door startled her, and she popped up on her feet, adrenaline rushing through her veins. "For God's sake, it's just a salesman or one of Nana's old friends coming through town," she scolded herself on the way down the hall and across the living room floor. She opened the door to find Tyler standing there with a worried look on his face.

Her heart skipped a beat and then raced ahead, giving her another shot of adrenaline. Something was wrong with Nana. That was the only reason Tyler's blue eyes would be misting over.

"Granny is going to kill me," he said. "I've lost Sheba. Would you please help me hunt for her?"

"No, I won't" — she swung the door open and pointed to the rocking chair — "because she already found me. Come on in and claim the runaway."

Tyler shut his eyes for just a moment, then opened them again. "I'll have to be more careful. She must've slipped out when I went to work this morning."

"You do know that she's pregnant, right?" Monica crossed the room and picked up the cat. "I'd say that she's going to pop any day, and my bet is that there's at least three kittens in her belly."

"I thought she was just fat. I'm not a vet or an obstetrician." Tyler groaned. "I figured Granny had her fixed when she found her out by the road. What am I going to do with kittens?"

"Raise 'em up to about six weeks and then give them away. Since Winnie never let her outside, I wonder how she got pregnant." Monica handed the cat off to Tyler.

"Probably by sneaking in and out when Granny came over here to watch her soaps with Dotty," Tyler answered.

Sparks danced around the room like fireflies on a summer night when Monica's hands brushed against Tyler's arms. A memory of lying next to him the first night they had made love in the back of his truck flashed through her head. Fireflies had been flitting around that evening, and the stars had been bright in the dark sky. Folks said that a person never forgets their first love, and she sure believed them. Not one of the guys she'd dated had ever made her feel the way Tyler did.

"I'll take one of the kittens," she said. "I've always wanted a cat, but Mama was allergic. And I've lived in pet-free apartments since we graduated. I should be settled in by the time the kittens are ready to give away."

"Thank you," Tyler said. "One down and however many to go. I see you've got paint colors on the walls. Have you made a decision yet?"

"Nope." She'd forgotten how much she missed his friendship. Sure, she missed all the being-in-love vibes, but she missed being able to talk to him about anything and everything maybe even more. "What about your place? Have you decided?"

"Yep. I'm going with pale yellow walls. The place is small, and that would make it look really light, but first I've got to strip away the paneling. Why Granny put up that dark stuff is beyond me," he answered.

"Maybe because your grandpa liked it," Monica offered.

"Could be," he agreed. "From the pictures I've seen of the big ranch house they had, the walls were paneled with cedar. Sometimes, I wish I'd grown up on the ranch," he said.

"Not me." Monica shook her head. "This is as country as I want to get."

"I should be taking my runaway cat home," he said. "See you tomorrow?"

"Probably." She nodded. "I plan to check on Nana every day while I'm on vacation."

"Given any thought to that job offer?" he asked.

"A little. It's almost too good to pass up," she answered.

"If I'm the problem, then I promise to stay out of your way," he offered.

"You're not the issue with the job." For the second time that day, she crossed her fingers behind her back. Even though it wasn't the whole truth and nothing but the truth, it wasn't entirely a lie, either. The trouble with Tyler wasn't really working in the same huge building with him; she could be professional in that environment. It had more to do with the flutters in her heart every time they were alone together.

CHAPTER THREE

Monica had made the decision to paint all the walls the same color and had narrowed down her selection to either the palest blue that she could find or the light yellow. She was still undecided when she got to the hardware store. The blue reminded her of her favorite color on Tyler and all the good times they'd had when they both spent time with their grandmothers. It was a wonder the gate between the two properties hadn't needed a new set of hinges by the time they were grown.

Tyler had said that he was painting his walls yellow so the house would be light and sunny. That color reminded her of the shirt Tyler was wearing the night she caught him in the garage with Raylene Carter. Monica had kissed him just minutes before that, and then her world had fallen.

"No yellow for me. Every time I looked at the walls, I'd think of Raylene kissing him," she muttered.

"Well, hello," Tyler said.

He was standing so close to her that she could feel the warmth of his breath on her neck. She braced herself for the shivers that always chased down her spine when he was near and hoped he hadn't heard her mumbling about that night. There was no use in beating that dead horse anymore. She felt as if she had already dug it up on a yearly basis and kicked it multiple times.

"Hey," she said, nodding.

"Decided on a color yet?" he asked.

"I've narrowed it down to these. I want blue, but I can't decide if I want it to be as pale as the top swatch or maybe with a little more color like this one." She held up two pieces of paper.

"My mind was made up to use yellow when I came in here, but" — he rubbed his chin — "that blue reminds me of a summer sky, and all the fun we had back when we were kids."

"Me, too, so I'm leaning toward it. What does the yellow remind you of?" she asked.

"I can't put my finger on it, but it's not a good thing," he answered. "I don't guess I should paint a whole house in a color that makes me kind of sad, even though I don't know why, should I?"

"Your house. Your decision," Monica answered and then realized how curt that sounded. A good neighbor would be a little softer, both in words and tone. "I think I'll go with the palest blue on this chart. Like you say, it brings back happy memories, and it's a soothing color."

"Is it going to upset you if I decide to use the same color?" Tyler asked.

"Not at all. We can probably save some money by buying our paint all at one time. That way, we might not wind up with two partial gallons of paint when we're done." Monica got a whiff of his cologne, and a picture of him after the first time he shaved flashed through her mind. She'd shaved her legs for the first time the same day. She had little bits of tissue stuck to several places around her knees and ankles. He had the same on his face and angular jawline.

"Great idea." He nodded. "I think five gallons will do my house."

"That's what I figured for Nana's place, but I bet we can buy nine and get both jobs done," she agreed. "I still can't call it *my house.*"

"I'm three months ahead of you. It gets easier with time." Tyler picked up two gallons of paint in each hand and carried them to the counter. "If you want, we could patch holes in your walls tonight and start painting. Once we get them all patched, the first ones should be dry enough, we can begin rolling on paint. You planning on doing the ceilings?" he asked.

Monica shook her head. "Probably not."

"Me, either."

In one sense, it seemed strange to talk to Tyler — even about paint — after all these years. But in another, it was a warm, comfortable feeling to have him back in her life, even if it was just as a neighbor.

Neighbor, my butt! Dotty's voice was clear in her head. *You can't ever be just a neighbor with Tyler. There's too much history.*

Watch me, Monica argued. *I'm just as bullheaded as you are.*

She picked up a bucket of paint in each hand and followed Tyler. "I'll need five gallons in this color," she told the guy behind the counter as she laid the color card on the top of one of the cans.

"Four for me," Tyler said. "I'll owe you for half of that gallon, or I'll buy you dinner one evening for my part."

"Give me about twenty minutes, and I'll have them done for you," the guy said.

"Thanks," Monica said. "I'll go find a roller and pan and some drop cloths while you get that done."

"Me, too," Tyler said.

Bells was a small town where rumors were the bread of life for some folks. Monica could have put money on a bet that Nana would call her before she even got home, asking if she and Tyler had made up, and if it was time to get her blue dress pressed and ready for the wedding.

Sure enough, Dotty got the phone call while the last buckets of paint were on the shaking machine and rushed over to Winnie's apartment to tell her.

"I already know," Winnie said with a grin when Dotty pushed the door open. "Bertie went to the hardware store to get paint to redo an old antique cradle she found at an auction, and she saw them together."

"Gracie called me. She works at the checkout counter. She said one of them bought five gallons, and the other one got four gallons of the same color paint," Dotty said. "That has to mean they're going to work together to get our houses redone."

"Pale blue," Winnie added. "Looks like they aren't going to need our help in getting things ironed out between them."

"That's where you're wrong. They'll go way too slow if we leave it totally up to them. I saw a commercial this morning, and there was a limo in it. I think you and I should go to the alumni banquet on Friday night. I'll hire us a limo to pick us up, and then we can go by our old places and get the kids," Dotty said.

"And they'll go in together." Winnie clapped her hands. "That will make everyone think they're back together."

"And the rumors will have it that they're dating," Dotty added with a big grin on her face.

"Think that will give them a little more of a push?" Winnie eased down on the sofa and motioned to the bowl of chocolates that she gave out to the staff and visitors.

Dotty took a Kit Kat and unwrapped it. "We got to do what we can to help this along. They need to kiss and get over what happened ten years ago. They'll think we just want to get all the use out of the limo that we can."

"You could wear your blue dress to the banquet," Winnie suggested. "The alumni banquet and dance *is* a dress-up affair."

Dotty popped the candy bar in her mouth and shook her head. "Gladys will be there. She always goes, and she never wears the same dress two years in a row. I want something new and all blinged out, as the kids say these days."

"Don't talk with food in your mouth," Winnie said. "What does it matter if Gladys is there?"

"I can't wear my dress to the alumni banquet and then to the Mother's Day party, too. She'll make a snide remark if I do, and I'd just have to slap her if she did," Dotty answered.

"And that would get you thrown out of Pecan Valley." Winnie sighed. "Which would mean I'd have to take up for you and wind up getting kicked to the curb, too. So, I guess we'll wear the matching black pant-suits we've worn for the past five years."

Dotty shook her head again. "I vote we make Monica take us shopping tomorrow for new outfits. I'll offer to buy her something sexy if she'll drive us and go with us."

"Did you bring your girdle when you moved in here?" Winnie asked.

"Hell, no! I burned it along with all the pantyhose and thigh-highs in my underwear drawer and felt downright liberated," Dotty answered. "I'm going to shop for something with an elastic waist and flowing top. That should cover up a multitude of fat cells."

"Sounds good to me," Winnie agreed. "When are you calling Monica?"

Dotty grabbed two more candy bars and pulled her phone out of her pocket. "Right now. You call Tyler and tell him that he's going to his ten-year class reunion."

"What if he says he doesn't want to go?" Winnie asked.

"Tell him that Monica will be there," Dotty answered.

"What if she says no?" Winnie picked up her phone and scrolled down through her contacts.

"Quit being negative. Together, we could sell a coffin to a dead man. This is a piece of cake." Dotty touched the right name on the phone screen and hit the button to make the call.

"Hello, Nana, is everything all right?" Monica asked.

"Where are you?" Dotty asked. "I hear road noises."

"On my way home from the hardware store. I bought paint to redo the walls," she answered, "but I bet you already knew that didn't you?"

"Yes, I did. *You* couldn't sneeze in Bells or Luella, Texas without everyone in town wondering if you've been in a dusty old barn making out with Tyler." Dotty laughed.

"Nana!" Monica gasped.

"Well, it's the gospel truth. Did you just buy the same color paint with him, or did you sneeze a few times?" Dotty asked.

"Paint only," Monica answered.

"Y'all goin' to work on the houses tonight?" Dotty asked.

"Yes, we are. Are you disappointed that I'm changing the color of the walls?" Monica asked.

"I don't care if you paint them turtle-crap green. It's your house now." Dotty smiled at her own joke. "I called to tell you that me and Winnie need you to pick us up tomorrow morning. We let the alumni banquet and dance sneak up on us, and we need to go shopping for new outfits. We'll have lunch while we're out, and I'll even spring for a new dress for you."

"I hadn't planned on going," Monica said. "When is it?"

"Friday night, and it's your ten-year reunion, and that's a big thing," Dotty told her. "Raylene is going to be there. Are you going to let her ruin another night for you?"

"How do you know Raylene is going?" Monica asked.

Dotty unwrapped one of the small candy bars while she talked. "Honey, I know everything, except why Eve ate that apple. I could strangle her for that. Ain't no snake, four-legged or two-legged or even no-legged, could talk me into goin' against what God told me not to do."

"I don't doubt that for a minute, Nana. I'm at the house now. What time do you want me to be there?" Monica asked.

Dotty smiled. "Nine o'clock, and you will go with us to the banquet, right?"

"Yes, but if Raylene gets all up in my face . . ." Monica paused.

"I'll knock her on her ass if she does." Dotty finished the sentence. "I'm old, so they won't put me in jail, and besides, it would be fun. What's that song I hear in the background?"

"It's Miranda Lambert singing 'Storms Never Last.' I made a playlist of songs I like to listen to on the commute to work," Monica answered.

"She sang that at the Opry," Dotty said. "You need to pay attention to it, girl."

"Yes, ma'am," Monica said. "Anything else?"

"Nope," Dotty said. "Just be here at nine, and we'll tell the staff that we won't be back until after lunch. Bye, now."

"See you tomorrow," Monica said and ended the call.

Monica sat still and listened to the last half of the song that talked about storms not lasting forever. Then she turned off the engine and swung the car door open. As an afterthought, she pulled the CD with her playlist on it out of the dash and tucked it into her purse. If things got awkward tonight, music just might help. At the very least, it would give her and Tyler something to talk about.

With one hand, she grabbed the bag with the painting supplies from the back seat and picked up a can of paint with the other one. A gentle breeze wafted the scent of either Tyler's cologne or shaving lotion over to her, and just the fact that she recognized it said there was still a lot of chemistry between them.

Whatever happened to "out of sight, out of mind"? she wondered as she led the way into the house.

"I'll take two more cans inside and come back for the rest," Tyler said, "and then I should go over to my place and get changed into painting clothes."

Monica looked down at her khaki shorts. "I should do the same."

"Hey, are you hungry?" Tyler asked on his way across the living room. "I can have a pizza delivered, and I've got beer at my house I could bring over."

It's not a date. He's just being neighborly, Monica thought.

"You bring the beer. I'll order the pizza.

Meat Lovers with extra black olives, right?" she asked.

"You remembered." He smiled. "Yes, that's great."

See, it's not a date. I'm paying for the pizza. We're just neighbors.

He brought in the rest of the paint, set it on the floor, and headed back out the door. "See you in a few minutes. I've got half a cheesecake in the fridge. I'll bring it over for dessert."

Monica did love cheesecake, but how did they get so friendly in such a short time? She'd avoided him for ten years, and now, they were just about where they had been when they were in junior high school — friends who did everything together. She wasn't sure she was ready for even that much but didn't know how to reverse things.

You went through all the stages of grief when Raylene caused that problem, the niggling voice in her head reminded her, *except acceptance.*

"Maybe being close to him is what I need to jump over that last hurdle and move on with my life. We've both changed in the past decade," she whispered as she went to her bedroom and changed into a pair of cutoff bibbed overalls with frayed hems and a faded orange tank top. She pulled her dark brown hair up into a ponytail and was on her way back to the living room when she heard a soft knock.

"Come on in," she called out.

Tyler pushed open the door, took a covered container of cheesecake and a six pack of beer to the kitchen table, and then turned around. A broad grin covered his face, and his blue eyes twinkled. "You wore that same outfit in high school the day we decorated this house for our graduation party. I thought you looked adorable then, and you still do."

"Thank you." She bit back a nasty remark about remembering the yellow shirt he had worn, and the skimpy dress Raylene had on the next night. "Pizza will be here in twenty minutes. We can probably patch the bedrooms while we're waiting."

"Or we could have a cold beer while we wait and catch our breath," he suggested.

Monica could hold her liquor fairly well, but the way Tyler jacked up her pulse, she didn't trust herself with even one beer on an empty stomach. "I'm saving my beer to have with my pizza. We've probably got time to stretch the plastic drop cloths onto the floors, right?"

"Probably so," Tyler said as he dug into

the bag on the table, brought out what they needed, and headed to the master bedroom. "I figured this one would be empty, because Granny's is. We could patch in here, and in the living room, then paint this bedroom tonight, and move the furniture from the other bedroom over here tomorrow night. That would fix it so we don't have to work around furniture."

"Sounds good to me." Monica took one of the drop cloths from him and unfolded it.

Working together, they had it taped down on the floor by the time the pizza delivery guy arrived. Monica paid him and took the box to the table, where Tyler was already seated.

See, it's not a date. If it was, he would have hopped up and held my chair for me.

She opened the box, took a beer out of the rings holding them together, and sat down across from him. As luck would have it, his bare knee touched hers under the table and sent a whole new wave of heat through her body.

Methinks the lady protests too damn much. There was no doubting that Nana's voice was in her head.

Tyler waited until she got a slice of pizza, and then he took one. "I've got a confession. I've kept up with you and your career and your dating history through my granny."

"I suppose neither of us had much choice about that, since they're like twin sisters, and they love gossip." Monica bit the end off her slice and took a sip of beer. "I love pizza and beer together."

"Me, too." He took a long sip of his beer. "Remember the first time we had beer?"

"Eighth grade, and we swiped it out of Nana's refrigerator and took it up to the barn on the old ranch place," she said.

"We thought we were drunk on half a beer." He chuckled. "I was terrified I'd wake up with a hangover the next morning."

"I was *terrified* that Nana would smell it on my breath. I wouldn't even hug her good night," Monica said. "She had to have known we took one of her beers, but she never said a word."

"I figure she told Granny, too, but I never heard anything, either. Guess they knew one beer wouldn't hurt us," he said. "Know what I remember the most?"

"What?" she asked.

"The way your kisses tasted after we'd had the beer," he answered.

She glanced across the table, and their eyes locked. Like so many times in the past, she knew what he was thinking, and had no doubts that he could do the same. When two people had spent as much time together as they had, ten years couldn't erase the bond.

Tyler blinked and looked away. He figured that he had pushed the memory card as far as he dared, so he changed the subject to the job at hand. "So, about living here. Are you going to take the master bedroom or continue to sleep on the twin-size bed in the spare room?"

"I'm going to use the bigger room so that I'll have the half-bath. I don't expect to have many overnight guests. When Mama and Daddy come out here, they bring their motor home and stay in it, and . . . ." She shrugged.

"My folks do the same, and neither of us have siblings, or nieces or nephews," he added. "I may turn the small bedroom into an office."

"I hadn't thought of that, but it's a good idea," she said with a nod. "If I remember right, that hole patch stuff dries in about an hour."

"Does that mean you've used it before?" he asked.

"Oh, yeah! In college, we had to be sure our dorm rooms were exactly as we found them. Painted tan with no nail holes, or we wouldn't get our deposit back. I worked really hard to patch up about a hundred nail holes," she answered.

Tyler would rather they talked about her past relationships. Had she found that none of them were satisfying, as he had? In college, he'd had a few fairly long-term relationships, but they never made him feel the way Monica did. Once he'd even called his girlfriend by Monica's name. That went over like a mouse in the punch bowl at a church social, and she broke up with him.

"It's not going to do itself," she sighed.

"Cheesecake before we start?" he asked.

"I'll have mine after we finish for the night," she answered. "Are you procrastinating, Tyler Magee?"

"I hate to paint," he admitted, "but I'm too tight to pay someone to do it for me."

"You are preaching to the choir. Maybe by working together, it won't be so bad. Want me to put on some music?" she asked.

"Long as it's country, I'd love that." He stood up with a groan. "If we get with it, we might get it all done by the time the weekend is over. Hey, did Dotty call and tell you that we're going to the alumni banquet on Friday night?"

"Oh yeah," Monica answered. "I think

they're playing matchmaker."

"Think it will work?" Tyler grinned.

"Probably not, but it will give them something to do." Monica smiled back, and for the first time since that fatal night, the warmth reached her eyes.

CHAPTER FOUR

Monica was a few minutes early that morning, but she had no doubt that Nana and Winnie would be wide awake and waiting for her. Four elderly gentlemen were playing dominoes around a table in the lobby, and six ladies were in rocking chairs on the other side of the big room. Their knitting needles made music as the women knitted what looked like baby caps. All of them looked up and smiled at her.

"Good mornin'." She raised her voice slightly so that everyone could hear her.

"Same to you," several of them answered.

"Dotty and Winnie have been dressed and waiting for an hour," one of the ladies told her as she passed by. "They're lucky women to have a granddaughter who will take them shopping."

Monica patted the lady on the shoulder. "I'm lucky that they let me go with them."

She crossed the floor and had started

down the hall when Tyler stepped out of Leona's office. "Hey," he said with a grin. "Do you like the blue walls as well this morning as you did last night?"

"Even better," Monica answered, and kept walking.

"Seemed like we should paint some white clouds up around the top of the bedroom so it would really look like a summer sky." He fell into step beside her. "I'm not following you. My office is this way, and I've got to get my briefcase. I've got a continuing education class in Sherman this morning."

"I've got one next week," she told him. "They're usually so boring, I have trouble staying awake."

"Yep," he agreed, "but to keep our license, we've got to do them." He stopped and opened a door with a key card. "See you this evening. You got the pizza last night. I'll bring burgers tonight. Mustard with no onions, right? And tater tots instead of fries?"

"I haven't changed, and thank you," she answered.

He grabbed a briefcase from his desk and waved as he headed down the hall in the opposite direction from where she was going.

"I really would like to work here," she muttered, and then realized someone was behind her.

"That's good news," Gloria said. "Stop by my office today and pick up an application packet."

Monica started to say that she hadn't made up her mind, but she clamped her mouth shut. "I'll be by when I bring Nana and Winnie home from their shopping trip."

"Great!" Gloria nodded as she knocked on an apartment door. "That really makes me happy."

Monica hadn't taken but a few more steps when Dotty and Winnie came out of her grandmother's apartment. Dotty was dressed in jeans, a T-shirt, cowboy boots, and her Stetson hat. Winnie looked about the same, but she had chosen tennis shoes.

Dotty slung her tooled leather purse over her shoulder. "We heard you coming. We're ready to go."

"And you both look just like ranchin' women." Monica grinned.

"She tried to get me to wear my boots," Winnie said, "but my feet would hurt at the end of the day."

"I can kick my boots off, and you're going to have to bend over to untie and tie those shoes a dozen times," Dotty shot back. "I might have sore feet, but you're going to have an aching back."

"If you two argue and fuss, we're going to McDonald's for lunch," Monica threatened.

"Why would you do that to us?" Dotty asked.

"If you act like children, then you get kid's meals," Monica informed them. "It's just the way it is."

"You're no fun," Winnie replied. "Don't you know that our bantering is what keeps us young? You should try it with Tyler. Speaking your mind is liberating."

"Tyler is still the same sweet guy he used to be, but he broke my heart, and all the bantering in the world won't put it back together again. We're neighbors and friends — if you use the word loosely." Monica led the way out into the bright sunshine.

"You ain't Humpty Dumpty," Dotty told her. "You don't have to glue the pieces of your old heart back together, darlin'. You can have a heart transplant and get a brand new one to start all over with."

Monica pushed the button on her key chain fob to open the car doors. "But then I'd have to take medicine to keep from rejecting my new heart."

"Shotgun!" Winnie called out and hurried to get in the front passenger seat.

"If you're in love, that's the medicine that works on a virtual heart transplant," Dotty said as she got in the back seat. "You can have the front seat, Winnie. I've got more room back here."

"Spoilsport," Winnie said.

Monica slid in behind the wheel and started the engine. "If y'all start slapping each other over the seats, I'm taking you right back to the center, and you can wear what you have on to the banquet."

"Yes, Mommy," Winnie said, laughing.

Tyler was one of the last people to make it to the conference center. He slipped into a desk in the back of the room and opened his briefcase. After a lengthy introduction, the instructor took his place behind the podium. He didn't waste any time but went right into a lecture on understanding the effects of opioids prescribed for pain management in the elderly.

Tyler tried to focus on what the man was saying, because there would be a quiz at the end of the two-hour class, and if he didn't pass it with at least seventy-five percent, he would have to take the course over again. And more than two hundred dollars would go right down the drain.

Visions of Monica in those cutoff bibbed

overalls, with her ponytail swinging back and forth as she rolled the paint on the walls, kept flashing through his mind. He had wanted to sweep her up in his arms and kiss her until they were both breathless, but it was way too soon for that to happen — if it ever did.

He was staring off into space and thinking about Monica when the instructor said, "The quiz for this class is on your computers. You have thirty minutes to finish it, and your grade will pop up after you hit 'submit'."

Tyler remembered most of the material from when he had taken a similar class his last year in school, but he was sweating when he hit the submit button at the end of the test. When eighty percent popped up, he heaved a heavy sigh of relief. That was the lowest grade he'd ever made on a test, but he had passed, and that meant he didn't have to retake the course.

"Little worried, were you?" the lady next to him asked.

"No, I was a whole lot worried," he admitted.

"There's a bunch of us going to have lunch together. Want to join us?" she asked. "By the way, I'm Paula Garber. I work with Dr. Avery here in Sherman."

"Tyler Magee," he said. "I work the day shift at Pecan Valley Retirement Center."

"Man, that's the job I'd like to have. My aunt is over there, and she loves it." She gathered up her things and headed toward the door. "Do you have to get back right now, or can you go eat with us and gripe about these classes?"

"I'd love to go. Where should I meet y'all?" Tyler finished putting his laptop away and snapped his briefcase shut.

"The Olive Garden. We'll save a seat for you," she said with a smile.

The restaurant was only a ten-minute drive from the place where the class was held. When Tyler arrived, he parked his truck and got out, only to find that he'd pulled in right next to Paula. She waved and motioned for him to follow her. It wasn't until they were in the lobby that he realized the seven other people were all women.

Paula went right up to the counter and told them she had reservations for seven, but could they add another person to that party. There Tyler was in a group of women, all trying to introduce themselves at the same time, when Dotty, Winnie, and Monica walked into the restaurant.

"Hey, Tyler!" Winnie yelled across the reception area.

"Granny? What are y'all doing here?" He left the circle of women and went right over to hug his grandmother. "I thought you were going to have lunch at a steak house."

"We changed our minds. You should come sit with us," Winnie said.

Tyler cut his eyes around to Monica, and their eyes locked. What must she be thinking, he wondered, to see him with so many women? At least, none of them had their tongue in his mouth or their hand down the front of his pants.

"I'd love to. Let me tell my colleagues that I won't be eating with them," he said, smiling.

Monica didn't return the smile, but she didn't turn around and walk out of the place, either, so he counted that as a win. He thanked Paula for the invitation and explained to her that his grandmother and her friends wanted him to have lunch with them.

"Maybe another time." Paula nodded and handed him a business card. "And if you decide to leave Pecan Valley, give me a call. I was serious about wanting to work there. I'd even start off with night shifts to get a toe in the door."

"Will do," Tyler said, "and I can sure enough vouch for the fact that it's an amazing place to work." He tucked the card into his shirt pocket and followed his new group of only three women to the back of the room.

Winnie and Dotty slid into one side of the booth, leaving the other side for him and Monica. He hesitated, but only for a moment, then sat down so close to her that their shoulders and thighs were touching. The chemistry between them sent sparks dancing like lightning bugs all around them. If Dotty and his granny could have seen or felt the electricity that he felt, they would both have been out in the aisle, singing a country song about second chances at love so loud that it would have drowned out the Italian music playing over the PA system.

"How did the shopping trip go?" His voice sounded a little hoarse in his own ears.

"They don't make clothes for sixty-year-old women anymore. Can't you just see me and Dotty in skimpy dresses cut down to our belly buttons and halfway up to our butts on the side?" Winnie complained.

Tyler's laughter was a little forced, but then, he felt like his thigh was on fire. "So, you've got more shopping to do this afternoon? Y'all going to be done by dark?"

"We don't have a curfew," Dotty told him, "but we're done now." She turned around just a little to face Winnie. "And Winnie Magee, sixty is so far in the past that you can't even catch a glimpse of it in the rearview mirror. At that age, we would have worn those kinds of dresses. We were still wearing two-piece bathing suits to the creek when these two young'uns were born."

"Yep, we were." Winnie laughed and then lowered her voice. "We finally did find something that suited us both in the last store we went into. I'm going to get double duty out of my outfit by wearing it to the Mother's Day party at the center."

"Not me," Dotty said. "I'm goin' to bring some bling and class to the party with my blue dress. It's going to look stunning with my crown."

Winnie tilted her chin up and looked at Dotty through her bifocals. "It'll look even better with my black pant set. Your dress is so fancy it will fight with the crown, whereas my outfit will enhance it."

"We haven't ordered yet," Monica warned them.

"What does that mean?" Tyler asked.

"Mommy here" — Dotty rolled her eyes — "says if we don't stop arguing, all we get for lunch are kids' meals from McDonald's."

Tyler's chuckle turned into a guffaw that

had the people around them staring. He unrolled his silverware and used the big green napkin to wipe the tears from his eyes. "Y'all have been at this our whole lives. I don't see it stopping now that you are" — he cleared his throat — "sixty years old."

"Then they'll be eating lots of McDonald's and walking to Sherman," Monica teased.

"I ain't walkin' nowhere," Dotty said. "I know how to call for a car or for the old people's shuttle to take me where I want to go if you're wearing your Mommy britches."

"Sounds to me like they're going to gang up on you," Tyler whispered. "If you need any help, just call me."

"I might do that," Monica said.

Doing so was tough, but Monica forced herself to concentrate on the menu. With Tyler's thigh and knee pressed against hers, that was no easy feat. When she finally laid the menu to the side, she noticed that both Winnie and Dotty were smiling like Cheshire cats, or maybe just old alley cats that had finally caught a house sparrow or a mouse.

She shivered at the image of the furry critter that popped into her head. She absolutely hated mice, and in the wintertime, one or two always found a way to get into Nana's house. That's why she wanted one of Sheba's kittens. By the time cold weather came around, the cat would be old enough to catch those wicked varmints.

"Cold?" Tyler asked.

"No." She shook her head. "I'm fine." She was practically sweating, even though the air conditioner vent was right above them.

"I'm Leon, and I'll be your waiter," a tall kid said. "Can I start y'all off with a daiquiri or maybe a glass of wine?"

"Just sweet tea," Monica answered.

"I'll have an Italian margarita," Winnie said.

"And I want a strawberry daiquiri." Dotty nodded. "Don't judge me, Monica! We just found outfits for the alumni party in two hours. This is a celebration."

Monica threw up both palms defensively. "No judging here. I'm just glad I'm driving if you two are drinking."

"Sweet tea," Tyler told the waiter and then turned to Monica. "Thanks for being their designated driver today. Where are y'all going after we finish lunch?"

"To the grocery store," Winnie answered for both of them. "We both need to stock up on candy and stuff to hand out to the staff and visitors."

"That's sweet of you," Tyler said.

"They have ulterior motives," Monica whispered. "They're trying to buy votes for the Mother's Day crown. Everyone that comes in their room leaves with a piece of candy or something to eat."

"If the way to a man's heart is through his stomach, then the way to that crown is through bribery," Dotty told them.

"And we ain't a bit ashamed to do it, either," Winnie added.

"What if one of you gets the most votes and wins, and the other one is the loser?" Tyler asked.

"We have a plan," Winnie said, and went on to tell him their idea. "That way we share custody of the crown, and we can each wear it a week at a time."

Monica rolled her eyes. "I bet that works out just great."

Tyler just shook his head. "You might wish you'd never applied for a job at the center."

Monica shot a look his way. "How did you know?"

"Gloria called me. She's very excited," Tyler answered.

Their drinks came, and Dotty took a long sip of hers, then narrowed her eyes at Monica. "I bet the whole center knows by now. You should have told us first."

"I just made up my mind this morning, and I haven't even picked up the application packet," Monica defended herself.

"Well, then we'll tell all our friends that you were thinking about it, and we talked you into it over lunch," Winnie said.

"Lord, it's worse than raisin' kids." Monica raised her glass in a toast. "To success in our shopping. To me making up my mind about the job offer. To having half the house painted."

Winnie touched her glass to Monica's. "To good times with friends and family."

Tyler went next. "To neighbors."

"To all of the above." Dotty clinked her glass with the other three.

Monica parked in front of the house just in time to see Sheba jump onto the porch swing. "You rascal," she muttered as she got out of the car and made her way across the yard. "How are you getting out of Tyler's house?"

Sheba meowed loudly, hopped down, and rubbed around Monica's legs.

"Don't give me that sad story," Monica fussed at her. "I've got enough problems of my own. I've got to deal with my grandmother and Winnie, and with these unresolved feelings I have for Tyler." She unlocked the door. Sheba beat her inside the house and curled up on the rocking chair. "There, I admitted it. I still have feelings for him. He still makes my pulse race when he sits next to me in a booth and takes my breath away when he looks at me with those sexy blue eyes."

She laid the job application packet on the table. "I'll look at you tomorrow. Gloria said I've got until Friday at five to get it back to her."

A rap on the door told her that Tyler was home. He still did the same *rat-a-tat-tat* that he'd done in high school. She would bet dollars to cow patties that he still had the same ringtone on his cell phone, too. But then, she had never deleted his phone number or changed "I Love the Way You Love Me" by John Michael Montgomery as the ringtone for his number on her phone, either.

"Come on in," she called out, "but don't let the cat out."

"I was careful this morning when I left," Tyler groaned. "I guess I'd best go through the house and figure out how she's escaping. Are you ready to start painting again?"

"Soon as I change clothes."

"Then I'll be back in ten minutes. Come on, Sheba, or maybe I should call you Houdini or Ghost. Seems like you can walk through walls." He picked up the cat and started for the door. He stopped in the middle of the living room, turned around, and said, "And just to keep things transparent, I had never met those women that I was with at the restaurant until today. They were in the class I took, and they invited me to go to lunch with them, probably because one of them wants to know if a position for a PA comes up at Pecan Valley."

Monica couldn't have wiped the smile off her face if she'd sucked on a lemon. "Thank you for that, but what you do is your business, Tyler."

"Just wanted you to know." He closed the door behind him.

Monica had been so angry that night she'd caught Tyler and Raylene together that she had never thought about how it must have affected him. This evening, for the first time, she put herself in his shoes. Surely, he knew he'd done something totally stupid and couldn't undo it. His heart must have been hurting as badly as hers when she refused to see him or talk to him that whole summer.

"No!" She stomped her foot. "I'll recognize that he was in pain, but not as much as I was."

She finished getting dressed in her paint outfit and was carefully putting the drop cloth down in the bathroom when Tyler knocked once on the door and then came on into the house. "I'm working in the bathroom," she called out. "This shouldn't take long, and then we'll move on to the kitchen."

"You might be surprised about the timing." His voice got louder as he came down the hallway.

Her breath caught in her chest when she looked up and realized he was standing in the doorway. The same hunger she had been feeling in her heart was evident in his eyes.

"Taping off a small area like this . . ." he started.

"Not if we work together." She was surprised that she could utter a word. Even wearing paint-stained denim shorts and a ragged tank top, he was so sexy that it took her breath away.

Monica pointed to rolls of blue painter's tape on the vanity. "If you'll do the ceiling, I'll take care of the baseboards."

She started to bend down to tuck the drop cloth into the corner, and her bare feet slipped on the slick plastic. One second, she was grasping for anything to brace her fall and hoping she wouldn't hit her head on the edge of the tub, and the next, two strong arms were around her and lifting her up.

Her heart thumped hard against Tyler's chest, but then she could feel *his* heart through both of their shirts, and it was keeping time with hers. She tried to tell him thank you, but the words froze in her throat when she looked up into his eyes. She knew and felt that starving look, and barely had time to moisten her lips, before his mouth closed over hers. Her arms found their way around his neck as she pressed her body more tightly against his. Her head was reeling and her hormones whining for more, and they were both panting when the kiss ended.

"Neighbors?" she gasped.

"Kissin' neighbors." He grinned.

"Do we need to talk about this?" She realized that his arms were still around her shoulders, and her fingers were tangled in his thick, dark hair.

"No, we just need to dream about it tonight," he answered as he released her and took a step back.

"I can almost promise that."

CHAPTER FIVE

Monica spent the entire day on Thursday going through her apartment in Denison, making a list of what she planned to keep and what she planned to donate to a local women's shelter. Then she called a moving company. They had an opening the very next morning, so that meant she had to pack fast, but first, she called her grandmother.

"Nana, I won't be by today. The moving people can get to me tomorrow, and if I don't take that time slot, it'll be weeks before they have another free time," she said.

"What are you talking to me for then?" Dotty said. "Get off this phone and get busy. You stayin' in the apartment tonight or coming back home?"

Monica smiled at that last word — _home._ "I think I'll stay here, but don't worry, I'll be ready for the alumni party tomorrow night."

"You better be. I've hired a limo to take us," Dotty said.

"Nana! I've got a car. You don't have to pay for a limo," Monica scolded.

"I don't have to do anything but die and pay taxes, and now that you own the house and the land it sits on, I don't even have many taxes to pay. I've made a deal with God not to take me until I rock my first great-grandbaby to sleep a few times, so I ain't dyin' for a long time." She sighed.

Monica's smile got bigger. "You can't guilt me into getting married and having babies."

"Oh, well" — another sigh — "it was worth a try, and darlin' girl, I will spend my money however I want to. Now, go pack. I'm ending this call."

Monica started to say something else, then realized that Dotty had indeed broken the connection. She picked up her purse, locked her apartment door, and started to her car. She had just slid in behind the wheel when her phone rang. She closed the door, fished the phone out of her purse, and answered on the fourth ring.

"I was going to tell you that I love you and goodbye," she answered.

"Well, that's good news, but I'd just as

soon you didn't tell me goodbye," Tyler drawled.

Heat gathered on the back of Monica's neck and rushed around to flush her cheeks, turning them scarlet. "I thought you were Nana. She hung up on me."

"Somedays, I just can't win." He chuckled. "I was calling to tell you that I have to work a double shift, so I won't be home until midnight. We were planning to do some work on my house tonight."

Monica explained that she was in Denison at her apartment. "This works out pretty well. I was feeling guilty, because I couldn't help you out with all this fast packing and moving I have to do."

"No guilt trips," he said. "We'll get my part done next week, or maybe over the weekend. Are you still planning to go to the alumni?"

"Nana hired a limo. She would never forgive me if I backed out." Monica sighed. "I'm not looking forward to going. Have you ever been to one of these things?"

"No, I haven't," he said, "and I wouldn't be attending this one if Granny hadn't insisted, and if you weren't going. Leona is calling on my office phone. See you tomorrow. Have fun packing. If I didn't have to work, I'd offer to help you."

"Thanks." Monica ended the call, crossed her arms over her steering wheel, and laid her head on them. She inhaled deeply and let her breath out slowly several times, then straightened up and started the engine. It was going to be a long day, but she always got her best thinking done when she was working, and she had a lot of that to do — starting with that kiss the night before.

Everything had been moved into her house by five o'clock the next day, but the place looked like a hoarder's nest with boxes stacked in every corner. Monica grabbed a quick shower, put some curls in her hair, slapped on a little makeup, and was zipping her dress when the limo rolled up in front of her house. She picked up her evening clutch and opened the door to find Tyler with his hand raised, as if he was about to knock.

"Well, don't you clean up nice," she said.

His shirt matched his blue eyes, and his black suit showed off his broad shoulders. "Thank you, ma'am. Granny told me you were wearing blue tonight. I know it's not a prom, but I wanted us to match, and" — he eyed her from head to toe — "you are stunning."

"Thank you," she said.

He opened the screen door and handed her a corsage of white baby roses. "This is for you. Want me to help pin it on your dress?"

"That's so sweet, Tyler." It was on the tip of her tongue to say that nothing could make up for their senior prom, but the words Nana had said about a new heart came to mind. "And yes, please, but you'd better do it in the limo. We'll never live it down if we cause Nana and Winnie to be late."

"This is really a big deal for them," he agreed, "but I don't know if it's because they're going to the alumni or if it's because they conned us into going with them."

"Probably a little of both," Monica whispered as she got into the limo.

"Well, don't you two look just gorgeous," Winnie said, grinning.

"We could say the same thing about y'all." Tyler returned the smile. "Think the folks can handle all of us coming in at once? All these beautiful women surrounding me might blind them."

Dotty giggled like a schoolgirl. "I hope it does, and that they all are struck plum speechless when we walk into the banquet room."

"Now, pin that corsage on Monica's

shoulder," Winnie bossed. "Another block or two, and we'll be there."

"How are we getting home?" Tyler asked.

"The limo will be waiting right here to take us back home when we are ready," Dotty said. "I hired him for the whole evening. I want people to gossip about us arriving in style."

"Nana!" Monica scolded, but secretly she hoped that Raylene saw the big, black stretch limo and was just a smidgen jealous. No, that wasn't right, she hoped the girl was a whole lot jealous. She wouldn't even mind seeing the hussy turn slightly green with envy.

About the time that Tyler finally got the corsage on right, the limo came to a stop in front of the cafeteria. The driver got out and opened the door to help the ladies out, then stood to the side when Tyler stepped out onto the parking lot.

"I'll be right here when y'all get ready to go home," he said.

"Thank you, Freddie," Winnie said.

Dotty hooked her arm in Winnie's, and the two of them strode through the cafeteria doors as if they were royalty. "Let's see Gladys outdo us tonight," Dotty whispered.

"Nana, that's not nice," Monica said.

"Gladys isn't nice," Dotty said. "She just

puts on airs to make everyone think she's a sweet old lady, but down under, she's a real . . ."

"Whoa!" Monica held up a palm.

"I was going to say that she's a witch. I bet there's a special broom that she rides parked in her bedroom closet," Dotty said.

Tyler tucked Monica's arm into his and laid his hand over hers. At his touch, she forgot all about the elderly ladies and niceties and even the vision of Gladys riding a broom around Pecan Valley Retirement Center. She even forgot about Raylene Carter, right up until they were in the cafeteria, and she spotted the *witch* — that seemed like a good word, since Nana had used it — across the room in a circle of the girls who had been the most popular in high school.

"Ignore them," Tyler whispered.

"Find your tables," Dotty said. "They're set up from left to right according to the year you graduated. Ours is way over here to the right, and these days, we only need one table. There aren't many of us left, and most of them don't come out to this party, so we get a couple of tables that cover several years."

Dotty and Winnie veered off to the table marked 1950 through 1960. Tyler ushered

Monica to their area and pulled out a chair for her. She sat down and took in the whole room. She'd eaten lunch in this very room for thirteen years. As juniors, she and Tyler had worked here one Friday when school ended until after midnight, getting the place decorated for the prom that they were responsible to put on for the seniors.

"Putting on the Ritz," she said.

"We fought hard for that theme, didn't we?" he said. "Some of the other kids on the committee wanted to do Mardi Gras."

Raylene had been the top contender for the Mardi Gras theme. Monica had wondered at the time if Raylene was going to want a float for a picture backdrop, and if she planned on showing off her boobs to get a string of bright-colored beads.

"If everyone will take a seat, we're going to ask the Reverend James McEntire to say grace for us before we are served our supper," an older lady with gray hair said from behind the lectern that was set up at the end of the room.

Monica turned to Tyler. "I'm not surprised that James is a preacher. Are you?"

"I always figured he'd go into the ministry or else be a missionary, so it doesn't shock me at all. Granny told me that he was preaching at a big church down in Houston, but that was a few years ago. He might be somewhere else by now," Tyler told her, as all around them the noise of chairs being pulled out from tables mixed with the sounds of folks still catching up with each other.

James took his place behind the lectern, and in a big, booming voice, said, "Please pray with me."

All heads bowed, and the buzz of dozens of conversations ceased. Monica tried to keep her thoughts on the blessing James was bestowing upon the gathering and the food, but Tyler was just too close for her to think of anything but him.

"Amen!" James said.

Tyler leaned over slightly and whispered, "Eat supper."

"National Anthem and then 'play ball,' grace and then 'eat supper.' That's pretty clever, Mr. Magee," Monica said with a smile that quickly faded when she saw that Raylene had taken a seat right across the table from them.

"Hello, Monica," Raylene said and then focused on Tyler. "Hi, Tyler. Y'all look great. Neither of you have changed much since high school."

Monica was speechless for a few seconds. Raylene was still a tall blonde with blue eyes, but something about her was totally different. There was a softer look about her eyes, and she was wearing a fairly modest purple dress that evening. Her wide, gold wedding band revealed that she was married, so Monica scanned the room to see who was still standing. The Reverend James took the last few steps toward their table and bent down to kiss Raylene on the forehead.

"Thanks for saving me a seat, darlin'," he said. "Hello, everyone. I'm glad to see such a good turnout from our class this year."

Several people around their table began to talk, giving Monica a chance to nudge Tyler on the shoulder and ask, "Did you know that . . ."

He shook his head. "Guess Granny forgot to mention it."

Raylene caught Monica's eye and smiled. "I'm glad to see y'all back together."

"Thank you," Tyler and Monica said at the same time.

"I don't see rings, so I guess you haven't . . ." she started.

"No, we haven't," Monica quickly answered. "How long have you been married?"

"Three wonderful years." James whipped out his wallet and flipped it open. "This is our eighteen-month-old daughter, Anna Ruth."

Monica glanced down at the photo of a little blond-haired girl with big blue eyes. "She's beautiful," she said.

"We think so." James looked at the picture for a couple of seconds before he put his wallet away. "I'm just glad she looks so much like her mother."

"I don't know where to start, but . . ." Raylene sighed and looked over at James.

He put his arm around her and kissed her on the cheek. "Just spit it out, darlin'. You'll feel better when you do, and you know it."

She laid her hand on the table, and James covered it with his own. That seemed to give her courage, because she inhaled deeply and said, "I'm so sorry for all the pain I caused both of you ten years ago. What I did was inexcusable, and I don't deserve your forgiveness. I can't undo what was done, but if I could, I would."

"What made you . . ." Monica started to say.

James butted in. "This has been disturbing her peace for years. She's started to call each of you on the phone several times, but we prayed about it, and she felt that she needed to talk to you face to face. That's one of the reasons we decided to attend this affair tonight. We're so happy that y'all are here."

If you don't forgive, then Jesus won't forgive you. Nana had preached those words to her ever since she was a child.

"When I met and fell in love with James, I realized what kind of person I had been, and how much I needed to change. I'm a pastor's wife now, and I've traded in my old, messed-up, ugly heart for a new Christian one," Raylene said with a sweet smile. "I put myself on the same twelve-step program that AA uses, and I'm trying to make amends with everyone I've hurt. Y'all are the last ones on my list, and it feels good to apologize."

"Forgiven," Monica said.

Tyler closed his eyes for a long time. Monica didn't know if he was praying or if he was figuring out a way to poison Raylene, but when he opened them, he nodded across the table. "I accept your apology."

"Thank you, both." Raylene's smile got even bigger. "That's a big weight off my shoulders and off my heart."

If Raylene can get a new heart and a new start, you can. Nana's voice was loud and clear in Monica's head.

"They're bringing our food." James nodded toward the servers coming their way.

"Let's forget the past and talk about the present. Where are y'all working these days?"

"I'm a physician's assistant at Pecan Valley Retirement Center," Tyler said.

"And I work as an RN in one of the nursing homes in Denison," Monica answered, "but I've applied for a job at Pecan Valley and hope to move there. My grandmother, as well as Tyler's, are living there."

"I didn't think those two would ever leave their homes," Raylene said.

"We didn't, either." Monica leaned over toward Tyler to give the server more room to set her plate of food down. "We've been working to get the two places cleaned out and ready for us to live in."

"Well, good luck with that," James said, and then turned his attention to one of their classmates sitting beside him.

"Thanks," Monica said, and concentrated on her dinner.

Tyler didn't taste a bite of the steak dinner that was served that evening. His tie felt a little too tight, and even though the room was nice and cool, he removed his jacket and hung it over the back of his chair halfway through the meal. He tried to listen to the speaker, who had been chosen distinguished alumnus of the year, but his mind kept going back to graduation night. Raylene had ruined his life for ten years, and yet she had gotten his acceptance of her apology in less than ten minutes. Somehow, that didn't seem right.

Are you going to let her continue to have power over you, or are you going to move on? His grandmother's voice was so clear in his head that he checked to see if she was still across the room with the other elderly folks.

"I'm glad that I didn't bore you so badly that you snored," the speaker said with a laugh. "I've been asked to tell everyone that we will be moving over to the gym at this time for our dance. First, though, would the graduating class from five years ago and the one from fifty years ago please stand up?"

Folks from each side of the room got to their feet.

"Let's give a big hand to the graduating class from five years and the one from fifty years ago, who collaborated and did all the decorations." The speaker started the applause, which was even louder than the noise of all the chairs scooting back on a tile floor. When the clapping died down, some of the younger alumni headed straight for the gym. Several folks on the other side of the room sat back down, but Dotty and

Winnie wove their way through the crowd toward where Tyler and Monica were standing.

"Who are you dancing with tonight?" Monica asked.

"We're stayin' long enough to see you kids dance a few times, and then we're goin' home," Dotty answered, and then looped her arm in Monica's and lowered her voice. "I saw that y'all had to sit with Raylene. How did that go?"

"Better than you'd expect," Monica answered. "She apologized to both of us for all the trouble she caused."

"Well, butter my butt and call me a biscuit," Dotty said. "I never saw that one coming."

"Did y'all know that she married James McEntire?" Tyler asked.

"The preacher?" Winnie gasped. "God almighty, Dotty! We've fallen down on our job of finding out things first! We've done got old!"

Dotty laid her hand over her heart. "I'm speechless."

Tyler slipped his arm around Monica's shoulders and took a step away from the crowd. "Shocked us, too, but Granny, you and Dotty aren't ever going to be old."

Winnie followed him. "Thanks for that,

but seeing all those kids who graduated five years ago reminds me that I'm not a spring chicken anymore. But we won't dwell on that right now. I would like one slow dance with my grandson before me and Dotty go home."

Dotty followed along beside Winnie. "You better make it pretty quick. This Cinderella is getting tired."

"Long as our limo don't turn into a pumpkin, we're fine," Winnie told her. "You might even find someone to dance with a couple of times."

"Hmmph," Dotty snorted. "I can't very well dance with an old man in a walker."

"I'll dance with you, Nana," Monica offered. "We did some fancy stepping to some good old country songs last Christmas in your living room. I bet we can show them all that we can outdance any of them."

"Yes, we did, and yes we can," Dotty agreed.

Tyler recognized the song, "My Girl," coming from the gym before they even entered the lobby and made their way to one of the tables that were shoved up against the walls.

"Too bad, this one's almost over," Winnie said.

When Tyler recognized the next song, he

extended his hand toward his grandmother. "I think this one is for us."

Winnie smiled up at him. "I believe you're right."

He did a slow country waltz with Winnie as the DJ played Zac Brown's "Grandma's Garden." The lyrics talked about the singer's grandma telling him that he would be sure to reap what he had sown.

"So, how's things going with you and Monica?" Winnie asked when the song ended and Tyler was escorting her back to their table.

"Better than I could have hoped," he answered.

The next song was Trace Adkins's "Honky Tonk Badonkadonk." Dotty hopped up from her chair and pulled Monica to her feet. "This one is for us, darlin' girl."

Before a minute had passed, everyone in the room had stepped back and given Dotty and Monica the floor. Dotty did a hip roll and slapped her butt when the lyrics said that no one could blame her for what her mama gave her. Everyone in the crowd applauded and whistled.

Tyler could hardly believe his eyes as he watched the show. He was afraid to blink for fear he would miss one of Monica's moves. He remembered that song from when they were teenagers, but good lord, he had never seen her move like that.

When the song ended, and she and Dotty made it back to the table, he grabbed Monica's hand and said, "This one, no matter what it is, belongs to me, and all the rest of the songs this evening, as far as that goes."

"Why's that?" Dotty asked.

"Because after that performance, every guy in this place is going to want to dance with Monica, and I'm not willing to share." He grinned and then leaned over closer to Dotty. "I can see those old guys over there in the corner eyeing you, Dotty. They might be interested in your badonkadonk."

"Then it's time to go home." Dotty stood up.

"I've had my dance, and I'm sleepy." Winnie covered a yawn with her hand. "The limo will take us home and will be waiting at midnight when this shindig ends to drive you kids."

"Thanks for that," Tyler said. "I guess that means we can drink?"

"If you can find anything stronger than punch or root beer, steal some for me." Dotty looped her arm in Winnie's, and the two of them disappeared into the dimly lit room.

Tyler led Monica out on the floor to the familiar first sounds of the guitar music playing "Tennessee Whiskey." He pulled her close to his chest and sang the lyrics with Chris Stapleton when he talked about her being as smooth as Tennessee whiskey and as sweet as strawberry wine.

Monica joined him when the words said that he'd looked for love in the same old places and found the bottom of the bottle always dry.

"Did you really?" he asked.

"A couple of times, but I didn't like the hangover," she answered. "How about you?"

"Same story."

They danced twice more, and then Tyler asked, "Have you had enough of this party?"

"Yes," Monica said without a moment's hesitation.

"Reckon the limo is back?" he asked.

"If not, we could wait outside," she suggested.

When they left the gym and saw that the limo wasn't anywhere in sight, she sat down on the curb and removed her shoes. "These things are killing me."

"You look just as beautiful in bare feet." Tyler sat down beside her and wrapped an arm around her shoulders. "It's a beautiful night. Just look at all those stars."

"Tell me about senior prom." She laid her head on his shoulder.

"I'd rather not go back there," he said after a full minute.

She raised her head and locked her brown eyes with his crystal-clear blue ones. "I need closure, and that's part of it."

"I was totally miserable," he said without blinking, and went on to tell her what Raylene had said about just using him to get back at her. "I took her home at ten-thirty, and until tonight, I never spoke to her again."

"Thank you." Monica laid her head back on his shoulder.

"We had our early graduation party at Dotty's one weekend, prom was the next Friday night, and then we graduated the week after. That time, and the summer months before college, were the worst days of my life," he admitted. "I never told anyone what happened at prom. I was too embarrassed."

"Nana told me basically the same thing that Raylene said about a new heart. Do you think that's even possible?" Monica asked.

The limo drove up before Tyler could answer. He picked up her shoes, got to his feet, and extended a hand to help her. When she put her hand in his, he hoped that meant she was trusting him just a little. The limo driver held the door for them, and Tyler stood to one side so that Monica could climb in first.

He slid into the seat beside her, then leaned over and kissed her on the forehead. "I believe that about a new heart, but I call it a second chance. Are you going to give me one?"

"Depends on whether you're willing to give me one," she answered. "I wouldn't even answer your calls or let you explain, and I've harbored these horrible feelings for years, so I don't deserve another chance, either."

"I was the initial guilty party." He drew her close and tipped her chin up with his knuckles. "But I promise it won't ever happen again."

"That's good enough for me." Her dark lashes came to rest on her high cheekbones.

His mouth met hers in a string of long, lingering, passionate kisses that didn't end until the limo driver opened the door. They both broke away with a chuckle, and Monica said, "I didn't even know we had stopped."

"Me either," Tyler said, "but technically, the vehicle stopped, not us. I hope that this time, we never quit."

"Me, too," she whispered.

CHAPTER SIX

Monica groaned when she awoke on Saturday morning and remembered all the boxes that had to be unpacked. She sat up in bed and squinted against the bright sunlight pouring into her room through the bare window. A shadow blocked the sun for just a moment, and then she realized that someone was mowing the lawn. She frowned and tried to remember if Nana had mentioned hiring someone to take care of the yard on a regular basis.

She crawled out of bed and crossed the hardwood floor to see Tyler on a riding mower, making circles around the house. His lawn was already done, and there was Sheba, sneaking out from under his house and making a mad dash across the lawn.

Monica hurried to the front door and let the cat inside. "You're going to be in big trouble, girl."

Sheba curled up in an open box that still

had a fluffy throw in the bottom and began washing herself.

"There must be a place somewhere in the floor big enough so you can shimmy down and crawl out. Now all Tyler has to do is figure out where it is and close it up." Monica moved through the maze of boxes and went to the kitchen to make herself a cup of coffee. When it was done, she carried it to the living room and sat down on the end of the sofa.

"This is all going too fast, Sheba," she muttered. "I can't get over ten years of trust issues in one week, not even with a new heart. And yet, when I'm with Tyler, it's like the past decade has been erased. I feel as if we're throwing out the bad memories and keeping the beautiful ones as we start all over."

The cat let out a long, pitiful meow.

"I wish I spoke cat language, so I'd know if you are agreeing with me or telling me to suck it up and quit worrying." Monica went back to the kitchen to make herself another cup of coffee.

The lawn mower stopped about the time the coffee finished dripping, so she poured a tall glass of sweet tea for Tyler. She heard him coming across the porch and realized that she was wearing a faded nightshirt with

Minnie Mouse on the front. She tugged at the bottom, trying to cover her underwear, but it was useless, so she took off at a dead run to her bedroom and jerked on a pair of running shorts, a bra, and a T-shirt.

This is crazy, she thought. *He's seen me naked before, and most of my body was covered by that shirt.* She dashed back to the living room to let him inside.

"Good mornin'." Tyler wiped sweat from his brow with a red bandanna.

She threw the screen door open. "Come on in. I've got a glass of iced tea ready for you. Thanks for doing my yard."

"You're welcome." His eyes grew wide at the sight of all the boxes. "Where are you ever going to put all this stuff?"

"Probably a lot of it will be repacked and put in the garage. I had to pack in a hurry, so there's not as much here as it looks like," she explained as she made her way to the kitchen and brought back his tea and her coffee. "We need to talk."

Tyler sat down in the rocking chair and took a sip of his tea. "Those four words kind of scare me."

Monica sank down on the buttery-soft, leather sofa. "Do we need to slow this thing between us down? I'm afraid that we're going too fast."

Tyler drank down half of his tea before he answered. "I had given up hope that we could ever have a future together." He paused for a long time. "I don't want to slow anything down, but since it was my stupidity that caused our problem, I'll abide by your wishes. Just tell me what you want."

At that very moment, Monica wanted to go to the courthouse on Monday and buy a marriage license. Common sense told her that was an insane idea. Her heart said that no one was perfect, and that she and Tyler had both made mistakes. His was letting Raylene talk him into going to the garage with her when he knew what kind of girl she was, and hers was not fighting for what she and Tyler had.

"I'm at a crossroads," she said.

"That reminds me of something." He pulled his phone out of his pocket and hit a few keys. "This song is about a man who's got two loves in his life and doesn't know which one to choose. I've got two loves in my life . . ." He hit the play button, and Vince Gill began singing, "Which Bridge to Cross."

Monica didn't realize she was holding her breath until her chest began to ache. If Tyler was playing that familiar song, then he must have another woman somewhere in the background.

He cleared his throat and repeated, "I've got two loves in my life. One is from the past, and one is sitting here with me. They're both the same person. Do I burn the bridge from the past and cross one into the future? Or do I burn the bridge to the future and be happy with the good memories from our past? It's totally up to you, Monica. We can be neighbors. We can be friends. We can stay on this fast train, or we can slow it down to a crawl. You make the call, and I'll abide by it."

When the lyrics of Gill's song said that the heart only knows what feels right and talked about reaching a decision and getting on with the rest of his life, tears filled Monica's eyes. By the time the last note was played, Monica had made up her mind. She picked up her phone from the back of the sofa and brought up "Love Can Build a Bridge," by The Judds.

"This is what I've been thinking about. It's an old one, but I remember us listening to it a few times," she said.

Tyler stood up and extended a hand to her. "I think I've got my answer about which bridge to burn and which one to cross, but I'd like to hear you say the words."

She put her hand in his, and he drew her

to his chest for a slow waltz around the boxes. "Let's burn the past and ride that fast train toward the future."

Monica sang with the lyrics, agreeing that the first step was realizing it all began with them. Tyler joined her when the words said that when they stood together, they could do anything. They danced until the song ended, and then he tipped her chin up and kissed her.

Only two people existed in the whole world in that moment — Monica and Tyler. Peace surrounded her like a warm blanket on a cold night, and she knew she'd made the right decision. No matter where this fast train took them, she would be on it with Tyler.

"Like it says, our finest hour is when we stand together," Tyler said.

"Let's don't let anything come between us ever again," she whispered.

Before he could answer, Sheba gave out another long meow that sounded as if she was in pain.

"What was that?" Tyler asked.

"I think we're about to have kittens." Monica could have tossed the cat out in the yard for ruining the romantic moment.

"What's she doing over here?" Tyler asked.

"I watched her come out from under your

house through the crawl space and book it over here this morning. I let her in so she wouldn't be around the mower." Monica moved away from him and around a couple of boxes. She dropped to her knees and motioned for Tyler to join her. "Evidently, she wanted to have her babies over here. Look! There's already two of them. One looks just like her and the other one is black and white. Do you think there will be more?"

Tyler knelt down beside her and put an arm around her shoulders. "Does this make us parents?"

"I'm not sure how the family tree goes with cats, but if this is the whole litter, I'll take them both," Monica answered. "It would be a shame to separate siblings."

"I should go find whatever hole she's getting out at and fix it before I take her home," Tyler said. "Did you ever wish for a brother or sister?"

"Just every day of my life," Monica answered. "Did you?"

"Yes, I did," Tyler answered. "Remember when we used to play that game about naming our kids when we got grown?"

Monica nodded. "The boy was going to be either Creed or Logan. The girl was going to be Sophia or Stella. I still want a big family someday. I don't want to raise an only child."

"Me, either." He took her hand in his and gave it a gentle squeeze. "I guess that's a stop on down the road for the train, though, isn't it?"

"Yep," she said. "For now, we've got two kittens to raise."

"I don't want to leave, but I should get on over to the house and figure out where that hole is. If she can get through it, then possums, raccoons, or rats could get in the house. Want to come with me?" he asked.

"Sure." She nodded. "I should get an idea of what all we're going to have to do to get your place ready, and I can help find Sheba Houdini's secret."

"That sounds like a video game." Tyler chuckled and helped her to her feet.

"Maybe we should sell the idea to a children's publisher. The cat keeps getting out, and the possum keeps coming into the house. Oh my! How does the child figure out how to keep one out and the other one in," she teased as he kept her hand in his and led her outside.

Winnie's house was an exact replica of Dotty's, except for a few minor details like white countertops in the kitchen instead of blue, and paneling on the walls. But now the walls were covered with nail holes where Tyler had removed all the old wood.

"This is going to take a lot of patching," Monica said.

"I know," Tyler groaned. "The paneling was put up with nails, and you can see that they used lots of them. I've called a crew to come in here and put up new drywall and get it ready to paint."

"Sounds like a good plan to me," Monica agreed. "Is there somewhere you don't want me looking?"

"I'll take my bedroom and bathroom," he answered. "You can check out everywhere else. I can't imagine where a hole big enough for her to get through might be, but evidently there is one."

Monica looked under the kitchen sink, and everything was all right there. The second place she tried was the cabinet beside the sink. When she opened the door, she found a possum curled up asleep on the bottom shelf. The animal didn't take but a few seconds to scurry down a hole and disappear under the house.

"I found it," she called out.

Tyler came running from the bedroom and dropped to his knees. "I wonder why the flooring is . . . oh, I remember now. Granny had the whole house replumbed a few years ago, and the plumbers had to take up the flooring in a couple of cabinets. Look!" He pointed. "They forgot to screw this floor back down."

"And this is where she stored her cast-iron skillets," Monica remembered. "The weight of them would have held the flooring down. I can see where the board slipped forward when Winnie moved the skillets, but how did Sheba open the door?"

"The catch is broken," Tyler said. "I'll get a drill and some screws and fix it. Then we can bring her and the kittens back over here. Thank goodness you saw her coming out from under the house."

"Like the song says, we can do anything together." Monica smiled.

"Yes, we can," Tyler said, and leaned over to brush a sweet kiss across her lips.

CHAPTER SEVEN

Everything was going so well in Monica and Tyler's relationship that, by the end of the next week, she had dismissed the feeling that the other shoe was about to drop. She had turned in her application packet to Gloria, and that Friday, she dressed in a cute little pink suit for her interview. She slipped her feet into white shoes with a chunky heel and then checked her reflection in the long mirror at the end of the hall.

Seeing Tyler's vehicle in front of his house, and a cute little sports car beside it, didn't send up any warning flags. Tyler had said he would be going in late that morning, because the drywall guys were coming, and he needed to be there when they arrived. Evidently, one of the workers drove a fancy car, Monica thought. She hesitated on the porch, took a deep breath of the fresh morning air, and then headed to her own car.

A movement in her peripheral vision made her jerk her head around to see if Sheba had gotten loose again. Her heart did a nosedive into the dirt when she saw a tall, blond-haired woman backing out of Tyler's house with him in tow. The screen door was halfway open, so Monica got the full impact of the woman wrapping her arms around his neck, pulling his face down to hers, and locking onto his lips.

Monica felt like she was watching a car wreck. The whole scene was horrible, but she couldn't force herself to look away or even blink. The kiss ended, and the woman walked slowly out to her car, got behind the wheel, and put on a pair of oversized sunglasses. She stuck her arm out the window and waved, and then left a dust trail behind her.

Tyler stepped out onto his porch, saw Monica, and started toward her, but she managed to get to her car, get in, and drive away before he could reach her. Her phone rang several times while she drove to her interview, but she ignored it. She didn't want to talk to him, not yet. Had that blonde spent the night in his bed? Had she just showed up, or had he called her and invited her to his house? How many more women from his past would she have to deal with?

When she got to the parking lot in front of the assisted living center, she laid her head on the steering wheel and tried to talk herself out of even going in for the interview. She couldn't live beside Tyler, or maybe even with him in the future, and be content with his old girlfriends popping in and out of his life.

Maybe it was a one-night stand that you weren't supposed to see or know about, the pesky voice in her head suggested. *This is the second time you've caught him with another woman. Wake up and realize that he's trouble.*

"No!" she yelled, raising her head.

Her phone rang again, and this time, she fished it out of her purse. "Might as well get it over with," she muttered.

"Hello, Tyler."

"We need to talk. I'm a block away, and you have ten minutes before your interview with Gloria," he said.

She ended the call and got out of her car. When he pulled into the lot, she was sitting on a park bench under a huge pecan tree in front of the building. He got out of his vehicle and sat down beside her.

"You've got eight minutes. I need one to

walk from here to Gloria's office," she said.

"I was in a relationship with that woman you saw two years ago. Her name is Audra. I met her in college, and we were together for a year. We broke up because she wanted to get married, and I couldn't commit to that. I was still in love with you, and I didn't have a whole heart to give to anyone." He raked his fingers through his hair.

"Did she spend the night with you?" Monica asked.

"No! Hell, no!" Tyler shook his head. "She came by the house . . ." He paused.

"Just to kiss you?" Monica checked her phone for the time.

"No!" His voice sounded like he was bewildered. "She showed up about five minutes before you saw us together. She said that she hadn't gotten over me and wanted to know if we might start things up again. I told her all about you, and how you were the reason I couldn't commit to more with her in the first place. I don't know why she kissed me, but please know that she did that, not me. But" — another pause — "I'm glad she did."

"Really? Why's that?" Monica asked.

"Because I felt nothing. No sparks, no chemistry. Not one single thing like I feel when we kiss or even when you just touch my arm or my hand," he admitted. "I had to talk to you right now and explain."

How would you feel if one of your old boyfriends came back and kissed you? Nana's voice was back in her head. *Give that some thought before you go off all half-cocked and end it with him.*

As if he could read her mind, Tyler said, "I'd be seeing red if the roles were reversed here. I can only imagine how you are feeling right now — especially after that fiasco ten years ago. Please, trust me when I say that I would never do anything to jeopardize this second chance we have."

If you want something bad enough, you'll fight for it. Nana's advice came back to mind.

"Now, it's my turn." Monica glanced at her phone again. "I don't know how many of these beautiful women you've got hiding in your past. I don't want to know, but I'm very much aware of the few relationships I had that didn't work out for me. I do trust you, Tyler, and I've got a remedy for this problem. We'll move in together. My house is already put together, so let's live in it. We can furnish your house with the furniture you bring from your rental property and use that place for our guest house. When my folks or yours come to see us, we'll have room for them, or if Nana and Winnie want to get away from here for a day or two, like at Christmas, we can let them stay there. Now, I've got to go to my interview. Think about it." She stood up and smoothed the front of her skirt.

"I don't have to think about it." He grinned. "I'm ready, but what good will living together do when it comes to old relationships?"

"It's quite simple. If one of your women comes to the door, I can kick her off the porch and send her on her way," Monica answered.

Tyler stood and wrapped Monica up in his arms. "I love you."

"I love you, Tyler Magee. I can't remember a time when I didn't." She hugged him back. "Wish me luck with this interview."

"You don't need it, darlin'," he said as he lowered his lips to hers.

CHAPTER EIGHT

"How do I look?" Dotty asked Winnie.

"Like an oversized blueberry." Winnie giggled. Dotty gave her a dirty look. "I'm going to change into the black outfit I wore to the alumni banquet. I won't have a bit of confidence in this thing after that ugly remark."

"Dotty Allen, the day you don't have confidence hasn't dawned yet," Winnie told her. "The black looks better on you, anyway, and our new things are more stylish. That blue dress is more than five years old, and it looks like something an old woman would wear, or maybe be buried in."

"Good God, Winnie!" Dotty gasped. "I'm going to give the dress away if it makes you think of funerals."

"Give it to Gladys," Winnie said, giggling.

"She could never fit into it," Dotty said as she pulled the dress over her head and put on the black pants outfit. "This will look better with my crown, anyway. Now, how do I look?"

"Like you could dance to that badonka-donk song and take Henry away from Gladys," Winnie answered.

"I always say it'll take a man with his own teeth, his own hair, and who doesn't have to use a walker to bounce my bedsprings." Dotty hooked her arm in Winnie's and said, "Let's go knock 'em all dead."

"That might not be the right thing to say when the youngest one in this place is over seventy," Winnie told her as they walked down the hall together.

The dining room was decorated with balloons and ribbons, and there were two long tables laid out with all kinds of finger foods. The crown was perched on a shelf under a banner that said MOTHER OF THE YEAR.

"There it is," Winnie whispered, "just waiting for them to announce my name."

"Or mine," Dotty reminded her.

"Hey, don't y'all look amazing." Monica crossed the room and hugged both of them. "Guess what? I got the job. Gloria called me this morning. I go to work in two weeks. I called my supervisor at the nursing home, and they agreed to let me use my vacation days for my two weeks' notice, so we've got that time to work on our guest house."

"Guest house?" Winnie asked.

Tyler walked up behind Monica and slipped an arm around her waist. "Did you tell them yet?"

"I told them that I got the job, but not about the other," she answered.

"What other?" Dotty's eyes widened.

Before Monica could answer, Gloria tapped on a glass with a spoon to get everyone's attention. "I'd like to ask everyone to find a seat so we can begin. First of all, thank you so much for coming out to our Mother's Day celebration. It's so good to see so many here this year to enjoy spending time with all the mothers and grandmothers that live at Pecan Valley. Before we begin, I'd like to announce that Leona, our RN, will be retiring in two weeks, and we've hired Monica Allen to step into that position. I won't say take her place, because Leona can't be replaced. Monica, would you stand up, please, so everyone can put a face to the name."

Monica blushed slightly as she got to her feet. Dotty started the applause, and everyone else joined in.

"Thank you," Monica said when the noise died down. "I appreciate that, and hope that I can do half the job that Leona has done." Then she sat back down.

411

"Now for the moment we've all been waiting for," Gloria said. "We'll crown our Mother of the Year, and then we invite all of you to enjoy the food, stay and visit as long as you want, and come back to see us often."

Dotty reached over and grabbed Winnie's hand. "This is it. We're goin' to win," she whispered.

"We tallied up the votes twice to be sure that we got this right, and we had a tie this year, so we asked all the staff members to vote one more time for either of these two sweet mothers," Gloria said. "And the winner of this year's Mother of the Year contest is Minnie Mason."

Winnie started to get up out of her chair, but Dotty pulled her back down. "She said Minnie, not Winnie."

"Well, crap!" Winnie said, "and to think of all the money I spent on candy bars."

Minnie, a little round woman with short, kinky hair dyed red, made her way to the front of the room. Gloria put the crown on her head and then led her down a stretch of red carpet as the background music for "Miss America" played.

"Crown is all buried down in that silly-looking hair," Dotty complained. "And her pink dress doesn't do a thing for it."

"That's one of them funeral dresses," Winnie whispered.

"We should sneak into her room tonight and steal the crown," Dotty suggested in a low voice.

"Nana!" Monica scolded.

"I just want to be a queen one time," Dotty said, pouting.

"Well," Winnie huffed. "The fact that you got the job, and we get to see you every single day, kind of takes the stink off this moment."

"Thank you for that," Monica said.

"And we do have other news." Tyler took Monica's hand in his.

Dotty couldn't think of a thing better than winning that crown, but she sighed and focused on the two of them. "Well, spit it out!"

"We're going to live together in my house and fix up Tyler's as a guest house," Monica told them. "That way, you two can come stay a few days over holidays with us."

"Oh my!" Dotty's hands went to her cheeks. "Sweet Jesus and all the angels in heaven. My prayers have been answered. What made you decide to do that?"

Winnie grabbed Tyler around the neck and hugged him tightly. "Yes! Whatever made you decide to do that?"

"Well, it all started ten years ago, when I

caught Tyler in the garage with Raylene Carter, and then a few days ago when . . ." Monica went on to tell the story of the woman who'd kissed Tyler.

"But what has all that got to do with living together?" Winnie asked.

"Nana told me that if I want something bad enough, I might have to fight for it," Monica explained. "I figure if some hussy comes knocking on my door looking for my boyfriend, I'll be waiting, and I can kick her off the porch. If she comes up with her hands knotted in fists, I'll know that it's time to fight for what I love."

Dotty and Winnie both broke out in laughter.

"That's my girl. When's the wedding? I need to shop for a new outfit." She cut her eyes around toward Winnie. "One that doesn't look like a funeral dress."

Winnie clapped her hands. "I just love that you two have made up, and you called him your boyfriend. I've waited ten years for this day. When is the wedding?"

"We're taking it slow and easy," Tyler said, "and we haven't talked about a date yet."

"We've got to see if we can stand each other before we talk marriage," Monica told them.

"Oh, honey, that's not going to be a

problem. You've been in love your whole lives," Dotty told her.

"You're right about that." Tyler leaned over and kissed Monica on the cheek.

"Amen!" Monica agreed, looking into his eyes.

EPILOGUE

Six months later

Snow covered the ground and was still coming down the December day when Monica went to the little white brick church in Bells. Winnie and Dotty were riding with Ginger in the car behind her. Pink sponge hair rollers covered Monica's head, and she prayed that her thick hair would be dry when her mother removed them. She parked right beside them at the backside of the fellowship hall, and all four women waded through snow that came up over the tops of their boots to the doors that led inside.

"Nervous?" Winnie asked as they kicked off their boots and headed across the room.

Monica stopped and stared. The room had been transformed into a beautiful reception hall, decorated with poinsettias in the middle of each table, and a fully adorned Christmas tree in the corner with wedding gifts under it. "Mama, this is beautiful. It's like a Christmas fairy tale."

Ginger gave her daughter a sideways hug. "Honey, I was tickled pink when you and Tyler decided to have a Christmas wedding. I've had so much fun helping get all this together. Wait until you see the sanctuary."

"I should have been in on all this," Monica said with a smile.

"We got it done, darlin' girl." Dotty made it a three-way hug. "And we enjoyed every minute of it."

Winnie joined in the embrace. "We loved doing this for our grandkids, and besides, y'all had to work through yesterday in order to get days off for your honeymoon in the Colorado mountains."

"But we expect less skiing and more baby making while you're up there." Dotty patted her on the back.

"Nana, you've got to learn some patience." Monica smiled.

"Honey, I'm eighty-six years old and staring eighty-seven right in the eyeballs. Patience is not in my basket of fruits of the spirit at this age," Dotty said.

"Hmmph," Winnie snorted. "When they were passing out patience to all the little baby girls that was born in the year we were, you told them, 'I don't want any of that crap. Just give me a double dose of sass.'"

"And it's done me a lot more good than all that other stuff," Dotty shot back at her, and tugged on Monica's hand. "Now, let's get on to the sanctuary for a quick peek, and then you've got to get dressed. You're getting married in two hours, and Ginger swears it will take an hour of that to get your hair fixed so the veil will fit just right."

"Oh, Mama," Monica said as they made a slow walk down the center aisle. "This is my dream wedding. Fluffy white pew bows with red poinsettias, candles everywhere, and a Christmas tree instead of an arch."

"I couldn't have done it without these two." Ginger waved to include Winnie and Dotty.

Tears dammed up in Monica's eyes, but she refused to let them spill out. No way was she going to ruin her makeup. "All right, let's go get dressed before I start crying."

Monica's white velvet dress, with its train that trailed over the floor, hung on a tall hook. Even looking at it, she couldn't believe that her day had come. She and Tyler would spend their first night together as a married couple in a cabin in Colorado.

But there are more nights to a marriage than just the ones in a honeymoon, and I want to be married to Tyler, not just have a wedding, she thought.

"Okay, sweetheart," Ginger said. "Sit down right here, and let's get those rollers out of your hair while Winnie and Dotty get dressed."

Monica sat down on a velvet stool in front of the vanity and watched her mother take the rollers out of her hair. "You've been doing this for as long as I can remember."

"With the same pink curlers," Ginger said, laughing, "just like the ones my mama used on my hair."

Monica realized for the first time how much she and her Latina mother looked alike. Ginger was a little taller than her daughter, and her eyes were the color of Yoohoo chocolate drinks, whereas Monica's were as dark as coal. But their skin tones were the same, and so was their facial structure. Monica hoped that, if she had a daughter, she would be blessed with thick black hair and blue eyes like Tyler's.

Ten minutes before it was time to walk down the aisle, her father, Kent, stuck his head in the door. "Is everyone ready?" he asked. "They're playing the music for your mother and Tyler's mama to walk down the aisle together."

"Almost," Monica said. "Just a couple more finishing touches." She brought out two tiaras that she had hidden in her duffle bag. "Nana and Winnie, you didn't get the Mother's Day crown at the center, but I want you to wear these today. They go with your pretty red dresses, and today I'm crowning you Grandmothers of the Year." She nestled the tiaras down into their freshly styled hair. "They are to thank you both for agreeing to be my bridesmaids."

"Now you're going to make me cry." Winnie grabbed a tissue and dabbed her eyes.

"Not me," Dotty said. "I'm going to wear this thing with pride and then put it on the shelf in my living room. Gladys and Minnie ain't got a thing on us. They might have Mother's Day crowns, but our grandkids are getting married, and we're going to get great-grands someday."

Ginger kissed Kent on the cheek. "I remember our wedding day," she said.

"Best day of my life. Then the next best day was when we had this gorgeous daughter," Kent said.

"You got that right." Ginger smiled at Monica and disappeared out into the hallway.

"Thank you for our crowns." Dotty picked up her bouquet.

"Thank you for being you and for forgiving my grandson," Winnie said as she straightened her back and adjusted her bouquet.

Monica blinked back tears as she took her father's arm. "I can truthfully say that this is the best day of my life, too, Daddy, but I think there are more even better ones in store."

"I can guarantee it," Kent said.

When the two ushers opened the doors into the sanctuary, the church was packed. Monica locked eyes with Tyler, and everyone and everything else disappeared. He met her in front of the altar and took her hand in his.

"You are stunning," he whispered.

"You clean up pretty good yourself," she said, and the two of them turned to face the preacher.

"Dearly beloved, we are gathered here today . . ." The preacher began the ceremony. "Who gives this bride?"

"No one," Kent answered, "but her family is willing to share her with Tyler, just as his family is willing to share him with ours."

"Family," Monica whispered as she handed off her bouquet to Dotty. "It's a beautiful thing."

"Yes, it is, and we are so lucky," Tyler said.

Vows and rings were exchanged, and then the preacher pronounced them man and wife. "You may now kiss your bride, Tyler."

Tyler bent her so far backward that her veil dragged on the floor behind her, and then he sealed the marriage with a true Hollywood kiss. When he brought her back to a standing position, he said, "I love you, Mrs. Magee."

"I love you," she told him, and they walked down the aisle as a married couple to the melody of "Love Can Build a Bridge."

ABOUT THE AUTHORS

Fern Michaels is the *USA Today* and *New York Times* bestselling author of the Sisterhood, Lost and Found, Men of the Sisterhood, the Godmothers series, and dozens of other novels and novellas. There are over ninety-five million copies of her books in print. Fern Michaels has built and funded several large day-care centers in her hometown, and is a passionate animal lover who has outfitted police dogs across the country with special bulletproof vests. She shares her home in South Carolina with her four dogs and a resident ghost named Mary Margaret. Visit her Website at FernMichaels.com.

Lori Foster is a *New York Times, USA Today* and *Publishers Weekly* bestselling author and a dominant force in the arena of sexy contemporary romance whose books have sold over 10 million copies. Visit her online at LoriFoster.com.

Carolyn Brown is an award-winning *New York Times, USA Today, Publishers Weekly,* and *Wall Street Journal* bestselling author with more than one hundred published books to her name and over 4 million copies sold. With a career spanning more than two decades and her books translated into nineteen foreign languages, she's known for writing heartwarming women's fiction, contemporary cowboy, and country music romances. She's a recipient of the Bookseller's Best Award, the prestigious Montlake Diamond Award, a three-time recipient of the National Reader's Choice Award, and a RITA Award finalist. Born in Texas and raised in Oklahoma, she and her husband live in the small town of Davis, Oklahoma, where everyone knows everyone else, including what they are doing and when — and they read the local newspaper on Wednesdays to see who got caught. They have three grown children and enough grandchildren and great-grandchildren to keep them young. For more information, visit Carolyn BrownBooks.com.

The employees of Thorndike Press hope you have enjoyed this Large Print book. All our Thorndike, Wheeler, and Kennebec Large Print titles are designed for easy reading, and all our books are made to last. Other Thorndike Press Large Print books are available at your library, through selected bookstores, or directly from us.

For information about titles, please call:
(800) 223-1244

or visit our website at:
gale.com/thorndike

To share your comments, please write:
Publisher
Thorndike Press
10 Water St., Suite 310
Waterville, ME 04901